D0355176

BEFORE

YOU

LEAP

NO LONGER PROPERTY OF
ANYTHINK LIBRARIES/
RANGEVIEW LIBRARY DISTRICT

ALSO BY KEITH HOUGHTON

No Coming Back

Gabe Quinn Thrillers

Killing Hope
Crossing Lines
Taking Liberty

BEFORE

YOU

LEAP

KEITH HOUGHTON

THOMAS & MERCER

This is a work of fiction. Names, characters, organizations, places, events, and incidents are either products of the author's imagination or are used fictitiously.

Text copyright © 2016 Keith Houghton
All rights reserved.

No part of this book may be reproduced, or stored in a retrieval system, or transmitted in any form or by any means, electronic, mechanical, photocopying, recording, or otherwise, without express written permission of the publisher.

Published by Thomas & Mercer, Seattle

www.apub.com

Amazon, the Amazon logo, and Thomas & Mercer are trademarks of Amazon.com, Inc., or its affiliates.

ISBN-13: 9781503938168
ISBN-10: 1503938166

Cover design by Stuart Bache

Printed in the United States of America

For Lynn,
my wife, my love, my life—who knows me better than I
know myself and doesn't hold it against me.

Preface

Don't ask me for the secret recipe.

Writing a novel isn't down to luck and providence. It's not about selling your soul or buying a golden ticket. I know, because I've tried both, and without much success on either count. It's more to do with blood, sweat, and tears, plus a hundred other emotionally charged components, all required to put aside their differences and come together at exactly the right moment. Imagine squeezing a lump of coal until it transmutes into a diamond.

The reality is, it's a complicated recipe, and no perfect formula exists. Imagination helps, but it can be a runaway train if left unchecked. The magic ingredients vary with each author, depending on cooking time and taste. Unquestionably, what is needed are oodles of patience and a bucketful of perseverance. Oh, and in my case, lots of caffeine. That's a no-brainer. Plus chocolate.

For me, writing a novel is a long, arduous ascent to the summit. It really is a wonder I ever get to plant my flag and admire the view. I am not one of those writers who can string together ten thousand words a day. If I am lucky, that takes me a month, dog and weather permitting. Nor am I able to stick to a strict story plan. It just doesn't happen. If I chalk out the plot, color the characters, stupidly get excited . . .

invariably the story will diverge, often drastically, taking me into areas I hadn't bargained on visiting. I can't tell you how many times I have fallen into the same trap of painting my protagonists into corners and expecting them to work their own way out, only to find them still sitting there weeks later.

Inventiveness is my lifesaver.

And so I set about writing this novel with the same unprepared, fingers-crossed abandon with which I approach all my writing.

Don't ask me how things worked out.

The proof of the pudding is in the eating.

Now, go feast.

Keith Houghton, Bonita Springs, Florida, November 2015

Prologue

O
ut here on the deserted highway, it's like a scene from one of those postapocalyptic movies. It's midday, but there's nobody on the interstate. No other vehicles and no other people anywhere in sight. We could be the last living souls on planet Earth—Kyle and me—as we drive north toward Tampa with the intense Florida sun baking the asphalt as far as the eye can see.

If only it were true, that the world was coming to an end. An uprising of the undead would be easier to live with.

Kyle laughs and tells me I'm a daydreamer.

He's not alone in this observation. Over the years, teachers, family, friends, and any number of well-meaning commentators have all arrived at the same damning conclusion: I have an overactive imagination, and one day it will get me killed.

Maybe today is that day.

As usual, Kyle goes one step too far. Not only am I a daydreamer, he says, I'm delusional on top of everything else—which is altogether something special, coming from him. This is Kyle, after all: the kid who is never satisfied with stealing one cookie. He has to take the whole jar and then brag about it afterward.

He glances at me from the driver's seat. "You do know this is seriously screwed up, right? You, me, *this*. It's so not like you, Greg. I'm in my element here, but you're way out of your comfort zone. Keep this up and you're in danger of becoming me."

He slams his foot down hard on the gas pedal. The engine screams, and the sudden burst of acceleration snaps our heads back against the seat. We're already doing eighty in a seventy zone, and his grip on the wheel is tenuous.

Kyle laughs again—his way of dismissing me—and the insane sound bounces around the car, hemorrhaging through the bullet holes in the rear window like bloodied confetti.

I have known Kyle for longer than I can remember.

He is everything I'm not. Salvation and damnation rolled into one. The definition of reckless. The result of a faulty gene. We couldn't be less alike. Sometimes I think that's the draw.

As if reading my mind, he murmurs, "Shadows only exist where there's light."

This is his mistake: he likes to think he's philosophical. But that's just some of me rubbing off on him. My argument is that he only knows what I've told him, and that repeating it back doesn't make him sound intelligent; it makes him as insubstantial as an echo.

Kyle rolls down the window and pokes out his head, like he's fifteen again and stealing his first automobile. His move causes the car to lurch. I steady the wheel with one hand, bringing it back into the middle lane. In the side mirror, Kyle's face forms a manic mask as the blast-furnace wind tries to tear it off.

Through bared teeth, he screams, "You can taste the heat!"

I feel like pushing him completely out the window.

This is Kyle's first visit to the Sunshine State. He's knocked out by the steam-room humidity and the steep angle of the light. The same way I was when I first came down here. Unlike him, I've had ten years to acclimate. The world has changed and taken me with it. But Kyle seems untouched by time. Like he's been locked in suspended animation, a boy in a bubble, back home in Michigan where we grew up.

"You're out of your mind if you think we're gonna get away with this!" he shouts into the wind. The words are torn from his lips, one by one, then gone.

My response is matter-of-fact. "You're the reason we're here, Kyle. I'm not the crazy one in this relationship."

Kyle says madness is like love—you don't realize you're in it until half of you is missing.

In the mirror, his grin is inhumanly wide, cartoonish, and there's an inappropriate amount of chirpiness in his voice when he calls, "Hey, man, don't kick the dog just because he howls at the moon." He proceeds to demonstrate, howling at the top of his lungs as we race along the empty highway.

Even with another man's blood staining his hands, he thinks this is a game. He thinks he'll win. But Kyle is a born loser.

I look at the dried blood on my own hands and marvel at how far I have fallen.

Kyle once said, *The way we come into this world isn't our call, but we can choose which way we go out. Fizzle or bang.*

He pulls his head back inside and turns his windblasted face to mine. "Hey, do you think we have enough gas to make it to Disney? We've never done Disney. I think I can feel a princess moment coming on."

It's hard to take him seriously with his hair blown back, looking like a mad professor who just blew up his science lab. But I do. I know Kyle is capable of very bad things.

A cancer has no conscience.

Even so, I can't help feeling our connection, in the same way that those cancerous cells were once a healthy part of the host.

I show him the gun, the only thing forcing him to follow my will. "No, Kyle. No Disney. Not today."

"Okay, then. Go ahead. Shoot me, Greg, if it makes you happy. I've made my peace. My aura is aligned. Death isn't the final deal here. Sure, it's the end of the road, but not the journey. I've got my ticket. My bags

3

are packed. So be it. I'm ready to catch the next train to transcendence if you are."

He spouts the whole spiritual-ascension thing like it's something he believes in, when the truth is he caught it on a TV show once, a long time ago. We both did. A forty-four-minute dissection of the human condition, plus commercials. Stuff we didn't fully understand back then. Still don't.

It will take more than one illuminating documentary to bring light to Kyle's darkness.

A half mile up ahead, red and blue sparkles lie scattered across the highway. Gems glinting in the midday sun.

"Take the next exit," I tell him.

"What happened to Disney?"

"Just do it, Kyle. Change of plans."

The off-ramp opens up, and we take the long curve toward the Sunshine Skyway, careening around the overpass with the tires squealing.

The rational half of me wants to end this now. To give up while we're ahead. It's gone too far. We've made a terrible mistake. As bad as this is, as unbelievable as this is, as impossible as this is, it's still recoverable.

No lost cause is ever worth dying for.

But the other half of me doesn't see any other way out.

We have done the unthinkable, the unforgivable.

Kyle is right about one thing: there is no way this can end well.

The rearview mirror is tilted in such a way that I can see the big guy on the backseat. His wrists and ankles are bound with silvery duct tape, with a noose of it pinning him to the headrest. Another strip is wrapped around his head several times, covering his seething mouth. I can see blood on his bare chest, deep-purple bruises beginning to welt on his cheeks, and one eye swollen and completely closed.

This is what happens when I let Kyle into my life.

"So, Greg, old pal," Kyle says as the road levels out. "What's the plan here? We just keep driving? What happens when we run out of gas? You think we can shake hands and walk? We shot at the police! They're not gonna be all chummy and forgiving about it. And what happens when you realize that the gun is empty? What then, man? Last I heard, Florida still had the death penalty."

Fizzle or bang.

I tell him I'm thinking. But my thoughts aren't coming easy. Mentally, I'm hauling myself through a bramble patch, catching on the barbs.

The truth is, I'm still in shock mode from what we've done. Still angry with myself for being a sheep.

Stony thoughts bleed through:

When we were kids, Kyle was always a bad influence. I never saw it. Or if I did, I ignored it. Now, my eyes are open.

"Think harder," he demands. "You're supposed to be the brains in this outfit."

I tell him to shut up.

"Just trying to grease the gears, man. Get those pistons firing."

A glance in the passenger-side mirror reveals something that resembles a mudslide chasing after us. It's a black-and-white tsunami, bull-dozing along the heat-hazed highway, layered with rubber, chrome, metal, and glass, and topped with blinking red and blue stars. The cavalcade has been on our tail for miles, flushing traffic off the roads and out of our path.

Jesus Christ. What have I done?

A toll station comes up, fast. It looks abandoned. Green lights all across, and each gate gaping open. No vehicles lined up. No underpaid attendants hanging out of the booths, wondering what maniac is going for the land-speed record. We sail through, leaving sparks. If a camera flashes, I don't see it.

Then we're charging across the long bridge spanning Tampa Bay, greenery succumbing to blue. It's a fantastic view. No land in sight. Just an endless tract of wave-whipped water and the sun-bleached pavement stretching out on stilts, disappearing over the horizon, like the road goes on forever. It's breathtaking. But it's lost on Kyle. His gaze is fixed on the humpbacked bridge rearing up in the distance like a monstrous sea creature rising from the depths.

With the car exceeding ninety, and with the window fully down, it's taking every bit of sophisticated engineering to keep the vehicle from colliding with the concrete barrier wall. It's like trying to thread a needle on a roller coaster. The car is weaving perilously in and out of the lane markings, its grip slipping and Kyle grinning, with just his bloody fingertips balanced on the wheel.

Crazy is what crazy does. No doubt in my mind.

Thunder roars directly overhead, and a police helicopter appears alongside us, dropping into a parallel course. Kyle lets out an expletive. A green-suited SWAT officer is hanging out of an open hatch, a sniper rifle tracking our breakneck dash.

Kyle leans over and waves at the sharpshooter. "Relax, old pal," he says to me. "It's just for show. They won't shoot knowing we have a hostage on board."

I half believe him.

The roadway begins its long ascent into the heavens, and we go with it, rocketing up the incline, the pedal jammed to the floor.

The Sunshine Skyway Bridge—aptly named on a day like this—is impressive. The longest span is a quarter mile of flat concrete, two hundred feet up, suspended between a pair of four-hundred-foot pylons. The view through the windshield is all blue sky and steel cables as thick as thighs. And our car is like a ballistic missile, headed for orbit.

"Who needs Disney when we've got this?" Kyle says.

Higher and higher we go, with Kyle's thin lips peeled back and his too-close-together eyes flaring wide. The police helicopter matches our ascent. One expertly aimed shot and the car will jump the wall, plunging us to our death.

We bounce onto the level summit and hit the homestretch at full speed.

Then Kyle stands on the brake.

The fierce deceleration jerks us forward against our belts. The back end fishtails. Tires shriek. Kyle wrestles with the wheel, arms as straight as pistons, but he can't prevent the right fender from crumpling against the low retaining wall. The impact jerks us sideways, and the car rebounds like a pinball and skids some more, twisting and turning, before coming to a juddering stop.

Kyle is cussing under his breath.

So am I.

Up ahead, the sea bridge is barnacled with Tampa police cruisers and granite-faced cops with their sunglasses on and their weapons aimed our way. In the ensuing silence comes the blast of a bullhorn, then:

"Get out of the car! Get down on the ground! Hands behind your head!"

Kyle bursts into a fit of ripsaw laughter and rolls out of the car.

I join him, shoving the gun in my waistband and out of sight.

Behind us, at the crest of the incline, the hot-pursuit tsunami has run aground, completely blocking any chance of retreat. A depressing mix of local cops, sheriff's deputies, and state troopers are using their car doors as shields and watching us along the lengths of their iron sights.

Snaking tracks of hot rubber stretch between us.

Over my shoulder, I hear Kyle ask, "What now, brainiac?"

Front and back, there's nowhere to go. Nowhere to run. No escape. For the second time today, we have reached the point of no return. But there is one route left open. One way out of this mess, to end this madness once and for all.

I see Kyle's eyes scan the police roadblock, see him cup his hands to his mouth, and hear him shout, "Stay back! We have a hostage here! Come any closer and he's dead meat!" He points at the police helicopter hanging in the air about a hundred yards out. "And call off your attack dog!"

For a moment, nothing happens. Then the helicopter pulls back, rotors slapping the air as it climbs higher.

Kyle turns to me and says, "Okay, let's get him out."

I open up the door to the backseat and rip away the duct tape pinning our hostage to the rear headrest, then grab him by the ankles. He tries to worm his way free, tries to kick my hands loose, but I keep hold. He's heavy, as heavy as a dead weight. With Kyle's help, I haul him out, stand him up, and between us we walk him over to the edge of the bridge. He doesn't go willingly. He resists, trying to wriggle out of our grasp, huffing and puffing, trying to hit us with his manacled hands. But he's as helpless as a bound hog. I don't blame him; he's had a taste of the madness.

Roughly, I sit him down on the knee-high wall and tell him to stay put, or else.

"Man, will you take a look at that view?" Kyle whoops, elbowing me playfully in the ribs.

"Stop it, Kyle."

"No, seriously, Greg. Folks would pay good money for a view like this." He elbows me again, this time harder. "Hey, I hope you remembered to pack the beer."

I decide that enough is enough. I can't take any more of Kyle's immature devil-may-care attitude. This is all his fault. He drove me here, to this. My life is over because of him.

Before I realize it, my hand is wrapped around his throat and I'm stepping up onto the concrete wall, hoisting him up there with me.

It's cool this high up, windy, as if invisible hands are trying to pluck us off the bridge. The wall is just inches thick, and the height is nothing short of dizzying. We're in the shade of a towering pylon that blots out the sun like a giant guillotine. Down below, on the sun-speckled water, pleasure craft and fishing boats ply the waves—white shards flecked with people dust. This is no place for the weak-kneed or the faint of heart, or for anyone in their right mind.

He tries to push me away, but I pull him back.

"Killing me isn't the answer," he squeaks from behind my fingers.

"What happened to you being ready to die?"

"I am. But I don't want it to be at your hand. Besides, you can't get rid of me this easily. I'm inside your head, man. You're stuck with me."

Kyle once said, *We're two sides of the same penny, forever bonded.*

Of course, Kyle is crazy.

"Go ahead, Greg. Deny it all you will, but you can't argue with chemistry. We share the same ancestral DNA, you and me. On a sub-atomic level, we're identical. Kill me and it'll be like killing yourself."

See what I mean?

My whole life has led to this point. This insane moment. Up here on the brink with Kyle. Him pushing. Me pulling. The same internal struggle that plagued me as a child. All those fragmentary memories have stacked up, with me wavering on the top, ready to fall . . . or to let go.

This is what it feels like to be a killer.

I shift my feet, and suddenly Kyle is teetering on the edge, sneakers scrabbling, his whole body hanging precariously over the blue abyss. My fingers around his scrawny throat are the only things preventing him from falling to certain death.

"Wait," he gasps. "You're forgetting our unfinished business. The hostage. He needs to pay for what he did. You need me for that. And I know exactly what to do."

Staring into Kyle's manic eyes is like looking at my own damned reflection.

"Greg, you gotta trust me here. This is my area of expertise. I know a way out of this. For both of us. We don't have to die today."

The wind blows at us, flapping noisily at our clothes.

It's all come down to just Kyle and me.

Two hundred feet up in the air.

Standing on the edge of the world, with only the twitch of a muscle deciding our fates.

Everything has come down to this.

"Trust me," he implores. "For old times' sake."

My grip starts to weaken.

"This better be good, Kyle."

He is choking, jagged blood vessels popping out on his eyes, but still he manages a lopsided smile.

You befriend a lion, and one day it'll bite off your head.

Chapter One

Three days earlier, I was clock-watching while Gus Toomey droned on about how much he loved his wife and how much he hated her for cheating on him, which was why I almost missed it when he said:

"If I fantasize about killing her, does it make me a bad husband?"

If I'd overheard him muttering it in a bar after a long night of devout drinking, I wouldn't have given it a second thought. I would have chalked it up to the usual sob story and left it at that. As it was, Toomey was seated in my office on the beach road, stone-cold sober and in complete control of what was coming out of his mouth.

He wanted me to know he'd been thinking about killing his wife, and he was fishing for my opinion on it. Worse still, he'd left his shock-and-awe reveal till the last gasp of his session.

Some people use therapy as a confessional.

It's not the first time I've heard similar words spoken to me in confidence, and it won't be the last.

When I first rented the private room in the community health center in Bonita Springs, I was startled to hear some of the things people admitted to: stalking, incest, fraud. One woman said she ate her own feces; another had sold a kidney for gin money.

No end of immoral revelations, and no end of sincere excuses.

In those days, youth and inexperience made it hard to keep my opinions to myself—until one day a young woman, whose boyfriend would be intimate with her only if she wore his dead mother's clothes, slapped me across the face for suggesting the first step in regaining her self-worth was to ditch him.

Are you kidding me? she'd spat with some venom before leaving in a whirlwind. *It's the only attention I get!*

Later that afternoon, I'd gotten an angry call from the boyfriend, telling me to keep my nose out of his business or else he'd chop it off.

Lesson learned.

These days, I keep a tight lid on my personal feelings and take most of what I hear with a grain of salt. People's lifestyle choices are their own. They don't always say what they mean, but equally they don't always mean what they say. My job is never to criticize or to apportion blame, and as for being judgmental, I have completely given up on it. I know most jumpers want to be talked down off the ledge, and so I give them the tools to reach the ground safely. What they do after that is up to them.

If I fantasize about killing her, does it make me a bad husband?

Toomey had spoken the words quietly, quickly, as though by saying them any louder he would have invoked evil or at the very least guaranteed himself a lengthy jail sentence.

And I almost missed it.

Ordinarily, when I'm with a client, I pay attention. Being distracted when I ought to be listening is not just bad manners; it's detrimental to both parties. Listening is my job, and I don't come cheap, so the very least I can do is focus when my clients speak.

But two things were competing here:

In the red corner, Toomey's underwhelming tale was one I'd heard repeated a hundred times previously and from a hundred Toomey clones. A broken record of blamelessness, where nothing is ever their fault, including the breakdown of their marriages. Denial bordering on the banal.

And in the blue corner, I'd arranged to meet with Zoe at Donovan's at 5:15, on the heels of my last appointment, and being on time was looking increasingly unlikely if Toomey had anything to do with it. Due to her work commitments, I hadn't seen Zoe in more than a week, and I missed her. I'm not embarrassed to admit it either. We are an item, and it feels good. The closer 5:15 came, the more my androgens were crawling the walls.

And that's why it took me several long seconds to process Toomey's disclosure.

During which time he said, "Give it to me straight, Doc. Don't hold back now. I'm a big boy. I can handle it."

Physically, he could. No doubt about it. Physically, Gus Toomey was a mountain of muscle squeezed into a jazzy Hawaiian shirt. The kind of muscle, I imagined, made solid by years of steroid abuse. He was in his late thirties, with one of those heavy brows that brawlers use as battering rams. He'd told me he was a bodybuilder, and he had big, nail-bitten fingernails that could poke holes in brickwork. Physically, Gus Toomey looked like a character straight off the pages of Homer's *Odyssey*, sitting here in his painfully tight short shorts. Mentally, it was a different story. Inside, he was a Grimm's fairy tale, in which he struggled with control issues, paranoia, and one or two bad habits. Mentally, he was as vulnerable as the rest of us.

Give it to me straight, he'd said. *I can handle it.*

For the past fifty-eight minutes, Toomey had tiptoed through his minefield, avoiding broaching the real reason behind his visit. Then, with the clock ticking, he'd handed me his unexploded bomb and expected me to defuse it in ninety seconds.

I wondered which wire of his I'd have to cut first.

"Gus, you do know it's against the law to seriously hurt someone?"

It's common sense, right? But you have to check. We're not all born with it. Some people will touch the flame just to prove the pain.

"Sure I do," he said, responding far too quickly, as most in his position do. But he didn't look sure, as most of them don't.

Unseen, I scribbled an exclamation point next to his name on my notepad.

In total, I've been doing talk therapy with the natives of Southwest Florida for almost ten years now. It's an interesting and rewarding job, and I like it. And I'm not just saying that because I get to hear offbeat confessions and other people's dark secrets. On more than one level, it satisfies a selfish need in me, and that's my own hang-up. It also means that for four days each week, I get to trowel toughening filler into all manner of fractures and cracks: underappreciated husbands like Gus Toomey; needy people in search of a little reassurance; anxious people with life-altering obsessions. I'm not a medical doctor and I don't command a six-figure salary, but I like to think I make a difference.

The bulk of my work comes in the form of referrals from family physicians. About a quarter of clients are random walk-ins right off the street, like Gus Toomey.

He'd been sitting in the easy chair facing me in the sunlit office for the better part of an hour—voicing the usual complaints about unreasonable life expectations—with no mention of wanting to do his wife mortal harm. In fact, up until his admission, I hadn't detected much in the way of hostility from Toomey. He'd come across as a likable-enough character with the usual emotional baggage accumulated by somebody his age.

Now I was beginning to think he regretted coming in.

"Gus, how long have you felt this way?"

"I guess since the first time I saw them together."

"Your wife and her lover?"

He nodded. "Yeah. Him and her. They were making out."

"In your home?"

"No. God, no. They were in his car, at the state park."

"Lovers Key?"

"Yeah. You know it?"

"I take my boat up there sometimes. It's a nice place."

"Not this time. It was after dark. The car windows were steamed up, but I managed to see enough of what I needed to see."

"You mean you followed them?"

"Damn right I did. Been doing it for months now. Each time it's either the beach or a hotel. The first occasion it was Lovers Key. I got pictures. The second time—"

I held up a halting hand. "You took photographs of them together?"

"With a night-vision filter."

"Why?"

"Otherwise the shots would've been underexposed."

"No, I mean why did you take the photos?"

He shrugged, and I got the feeling Toomey had done more than merely snap a few pictures.

"I guess, if it comes down to it, for proof against her in a court of law." It came out more as a question than a statement. He brought out his phone. "You want to see the pictures? I got them right here."

"No, thank you. That won't be necessary."

Toomey stuck out a ledge of a lip. He desperately wanted to share, to hear me empathize, to feel justified in his fantasies.

A problem shared isn't always a problem halved.

I knew better than to pick sides. Sometimes an innocent nod in the wrong place can lead to bad consequences.

"Well, that's a pity," he murmured, "because they came out pretty good." He offered me a brief smile. "Revealing, if you know what I mean? Maybe I'll e-mail you copies."

It wouldn't be a first.

"So, anyway," he continued as he stuffed the phone away, "I was at Home Depot yesterday. I needed new blades for my jigsaw. But I kept getting distracted, thinking about all the ways I could kill her. Next thing I know, I'm staring at the power tools, wondering which would cause her the most pain."

"What did you do?"

"I picked up one of those big industrial-sized wood chippers."

"Gus . . ."

"Doc, it's not what you think. It was on a special price reduction. It would've been remiss of me not to take advantage. Saved myself a hundred bucks on the regular price."

For a moment, I imagined the shrill mechanical whir of steel blades. Soft flesh succumbing to jagged rotors, tearing, shredding. Muscles pulping. Blood spraying. Bone splintering. Mrs. Toomey's spine-chilling screams as her husband feeds her feetfirst into the chipper.

I shook the gruesome image from my head.

The clock on the wall said it was exactly 5:00.

I closed the notepad with a snap. "Gus, I'm sorry to cut you off right here—"

"So don't."

"But I'm afraid we're out of time."

He fingered a money clip from out of his shirt pocket. "So let me pay for the extra hour. Just name it. I'm not done with you yet."

I got to my feet. "I appreciate the offer. But the money isn't the issue, Gus. I have a prior engagement. I'm sorry." I retreated behind my desk and opened up my planner. "But I promise we'll continue this at your next appointment. You've made real progress here today. Sharing is just the beginning. It's all about keeping things in perspective. We will work on this some more. Just don't do anything illegal in the meantime. Okay?"

"Sure, sure."

Another far-too-quick confirmation.

Toomey pushed himself to his feet and smoothed down his shirt. There were sweat patches under the arms and a distinct musky odor wafting my way. "Doc, you won't tell anybody we discussed this, will you?"

I looked up from the planner. "Like the police, for instance?"

"I was thinking more like my wife."

I smiled reassuringly. "Gus, listen to me. There's nothing wrong with having these kinds of fantasies. We all do. So long as you don't act on them, they're perfectly natural."

Toomey's eyes narrowed, and for a second I was unsure if he was despondent or desperate, or even dangerous.

I put a finger on the planner. "How does Friday, same time, sound to you?"

"Okay, I guess."

"You sure? If you like, I can call you if I get a cancellation before then."

"No, no. Friday will be great. Just pencil me in."

I pulled a business card out of a holder. "Here're my numbers. If there's anything at all you want to talk about in the meantime, don't hesitate. I mean it, Gus. Use me."

Toomey reached over, plucked the card from my hand, and slid it into his breast pocket without looking at it.

"We can fix this," I called after him as he let himself out.

But experience had taught me that people like Toomey hardly ever come back, and sometimes I got to read about them in the paper.

Nevertheless, I penciled his name in the planner.

Two minutes later, I was skipping down the wooden steps outside the health center, with not a single neuron dedicated to Gus Toomey and his wood chipper. My thoughts were focused solely on Zoe and where the rest of the evening would take us.

In fact, I was so absorbed in my thoughts of her that I barely noticed the gray-haired African American man leaning against the hood of a dark sedan, only fully registering his presence when he called out:

"It is you, right?"

I slowed automatically, squinting at him in the early evening sun-shine. He looked to be in his late sixties, thin, with one of those grainy faces that looks like it's been chiseled from a cinder block. He wore a black button-down shirt tucked neatly into black dress pants, with brogues shone to mirrorlike perfection.

"Excuse me?" I said.

"You're the guy I'm looking for. Greg Cole. Right?"

Now I stopped altogether, a few feet from my car. "Do I know you?"

He pushed himself up off the hood and strolled over. "Great picture of you in the brochure, by the way."

"Thanks."

"It says you do talk therapy."

"That's right. And if it's an appointment you need—"

He raised a halting hand. "No, thank you. The last shrink I saw bled me dry and almost cost me my marriage."

"Oh. I'm sorry to hear that." I took out my car keys and jangled them. "Well, if you're not looking to book an appointment, I really need to be on my way."

"Sure. I understand." But it didn't stop him blocking my path. "You youngsters are always rushing around. Always got to be someplace else, and usually in a hurry." He jabbed a thumb toward the service directory board standing at the corner of the lot. "For the record, you threw me a curveball with the listing."

"Oh?"

"Well, I noticed you changed it. Your name, that is. You swapped it around from Gregory Cole to Cole Gregory. Same in the brochure, too." He placed a hand on the trunk of my car. "I have to say, I like it. Gives you a well-heeled first impression. But I have to be honest with you. In my experience, most people change their name only if they're running away from something."

Suspicious, I looked sideways at him. "Who did you say you were?"

"Oh, excuse me." He dipped a hand in a pocket and rummaged around for a while, his tongue performing the same oscillations against his inner cheek. "Oh, here we go." He flashed an ID card. "The name's O'Malley. I work with the sheriff's office."

I went around to the driver's door. "Well, that's great. The sheriff's office and I have a good relationship. What's this about? Did I run another red?"

He dropped the ID back in the bottomless pocket. "Well, I don't know about that, and I certainly hope not. Running reds can be a very dangerous pastime."

"I was joking."

"I know. Actually, Mr. Cole." He paused. "Am I safe calling you Mr. Cole?"

"I think so. It's my name."

"But the service directory—"

"It's a mistake."

The sign maker had gotten it wrong. I hadn't noticed right away. How often does anyone actually read their own entry on an office listing? A month had passed before somebody had pointed it out, by which time people had already made repeat appointments with the receptionist to see Cole Gregory. It was an honest mistake and one I didn't reverse, simply because that would have meant losing face and maybe losing business. So the name had stuck. I'd even updated my online business presence to match it, with billboards around town showing a smiling Cole Gregory, your local talk therapist.

The man calling himself O'Malley nodded. "In your line of business, does it constitute a Freudian slip?"

"No." I popped the locks.

"But you are a psychiatrist, right?"

"Psychotherapist," I corrected. "There's a difference."

I could see he wasn't sure what that difference was. Not many people are, not at first. Incredibly, neither are some of those in the profession itself.

O'Malley smiled, revealing a gold molar. "To be perfectly honest, Mr. Cole, anything with the word *psycho* in the title gives me the jitters."

I pulled open the car door. "Then I take it you're not a Hitchcock fan?"

"Oh, on the contrary. Now that you mention it, *Vertigo* is my all-time favorite film. Jimmy Stewart is just sensational in that movie, don't you think? I never tire of his acting. That chase scene over the rooftops, and where he realizes Kim Novak is a fake: simply breathtaking. It's real life that gives me the willies."

I tossed my messenger bag on the passenger seat.

O'Malley came over and put a hand on the rim of the door. "Mr. Cole, do you mind if I ask you a quick question before you leave? I promise I won't keep you any longer than absolutely necessary."

I pulled at the door, but he resisted. "Which department did you say you work in?" I asked.

In my job, I am trained to observe, and something about O'Malley didn't feel right. As far as appearances went, he didn't fit the typical image of a Southwest Florida detective, at least none I had ever met. No summer suit with pastel shirt and loafers. No Ray-Bans hooked over his breast pocket. If anything, he looked like he'd just tap-danced his way out of a jazz-and-blues club.

"Actually, Mr. Cole," he began, "I believe I may have given you the wrong impression from the get-go."

"Oh?"

"I never said I worked for the sheriff. That would be untrue and an error on my part. It's true, on occasion, I do work *with* the sheriff, plus all the other police agencies, usually on an as-needed basis, but I'm not actually employed by them." He saw my developing frown and added, "Relax. I'm not here to hustle you, Mr. Cole. I'm a professional investigator."

"A private detective?"

"Going on thirty years. Fully licensed. And good at it, too, if I may say so myself."

Suddenly, I had visions of a disgruntled spouse keeping tabs on a philandering husband, and O'Malley spying on my office through binoculars, watching the comings and goings of one of my many male clients who confessed to an extramarital affair, only to swear his wife was oblivious, or worse still, fine with it.

"Please let go of my door."

Reluctantly, O'Malley unhooked his fingers.

I pulled the door fully open, climbed inside, and started the engine. "You do know I'm sworn to patient confidentiality?"

"That I do. And I'm the first to respect your Hippocratic oath. But I think our wires may have gone and gotten themselves crossed all over again. I'm not here because of one of your clients, Mr. Cole. I'm here to see you." He leaned in a little. "I need to ask you something."

I let out an impatient sigh. "You've got ten seconds."

He smiled toothily. "All I need is five." He drew a deep breath and held my gaze. "This is out of personal curiosity, Mr. Cole. Definitively, and without risk of any mix-up this time, did you kill your sister?"

Chapter Two

On a stormy night ten years ago, lightning had struck, splitting my world in half and changing the course of my life forever.

The day had started out innocently enough, with no hint of the tragic events that would unfold and brand themselves indelibly into my brain.

I'd gone about my business on that fateful day as usual, with no knowledge that my universe was on the brink of imploding.

Fancifully, I had thought I would feel the exact moment if anything ever happened to Scarlett, even if she wasn't nearby. Some kind of immense magnetic disturbance as our two hemispheres divided and went their separate ways.

I had thought I'd sense *something*.

But the sky had fallen and I'd slept through it like a baby.

When I'd woken the next morning, I'd done so in a dislocated world of dimmed daylight and diluted colors, a sodden world, feeling like I was a castaway on an alien planet. Knowing that the person closest to you in the whole world is dead can do that kind of thing.

My twin sister was gone, and life would never be the same again.

"What can I get you?"

It took a moment to refocus, and I rematerialized back in the present with cool sweat prickling under my arms and my heart jackhammering crazily behind my ribs.

This is how it is when I think too long and hard about Scarlett.

"You looked like you were having a moment there. Everything okay?"

The question came from a young bartender with a bushy beard and a trendy samurai bun.

"Yeah, thanks," I said. But the truth was, things were far from okay. I never intend to burden, and so I offered him a weak smile as way of compensation.

I was at Donovan's, in the thick of a happy-hour crowd, hoping to blend in with the fake-rustic atmosphere.

"Can I get you a drink?" he asked.

I pulled myself together and slid onto a high-backed stool, using my shirtsleeve to wipe cool sweat from my face. "Guinness," I said. My voice sounded reedy.

Donovan's is an Irish pub, a quarter mile from my office on the beach road. Actually, I'm lying. Donovan's isn't an Irish pub at all. It only pretends to be an Irish pub—or some homegrown designer's impression of one—complete with its clichéd lucky-clover theme and U2's greatest hits stacked high in the jukebox. Before it was a faux Irish pub, it was a fast-food outlet, and before it was a fast-food outlet it was an electronics store, selling cheap Japanese cameras made in China. I imagine there's a Donovan's clone in every touristy town, promoting old-country nostalgia and something altogether earthier than ourselves. For some reason, we all love the Irish, even when we don't have a drop of Gaelic blood in our veins.

I held on to the wooden bar top, comforted slightly by the feel of the grain, its solidity, and its connection with the ground.

Guardedly, I scanned the busy bar.

A soccer game was being shown on a big flat-screen TV in the adjoining lounge, drawing most of the attention.

I let out a superheated breath.

I didn't want to think about O'Malley's killer question, or his searching gaze as I'd driven out of the parking lot like the devil was on my tail. But I did. It was impossible not to.

Scarlett and I were more than close. We were inseparable. For us, it was all we knew. Circumstances had decided it for us long before we were old enough to know any differently.

I saw the bartender glance my way as he pulled a pair of glasses out of a drying crate, and I smiled weakly again.

He showed me both empty options. "Eight-ounce or sixteen?"

I pointed to the pint glass, then added as an afterthought, "Make that two."

He lined up the glasses and began the slow pouring process. *Don't rush the black stuff*, I thought. But he'd noticed my bloodless face and my stricken eyes, and he couldn't help being curious.

It's ridiculous, I know, that the merest mention of my sister sends me into a full-blown panic attack.

"Rough day?" he asked.

"Death in the family," I told him, hoping it would be enough to prevent him from delving any deeper. It usually works.

"My condolences."

Aptly, U2's "With or Without You" started seesawing from the speakers over the bar.

I got out my phone and checked the time—5:14 p.m.—then peered through the happy-hour throng toward the main doors, hoping to spy Zoe working her way over.

It's no coincidence we'd arranged to meet here.

Zoe and I first met at Donovan's six months ago. It was a birthday celebration. One of her colleagues had hit the big four-oh and wanted to drown his sorrows. He'd brought along a raucous crowd to help him achieve his goal. I was propping up the bar after a long day of picking at brains, minding my own business but happy to observe. It's what I do. I people-watch. I do it more than I should. Most of the time I'm not even aware I'm doing it. It sounds creepy, I know, but you won't find me hanging out in the park, loitering behind trees, or glued to a telescope, peering into people's bedrooms from a high window. I do it everywhere I go, because human behavior interests me, and because it takes me away from my own thoughts.

But people-watching can be dangerous.

I was ten years old when the guy in the local park came over and punched me in the face, for no apparent reason, his big fist falling like an iron meteor, knocking me off my feet. I'd blacked out under the force of the blow. When I'd regained consciousness, he was gone and so, too, was one of my front teeth.

At first, dazed and dumbstruck, I had no idea why he'd walked over and hit me; I was too busy bawling and running home with blood and tears streaming down my face. What kind of man goes up to a boy he doesn't know and strikes him in the mouth? It was only as I grew older and became more socially aware that I realized what had brought on his seemingly unprovoked attack. Absentmindedly, I'd been watching him yelling at his wife while she cowered over a bright-red stroller, trying to hush him, to stop him from waking the baby. He'd seen me gawking, and I was an easy target, rage giving way to release.

These days, I try to do my observing more discreetly.

So there I was six months ago, watching the partygoers here in Donovan's, subconsciously mapping out their movements and noting how the Big Four-Oh had interacted with each of his coconspirators, when a woman's voice had sounded at the bar:

"Save me?"

I had been so wrapped up in watching her colleagues trying to outdrink each other that I hadn't noticed her slide onto the stool next to me, or the fact that she was leaning my way and staring at me with big brown inviting eyes. Heat came off her, bringing with it an edible scent of pomegranate.

I'd blinked. "Save you from what exactly?"

"From doing something I'd regret, like starting a fistfight."

Then I'd smiled. She was small, almost petite. Five four, with short black hair styled in a pixie cut, and hands that didn't look like they'd seen much in the way of any hard labor, let alone bare-knuckled fighting.

Still smiling, I'd said, "It's a boisterous crowd all right, but you don't look like you need saving. I've been watching you. Take your pick—you can run rings around any of these players."

She'd glanced at her colleagues and muttered something that might have countered my remark before saying, "In my line of work, a girl needs to be two things: faster and smarter. It's the only way to get ahead without giving head." Then her dark eyes had swung back to me and an inquisitive eyebrow had hiked itself up. "So you've been watching me," she said. "Should I be concerned? Are you a psycho?"

I'd laughed. "You're only half-right." I'd kept my smile in place, trying to sound funny, before realizing from her expression that I didn't. "I'm a psychotherapist."

"All one word?"

"I hope so."

"Jesus. I'm sorry. I had high expectations there for a moment. Meeting a psychotic therapist sounds way more interesting, and I could do with the attention right now."

We'd laughed. It had felt good.

"Zoe, by the way." She'd stuck out a small hand.

I'd shaken it gently. "Greg."

"So, which is it—gay, straight, or undecided?"

"Excuse me?"

"Your sexual preference."

"I know what you mean. I'm just shocked you asked, is all."

"Hey, a girl needs to be informed. Right from the get-go. Life's too short to be indirect."

"Straight as an arrow."

"Perfect. Me too. How's that for a coincidence? Although I'm open to persuasion if the right deal presents itself. You know what I mean?"

I'd looked at her with one eyebrow raised.

She'd tittered, then asked, "You with someone, Greg?"

"I guess I could be, if this works out."

"Good answer."

"Thanks."

We'd clinked beer glasses together.

"Okay. Let's get this party started." She'd nodded at the Guinness warming in my hand. "Ready for another? Your glass is half-empty."

"Depends on how you look at it."

"Clever."

She'd gone on to summon the bartender and order drinks before I could protest. Not that I would have objected in any case. Zoe has this habit of getting her own way. It isn't textbook manipulation and it isn't brute force, but it accomplishes the same goal. Men are mules. On any given day, a woman like Zoe knows how to steer her mule in the direction she chooses, and we go along without too much fuss because the thought of tasting the carrot is too tempting to ignore.

So we'd chatted, our tongues lubricated by the black stuff, getting to know as much about each other as two people could do in a bar full of noisy partiers. Briefly, she'd told me what she did for a living—although it hadn't taken a brain surgeon to figure it out—and I'd told her about my therapy practice, after which she'd insisted on calling me Doc. I didn't object; it's what most people do.

Eventually, and to the tune of Van Morrison's "Brown Eyed Girl," she'd leaned into me and pressed her damp lips against my ear, whispering drunkenly, "Say, do you want to get out of here and go someplace quieter? I think my brain's about to melt."

"Sure. Anywhere particular in mind?"

"Bed?"

Like I was saying: straight for the kill.

From that night on, every weak molecule inside me was attracted to Zoe.

And drinking at Donovan's became something of a weekly ritual.

"Busy crowd tonight," the bearded and bunned bartender commented, refocusing me back in the present. "World Cup warm-up between Ireland and Belarus."

I raised my chin in acknowledgment, pretending I knew who or what Belarus was, and that soccer meant something to me other than a second-tier sport.

"You here for the game?"

I shook my head.

"Too bad." He placed a perfectly poured pint of Guinness on the bar top. "Promises to be a good one. All drinks half-price."

"Thanks." I wrapped my fingers around the cold glass. The shape of a four-leaf clover was carved into the thick foam head.

"Number two coming up."

I touched my lips to the froth and slurped some of the malty black stuff through it.

My phone rang on the bar top. I picked up, sensing the world's brightness control turn up a notch when I saw the name glowing on the screen. "Hi, Zoe," I said as I answered. "Where are you?"

"About to leave the office." She sounded slightly breathy.

"You're running late."

"I know, and I'm sorry."

"No worry. Your beer is just being poured." I took another sip of my own.

"Yet one more reason why I feel extremely bad about canceling."

Immediately, I felt my whole frame slump under the weight of her words.

In the six months since that first night with Zoe, for the most part it had been great. Nothing too intense. No expectations other than a promise to be ourselves and not to put undue demands on the other. Mostly, great sex.

I leaned heavy elbows on the bar top and unsuccessfully tried to keep the mope from my voice. "You can't make it?"

"Not tonight. There's been a development, and something's come up. I was meaning to call you earlier, but you know how it is."

"Okay. So, what about breakfast?" I tried injecting a little cheer into the words, but my real mood was tainting everything. "I'll bring coffee and crepes."

"You don't do crepes."

"But you do. And I can learn, or die faking it."

I heard her smile creakily. "You'd eat crepes for me?"

"On second thought, I may take a rain check on that."

"I can't, anyway. Not for the next day or two. Can you hold out until Friday?"

My runaway fun train came to a screeching halt.

"Let me check my planner." I took another slurp of the Guinness and savored it, deliberately taking my time and being childishly obstinate.

I don't know why it bothered me—Zoe canceling—as much as it did, but it did. Ordinarily, I can cope for a few days without seeing her. But O'Malley's intrusion into my personal life had put me on edge. His question had wormed its way under my skin and left me itchy. Zoe's company was the perfect salve. Only, I wouldn't be getting it now.

I took another long swig of the beer. It was cold enough to make an Inuit's teeth chatter. Then I wiped the creamy froth from my upper lip. "I can squeeze you in," I said, "just about . . . now."

"You're pissed."

"Disappointed."

"Doc . . ."

"Aw, come on, Zoe. I have a right to feel at least a little bit abandoned—it's been nine days, for Chrissake. But, hey, who's counting?"

One or two of the nearest patrons glanced my way, looking for the source of the infantile outburst. I turned and hunched over the phone.

In my ear, I heard Zoe say, "You sound like a lovesick teenager."

"Maybe I am. We made arrangements. You made a promise. Don't make me hold you to it."

"We don't do this to each other."

"Do what?"

"Pick a fight. We said we wouldn't do this, put pressure on each other to commit. Friday will be here before we know it. I will make it up to you, Doc. And *that's* a promise."

Voices sounded in the background with her, and I pulled back on my pushiness. Thinking of Scarlett had gotten me feeling more than slightly possessive, I realized, which was something I normally avoided being with Zoe. Possession implies ownership. I'd felt possessive over my sister, but I hadn't owned her, and I don't own Zoe. I'm not sure anyone could. I know her husband has no hold on her.

I took a mouthful of icy beer and washed down my sourness. "I'm being an unreasonable asshole, aren't I?"

"In a word."

"Just ignore me, okay? I've had a weird day."

"You're forgiven—we all have them. Listen, I hate doing this, but I have to go."

I forced a smile. Zoe is the epitome of conscientious. And that's what keeps us apart so often.

"Call me Friday?" I said.

"The minute I'm home."

I went to tell her how much I missed her, but she had already said her good-byes and hung up.

I pushed the cell back onto the bar top, wallowing in a self-pity that didn't quite stick.

"Happens to the best of us," the bartender said as he placed the second glass of Guinness next to the first. This time, he'd sculpted a smiley face into the froth. "They're either busy saving injured birds or can't find anything to wear. This one's on the house."

Chapter Three

Two hours after speaking with Zoe, I was standing next to my car in Donovan's parking lot, swaying dangerously and squinting at the setting sun, unable to make a decision or remember exactly what decision I was supposed to be making.

This is what happens to an overheated brain when you soak it in eight pints of beer in a short space of time.

"Now here's a pleasant surprise."

I pivoted unsteadily on my heels to see O'Malley approaching across the blacktop, brogues clacking against the asphalt.

"Is this some kind of a sick joke?" I demanded drunkenly. I even waggled a reproving finger to make my point.

"Funny," he answered, "but I don't hear anybody laughing. In fact, Mr. Cole, your sister's murder is a very serious matter, as you already know all too vividly. If you ask me, anyone who makes fun of something as tragic as a sibling's untimely death needs his brain examined. But you already know that, too."

I narrowed my eyes at him; I'd had way too much to drink, and he was talking too much. The two didn't mix very well.

"Who won the match?" he asked.

"Match?"

He nodded toward a chalkboard hanging on the wall next to Donovan's main entrance. "The advertised soccer game."

"You know what—I have no idea." I didn't; I'd been too busy pickling brain cells and feeling sorry for myself to notice. Vaguely, I had noticed an aftertaste of cheering and jeering and maybe the sound of a beer glass breaking.

"Now I wish I'd come down sooner," O'Malley lamented.

"You don't strike me as a soccer fan."

"I don't? Well, I'll be damned. Look at me, Mr. Cole. With a name like O'Malley, I'm as Black Irish as the Guinness."

I grunted and pulled at the door handle of my car, but the door refused to budge. I pulled harder, until my fingers sprang off, leaving the fingertips stinging.

"It's locked," O'Malley pointed out matter-of-factly. "Where'd you put the keys?"

I patted my pockets and screwed up my forehead, trying to remember something I couldn't.

It's not often I drink alone and even less often that I let myself get wasted. Usually, neither is in public.

O'Malley was watching with a slight hint of amusement. "Well, I'm guessing they must have confiscated them back in the bar. Come on—I'll drive you home." He reached out a helping hand.

I batted it away. "No, thanks. This constitutes borderline harassment, O'Malley. Right here." My finger was waggling again, aimlessly.

"Mr. Cole, you're clearly in no fit state to drive. In fact, I don't believe you could even make it on foot. Let me help you home. It's no trouble at all."

I stood my uneven ground. "What exactly are you doing here, O'Malley? This isn't on any tourist map. Have you been following me?"

"Nothing of the sort. Would you believe I just came to get a quiet drink with a friendly crowd? The hotel concierge recommended this place. You're the last person I expected to run into."

"I'll bet." I gave him a skeptical look to back it up. "Do you know how to jimmy a lock?"

"I'm not breaking into your car for you, if that's what you mean."

"It's just that I figured with you being—"

"A black man?"

"I was going to say, with you being a private eye you might know how to go about it. But never mind. I'll call a cab." I started checking my pockets again, hopelessly looking for my phone.

"Mr. Cole, let me give you that ride. My car's right here." He motioned to a black sedan parked a couple of spaces away. "It's the least I can do."

I heard a disapproving grunt gargle in my throat. "Then cut the BS and just level with me, O'Malley. Why would you even do it?"

"Because I'm the charitable kind."

"I mean, why would you even ask, earlier, about my sister?"

"Two reasons, I guess: I'm thorough, and I love a good mystery."

"Oh, that's right. You're a Hitchcock fan." I pressed a damp palm against the driver's-side window, tried to slide it down with brute force.

"Plus, we have something in common."

"Yeah?" I peered through the glass, as though O'Malley were mistaken and I'd see the keys dangling from the ignition.

"We both exhume people's skeletons for a living."

Now I turned with a scowl. "Who did you say you work for?"

"I didn't, I won't, and you know better than to ask. You're not the only one who enjoys client confidentiality. Now, come on—let's get you home before you make a fool of yourself."

I shook him off. "Show me that ID of yours again."

Sighing, he rummaged it out and handed it over.

I blinked at the card, trying to focus in the fading light.

"Please forgive the dubious close-up," O'Malley said. "I had a terrible stomach flu that day and wasn't at my best. Plus, I don't happen to be very photogenic, as you can see."

I squinted at the monochrome image engraved into the card. It was a standard driver's license photo showing a stony-faced man with brooding eyes and a suggestion of discomfort. Someone who didn't like being on the business end of a camera. "This license has a Jacksonville address."

"Which stands to reason, Mr. Cole, since that's where I live."

I looked up too fast and swayed. "Wait a second. Just . . . wait a second here. You came all the way down here from Jacksonville?" It came out like I was remarking on a physical impossibility, as though O'Malley had teleported to Bonita Springs.

"As a matter of fact, I did. First thing this morning. Booked myself into a nice hotel over on Trail's Edge for the night. I'm heading back first thing tomorrow. It's not that far, Mr. Cole. Six hours tops, including a couple of pit stops."

"Why?"

"Because when you get to my age, you are slave to your bladder."

"No, I mean why come here in person? Haven't you heard of the telephone?"

"Sure. But like you, I'm a people person. I work best doing business face to face. And you can only learn so much about a person from their social media profiles. Besides, there was the issue with your business name, how you swapped it around, and my client wanted to make absolutely sure it was you before he . . ."

"Before he what, O'Malley?"

He reached over and plucked the ID card from my hand. "Before I say too much and get myself in trouble. That's what. Now come on, Mr. Cole. Stop playing hardball and let's get you home. It'll soon be dark. It would be unchristian of me to abandon you here like this."

"It's a safe neighborhood, and I'd rather walk." I almost fell flat on my face with my first unsteady step.

O'Malley caught me and set me upright. He was stronger than he looked, solid, with fingers like spring clamps.

"Recognizing our limitations doesn't limit us," he said as he walked me over to his car. "It empowers us to try harder."

"Who said that? Confucius?"

"My wife. She knows all the one-liners and isn't afraid to use them."

He opened the passenger door, and I spilled onto the seat like a tipped bag of groceries.

The world spun, and I let it.

A minute later, we were headed west on Bonita Beach Road, driving toward a golden sky alchemizing into copper.

"This doesn't make us friends," I groused as I fumbled the sun visor down.

"I didn't expect it would."

"I won't be inviting you in for a nightcap."

O'Malley chuckled. "I guess I owe you an apology, Mr. Cole."

"Oh?"

"It wasn't my intention to ruffle your feathers back there, or at the office earlier, regarding your sister."

"You accused me of murder. Please consider my feathers entirely ruffled."

"I only asked the question. I didn't imply actual guilt."

"Semantics."

"Maybe. And maybe I need to work on my delivery. My wife says I can be a little too verbose at times. She says I could talk the ears off a brass statue."

"She sounds like a wise woman."

"She's the best. And I'm better for it. Anyway, the good news is, you were genuinely shocked by my question, and in my book that's a good thing."

"Thanks for the vote of confidence."

"I'm serious, Mr. Cole. I've been around the block a number of times. I've learned to read all the signs. The odds are, if you were guilty of your sister's murder, you would've shut me down and threatened me with legal action. Defamation of character and all that jazz. But you didn't. Instead, you clammed up and hightailed it."

I released a rattling breath. "There are no old heroes. And Eve says I'm allergic to conflict."

"Eve?"

"It's a long story. She's the reason I'm here."

"Ah, your date. The one you were rushing off to meet at the Irish pub. Your love interest."

"Not quite." I didn't bother correcting him, to explain about my platonic relationship with Eve, or to tell him that Zoe had stood me up and that's why I'd ended up drinking more than I should. "She says I employ diversionary tactics."

O'Malley nodded. "Women. They have all the answers. Puts us men to shame, don't it? I guess diversionary tactics come with the territory, you being a counselor and all. I'm betting you spend most of your time creating detours for your clients. Wouldn't surprise me in the slightest if some of that good advice wore off on you."

We slowed for the intersection with US 41, then stopped completely. Rush hour had faded with the daylight, but this crossroads was always busy, jammed with red and white lights running four ways.

"What made you choose Florida?" he asked speculatively.

"I'm sorry?"

"As opposed to staying in Michigan?"

Florida was Eve's idea. If I'd followed my own broken compass, I would surely have gone around in circles. *Plenty of off-axis people to fill your new psychotherapy practice,* she'd said. That's what Eve calls anyone who seeks the help of a counselor: *off-axis*. As though they are somehow a subset, which is strange considering Eve herself is often full tilt.

"The boating," I said in answer to O'Malley's question. "It's exceptional."

"You're right, I guess. You hear it said there are three kinds of people down here: golfers, boaters, and those who are running away from their past."

I turned my face to the side window, mainly because I didn't want O'Malley to pick up on my reddening cheeks. He wasn't too wide of the mark. I wanted him to be. I didn't want O'Malley to be right on the money with anything about me. But he was, and I couldn't change it.

The signal glowed green, and the bumper-to-bumper traffic started accelerating through the intersection. We went with it. Lights popped on in the strip malls as twilight painted violet brushstrokes on the coppery canvas.

"What's really going on here, O'Malley?" I blurted. "Who do you work for?" My tipsy impatience was out in front and leading the way. "Is it Murdoch? Is that what this is all about? This little masquerade. Is this Murdoch's way of playing with me? Did he put you up to this? Are you even a real private eye?"

O'Malley glanced my way. "Mr. Cole, we both know I'm not at liberty to discuss—"

"Bullshit!" It came out ahead of a belch, which lessened its severity. "What's in this for you?"

"Aside from an all-expenses-paid overnight stay and the promise of a fat paycheck when all this is over? Nothing. My only purview was to confirm your identity visually."

We turned off the beach road and onto Imperial Shores. The deepening dusk had transformed the leafy lane into a dark tunnel with an indigo crack running along the roof. We drove past the darkened American Legion and houses with their porch lights on.

I sat up a little straighter. It was an effort; my melon head had begun to feel squishy.

O'Malley slowed the car for the turn onto Esplanade Street. Then we followed the bend as it curled past quiet homes before pulling up to the threshold of a driveway belonging to a modest-sized dwelling sitting on a corner plot.

"Home sweet home," he remarked as the car came to a stop. "Looks like you found yourself a nice place here, Mr. Cole."

I blinked at the Spanish-style two-story house, with its creamy stucco walls and its olive-green shingles, wondering what Eve would think about my coming home drunk.

Before leaving Michigan's Upper Peninsula, Eve and I hadn't picked out a new place to call home. Where we ended up was based less on popularity and more on suitability.

Growing up on the rivers and lakes of the UP had left their mark on me, *in me*, and I couldn't picture myself anywhere arid. Plus, I wanted to start my own therapy practice, migrating my skills to a location wealthy enough to provide a respectable flow of troubled clients, but not someplace so upmarket that it would inundate me with boorish snobs.

Bonita Springs had delivered on both counts.

O'Malley was admiring the view. "It must be something else, living in paradise. I have to say, it's a far cry from my neighborhood. How much does a place like this cost these days?"

Luckily, I'd had money in the bank, and Eve had had an inheritance. Neither could have been considered a fortune, but together it was enough to put down a decent deposit and see me through the first year's rent for office space. And with what was left, I'd bought myself a boat.

"I'm guessing it backs onto the river?"

I opened the door. "Good night, O'Malley."

"Wait," he said. "There's something else you should know."

"I think we're done talking here." I started to get out.

"You'll want to hear this. It's about Zane Murdoch."

I froze, which isn't an easy achievement in Florida.

Even so, I had ice in my belly.

O'Malley must have seen the blood drain from my face, but it didn't stop him from pulling out his phone and bringing up an image on the screen. "Go ahead, Mr. Cole. Take it. Take a good look. Take as long as you like."

I did, with shaky fingers and the chill rising.

It was the picture of a man, taken outside, at a gas station on a rainy evening. He was standing at a pump, filling the tank of a black Subaru pickup truck. He wore a red plaid shirt over baggy jeans, and a permanent scowl I'd learned to know and loathe. He was older than the last time I'd seen him. Ten years older. My age. Fuller, meaner. But his identity was unmistakable.

"My client wanted you to see this," O'Malley was saying. "It was taken this morning, at the Sunoco in Gulliver, on US 2. You know the one?"

I nodded tightly, as though someone had their hands clamped around my head and was moving it back and forth against my will. The gas station was a few miles east of Manistique, my hometown, back in Michigan.

With hesitant fingers, I pinch-zoomed until the man's head filled the screen. I didn't want it to be him—Zane Murdoch—but even in the grainy magnification there was no mistaking his face. For years, that mean glare had tattooed itself on the inside of my eyelids, where it had stared at me, inescapable, whenever I'd tried to sleep. A face that had sneered at me all the way through the murder trial, with spiteful lips that had silently mouthed the words *I'm coming for you* every time our gazes had met.

The chill shook me visibly, and O'Malley saw it.

"How is this possible?" My voice sounded strained, distant, like it was coming from somebody bundled in the trunk. "Murdoch's serving a life sentence in Marquette."

"Was."

I glanced up, quick enough to make everything spin. O'Malley was watching my reaction like someone who had baited a hook with the juiciest worm and was keen to see what bit.

"You look surprised."

"Damn right I am."

"They didn't notify you?"

"Who?"

"The Schoolcraft County Prosecutor's Office."

"No. Should they have? No! No one's told me anything! What's going on here?"

"Somebody messed up. That's what. I thought you'd know by now."

I shook the phone at him. "What the hell kind of trick is this, O'Malley?"

"No trick, Mr. Cole. This is exactly what it looks like. And I'm sorry you had to hear it from me first. There was a recent petition against Mr. Murdoch's conviction, and in their infinite wisdom, the Michigan Court of Appeals vacated his sentence."

The chill frosted my throat.

"Mr. Murdoch was acquitted of your sister's murder on the spot and subsequently released with a full pardon and the promise of a hefty financial compensation package."

I tried not to let my jaw drop open, but the weight of O'Malley's revelation pulled it down and took my freezing stomach with it. "How?"

"To tell you the truth, I'm not in possession of all the facts. It's my understanding his lawyer presented new and incontrovertible evidence. Something the court couldn't ignore."

"Evidence? I don't understand. The guilty verdict was unanimous. Murdoch killed Scarlett." My breath was icy, and a foggy darkness had begun to creep into the edges of my vision, like blood soaking into cotton.

"Trust me, Mr. Cole, you're not the only one surprised by the rul-ing. I've read the court transcripts. It was a textbook slam-dunk of a case if there ever was one. Including yourself, you had several credible eyewitnesses testifying that they heard Mr. Murdoch make sincere death threats against you and your sister in the weeks and days before her murder. Then, after an anonymous tip, the police recovered what they believed to be the murder weapon in Mr. Murdoch's trash, wrapped in her bloodied shirt. Add that to the fact that he failed to offer an alibi for the night she disappeared and, like I said, it's a slam-dunk."

"Only now they've overturned his conviction."

"Sucks, don't it?" He reached over and swapped the phone in my limp grasp for a business card. "Here're my details. Like I said, I'll be staying overnight on Trail's Edge. It's not exactly the Ritz, but it comes with complimentary breakfast and make-your-own waffles, and that's a bonus for a guy like me. Give me a call if you want to meet up. Otherwise, I'll be heading home in the morning."

Wordlessly, I slipped the card into my pocket.

Then I leaned out of the car, facedown, and shuddered as regurgitated Guinness splashed the pavement.

Chapter Four

Well-wishers will tell you that wounds heal over time.
Don't believe them.

The only thing time heals is other people's memories. Surprisingly soon, they forget about your tragedy. They move on. They forget that your pain is as constant as your heartbeat.

Give it time, they say. *Things will get easier,* they say.

I can't remember how many times a well-intentioned family friend or a sincerely concerned observer assured me of this so-called "fact."

You'll get over it. You have a future. You'll be okay.

It's all a lie.

Just about the only piece of bereavement advice that made any sense had come from Eve. I have known Eve all my life, but before she entered into it on a permanent basis, I was fully withdrawn into my shell, not even leaving the house or taking calls. I guess you could say, in my own way, I'd already run away to another state: one of inactivity. In her youth, she, too, had experienced emotional trauma and survived a grief that mirrored my own. She'd seen me destroying my life and had felt compelled to act.

She'd said, *The best way to honor Scarlett's life is not to flush yours down the toilet.*

So we'd run away to Florida, to begin our lives anew, ending up here, on the Imperial River.

For ten years, it was the perfect getaway.

I'd blended in, become part of the community.

No one from back home knew we were here.

Until now.

I lingered in the driveway, with dark spots in my vision and frost in my throat, as the taillights belonging to O'Malley's car disappeared into the thickening dusk.

Partly, it was the beer making me light-headed and woozy. Mostly, it was the impact of O'Malley's revelation on my nervous system.

I dropped to my haunches, then onto my butt on the Bahia grass, then onto my back.

I knew what was coming. I knew it was unlikely I could stop it. It hadn't happened in a long, long time. But here it came: an old, familiar enemy.

Around me, the whole darkening world was narrowing, as though I were seeing it through a tunnel. Everything was trembling, made out of Jell-O. My ears were ringing, pulsating.

Any second now . . .

The darkness rushed in and, despite my vain effort not to hyper-ventilate, I blacked out. Right there, half on the sandy roadway, half on the coarse grass. My DNA winning out over logic, my self-preservation not in the least bit interested in saving face.

Chapter Five

I landed back in reality with a bump, beneath the black bowl of
night, with a sour taste of vomit drying on my lips and no idea
how long I'd lain here, unconscious of time and the universe
expanding.

Weakly, I staggered to my feet and waited for the world to take
shape.

I didn't go in the house right away. I looked around at the quiet
street instead, at its indistinct features concealed by darkness, trying
to force the alcohol out of my blood so that I had a fighting chance of
processing O'Malley's news.

His questioning my involvement in Scarlett's death wasn't what
bothered me. The matter of my innocence wasn't an issue. Even in my
inebriated state, I knew where I stood on that score. In time, even the
thought of Zane Murdoch being released was something I could learn
to live with. But it didn't mean I had to be happy about it. I didn't know
what kind of incontrovertible evidence had come to light—O'Malley
had neglected to say—but the Michigan Court of Appeals had accepted
it as unequivocal proof of Murdoch's false imprisonment, and I couldn't
argue with that. Sure, I could look into it, and probably would once my
head cleared, but it wouldn't make any difference. What haunted me,
what had me in a spin, aside from the Guinness, was the realization that

if Murdoch wasn't responsible for Scarlett's death, then somebody else was, and that all this time my anger had been misdirected.

I'd been hating the wrong man.

Hate is a strong emotion, and I tell my clients it's like Krazy Glue; it sticks to everything it touches. Don't use it unless you can handle it.

Of course, I imagined that Murdoch hated me with equal passion, and now that he was a free man, it was a problem—my problem—because the Murdoch I knew wouldn't settle for an apology.

In his shoes, would I?

I stopped feeling sorry for myself and went inside the house.

It was quiet in the hallway, dark.

I caught a glimpse of my Phantom of the Opera reflection in a mirror and hesitated, hands holding on to the hall table.

"You look dreadful. What happened?"

In the mirror, I saw the ghostly image of Eve approaching from out of the shadowy living room behind me. She had a tumbler of whiskey in one hand; the other was wrapped around her slim waist. Immediately, just the sight of her loosened up my neck muscles and chased harmful thoughts from my mind.

Eve is the best tonic for any hangover.

I smiled. "There you are."

In any light, Eve is classically pretty. I'm not just saying that because I'm her biggest fan, which I am, undeniably. Eve has the smooth physique of an art deco figurine, with green eyes so intense that they could be backlit. She's also got that Roaring Twenties thing going on—the slinky dresses, the chin-length bob, the sweetheart freckles—and she pulls it off to a T, effortlessly.

You would think that I, being a hot-blooded male, would be sexually attracted to her, especially living together the way we do. Don't get me wrong—I see her sexiness, but I have never looked at her that way, and I have never sensed it being the case for the way she looks at me. Eve has always been a good friend, and the unwritten agreement when we left Michigan was that we'd jointly fund the move, share a house, and split the costs, but we'd pursue our own interests, which included the opposite sex. She has never intimated that she wants anything more than what we have, and I respect that. You hear about some male/female friendships taking the next step, but we've always been happy with where we're at. I know our situation might sound quirky, but it works for us. Why ruin a good thing?

"I thought you were seeing Zoe tonight," she said. "Did something happen? Is that why you're home early?"

I sighed. "Apparently, something came up and she couldn't get out of it."

"You make it sound like it was an excuse."

"Maybe it was. I don't know."

"Is it her husband?"

Her question threw me. "No, it doesn't have anything to do with her husband."

Zoe's marriage is a sham. She doesn't use that word—she admonishes me when I do—but that's what it is, plain and simple. One of those loveless marriages where couples grow apart instead of together.

In counseling, I tell warring couples that their relationship is like a river. It starts out in a rush, full of energy and passion, but rapids and sometimes falls are to be expected before it reaches its calmer course. You need stamina for the long haul.

"Whatever it is, it has you shaking. Do you want to talk about it?"

I turned around to face Eve. "I'll be okay. Just feeling cold." I offered a reassuring smile, warming to her presence. On every level, Eve is my sanctuary, my touchstone.

Her nose wrinkled. "You smell of vomit."

"A little."

"You're drunk."

I smirked. "*More* than a little." I nodded at the whiskey in her hand. "Catching up?"

"Just a nightcap, then I'm off to bed." She swirled the amber liquor. "You know, speaking purely from a female perspective, Zoe wouldn't cancel without a good reason. She's not like that. She thinks too highly of you."

My smile flattened. "That's one way of putting it. Sometimes I wonder. Sometimes I think I'm just a convenience."

"And that's your cross to bear, Greg. You overthink things, always have. It's not her fault you obsess."

"Are you defending her?"

"Absolutely. We girls have got to stick together."

"Now I'm feeling totally ganged up on. Give me a sip?"

She handed the whiskey over. I closed my eyes and slugged some of it back, sending flames down my throat.

And I am transported instantly back to Manistique, age seventeen, dropped into a slow-motion memory of running through knee-high grasses with my sister on our way to the river, with its whiskey-colored water. Our river, that's how we thought of it. Ours, whose energy flowed through our lives. It's a blue-sky day, scratched by high cirrus. Raptors wheeling and cawing. The vibrant greens of early summer. And Scarlett glancing over her shoulder as she runs, giggling, cajoling, while strands of her long fiery hair blow across her face, forming red slashes on her lily-white skin.

I opened my eyes to find Eve studying me intently, one neat eyebrow cocked.

"There's something else," I said. "I fainted. Right outside on the street." I didn't tell her why; I didn't need an inquisition.

I love Eve like a sister. But she asks more questions than I have answers to.

Her expression softened slightly. "You blacked out? You haven't done that in all the time we've been down here. What happened?"

"I think I drank too much."

"You think?"

"Or not enough."

The wisecrack chased a little of the dismay from her face, but not much.

"You work yourself too hard," she said. "I've been saying for months you need a break."

"I'm okay."

"Not *my* definition of okay. Look at you—you're a mess. Now you're blacking out again?"

"Just once."

"Did something happen at the office? We both know anxiety is the trigger. The doctor said—"

"Eve, I know what the doctor said. He said the blackouts are incurable."

She shook her head. "No, Greg, he didn't. He said they were manageable, so long as you avoided high-stress situations. Don't tell me Zoe canceling was enough to make you black out?"

I was going to tell her about O'Malley, but something in me held up a red light, halting the flow.

Eve had her own problems, her own worries to deal with; she didn't need more of mine to wear her down. Besides, I wasn't even sure what O'Malley's visit meant, or if Murdoch would have the nerve to come looking for me. For now, the more I kept from her, the less she'd feel compelled to intervene.

"When was the last time you took any time off?" she said.

I leaned against the hall table, folding my arms. "I had a virus a couple of years ago."

"Sick leave doesn't count. I mean real time off. A change of scenery. A vacation." Eve caught me inflating my lungs, readying to release another sigh, and said, "Before you protest and give me twenty unarguable reasons why you can't take a break, just think about it. That's all I'm asking here. I'm not being unreasonable. I'm not being overly demanding. It's your job to think about the mental health of others. But it's my job to think about yours." She took the whiskey from my hand. "Look, we haven't had a break in years. I think it's time."

"Because I came home drunk?"

"No, because it's what normal people do. In a world where you are blinded by your masculinity, I can see the things you can only dream of seeing."

I snickered. "I'm not sure if you sound like a fortune-teller or a movie trailer."

"I'm trying to sound convincing. Anyway, it's your call. Summer's on its way, and you've always wanted to see Europe. There's nothing keeping you here."

Only the ghost of my dead sister, I thought.

But I didn't say it. I didn't need to; Eve had read my horror story from cover to cover.

"So, what's stopping you?" she asked.

"Aside from thirty needy clients? Seriously, my appointment book is full through Christmas."

"Only because you want it that way. It's how you shield yourself. But you're not the center of the universe, Greg. The world won't fall off its axis if you take a few weeks off."

Eve and her off-axis obsession. She kills me. "Can we talk about this some other time?"

"You'll forget."

"Yes, I probably will. But you won't." I took the whiskey back and drained it. "I don't want to argue when I'm drunk. I'm through with arguing. My clients depend on me, and there's nothing I can do about it."

"Okay."

"I really think it best if we don't do this right now. I mean it, Eve."

"You're the only one arguing."

I frowned at her. My head hurt. "Besides, what about your, um, thingamajig?" I flapped a hand, summoning help.

"My what?"

"You know—your agoraphobia thing?"

"What about it?"

I spread my arms. "Well, hello? It's what keeps you indoors all the time! Not that you haven't benefited from it. You've made a darn nice life for yourself here. It's comfortable. You have everything you need, the way you like. You make a good living from all those advertisers on that self-help blog of yours. Heck, you're a successful career woman! But you rarely leave the house, let alone fly anywhere, and you're talking about jetting off to Europe?" I huffed and gave her the empty glass. "It's never going to happen. Now, excuse me. I think I'm going to puke again."

Chapter Six

An out-of-place sound invaded my sleep, abruptly shaking me awake. Momentarily disoriented, I blinked at the sparks flying in my night vision, my heart rate quickened.

Fumbling, I felt around in the dark, reaching out for something familiar, a port in a storm. Everything felt tilted, like I was on a slant. I grabbed hold of the mattress, my pillow, the bedsheet dampened from the sweat lacquering my body.

I was safe, home in my bed, with a dull throb behind my eyes and a tongue as dry as old leather, my brain still pickling itself in alcohol.

I rolled onto my back, panting, staring at the ceiling fan silently going around and around above me.

As I often do, I'd been dreaming of Scarlett—this time, the two of us, teenagers again, furiously paddling kayaks downhill through rocky rapids, shouting taunts and challenging one another to brave the regions of greatest turbulence. It was an azure-sky day, cloudless. With towering trees on either side of the river. Black reflections. Cold water spraying in our faces. And Scarlett's blithe laughter stitching everything together. She was ahead of me, paddle blurring as her strong arms plied the white water, her long red hair trailing behind her like the tail of a meteor. In clipped words, she was daring me to pass her, but I was playing catch-up, breathing hard, struggling to keep pace with her as I had done in real life.

You're such a loser! she'd called playfully.

Takes one to know one, I'd called back, knowing that Scarlett was anything but a loser.

Sometimes, I wonder if her success was at my expense—if our parents' best genes had somehow skipped me and gravitated toward her. If they had, I couldn't blame them. If embryonically, she'd sucked up all the good stuff, leaving me to sweep up the debris left behind in her formation. Make something out of nothing. Cosmically, she was a shining star and I was a rocky ball in her orbit, warmed by her glow and looking less inhospitable in her astral light. A speck of dust with dreams of becoming a planet.

Sometimes, I'm surprised I exist at all.

In the dream, she'd leaned forward in her kayak and started pulling even longer strokes, increasing the distance between us.

Race you to the portage point!

Realistically, I'd stood no hope of catching her.

My dear sister was an oxymoron: the hundred-pound sapling with the might of an oak.

Better than me in just about everything, especially kayaking.

Race you!

Then the alien sound had invaded the dream, taking the shape of a sudden drop-off in the river. A thunderous waterfall, opening up from nowhere, and seemingly falling over the edge of the world.

And Scarlett had gone with it, slipping into the mist. One moment she was there, grinning over her shoulder, challenging, and the next she was gone.

I'm not sure if such dreams are restorative or just the mind's way of preventing memory loss.

The clock on the nightstand read 3:13 a.m.

And my heart was flapping around like a landed fish.

Cold sweat had paved the way for goose bumps.

I pushed myself to the edge of the bed, then rolled to my feet, padded into the bathroom, and emptied my bladder.

In the decade that has passed since Scarlett died, I've come to terms with her loss, but I still miss her, still wonder what life would be like if she were in it.

Would she be a successful writer or artist? Would I be a proud uncle?

Scarlett's memory still haunts me. But I have learned to live with her ghost, adapted to it. For a long time now, I have been able to function normally, to smile and laugh. No one would ever suspect that half of me is dead.

It hasn't always been this way.

At first, I was a wreck. I gave in to my grief. The overwhelming burden of simply living from day to day was crippling, crushing. I was inconsolable, useless, lost in my loss. A real piece of work.

I spent the best part of the worst year of my life existing as a pale ghost, drifting through the minutiae of each moment, indifferent to sunlight and the pull of the tides. *A lost cause,* they'd said. *Just leave him to it,* they'd said. *He should be ashamed of himself,* they'd said. All but Eve giving up on me, either moving on or moving out.

I scowled at my ghoulish reflection in the inky bathroom mirror.

You want to see what selfish looks like? There it is.

It's pathetic, embarrassing.

Survival isn't instinctive; it's reactive.

That's what grief does: It makes us think illogically, irrationally. It turns us temporarily insane.

Thankfully, I don't permanently inhabit my dark place anymore. But it's only a short trip away, and all it takes to send me straight back there is a song, a smell, a bad dream, or a throwaway comment from someone like O'Malley.

I rinsed my hands, ran tepid water into my mouth, splashed more over my face, then paused with the towel muffling my mouth as a bluish glow lit up the bedroom behind me.

Something had tripped the security light in the backyard, I realized. The harsh halogen glow was bleeding in around the blinds.

I flushed the toilet and padded back into the bedroom, still relatively unconcerned. Occasionally, an insect would crawl over the sensor, briefly breaking the beam and triggering the light. It would switch off automatically after a few seconds.

But when it didn't, my mouth folded into a frown.

I'd told O'Malley the neighborhood was safe, but that wasn't entirely true. The year before last, a spate of home burglaries had local residents on the lookout for what the police had said were opportunists trying their luck. A number of the riverside properties around here are vacation rentals or second homes owned by snowbirds from the north—my hometown crowd in search of a winter tan—which remain unoccupied for weeks and even months at a time. Soft targets for druggies and low-level criminals looking to steal and sell their way to their next hit. As a deterrent, the police had urged homeowners to install security lights and to be extra vigilant about leaving valuables outside after dark. Shortly after, the perpetrators had been apprehended and taken away, but the lights had stayed put.

And mine was still lit.

Either there was a raccoon in the pool doing lengths or someone was loitering in the yard.

My first instinct was to go over to the window, part the slats, and peer out, which I did.

Down below, the halogen lamp was burning up the backyard, filling the screened pool area with its bright, sterile light and turning everything beyond the mesh into an unfathomable blackness. But there were no ripples in the pool, not that I could see from this angle, and no signs of an animal interloper or anyone skulking around and helping themselves to my patio furniture.

But the light wasn't going off, which meant *something* was being picked up on the sensor.

Zane Murdoch.

The sudden thought of him turning up and breaking into my home sent a hot spike spearing though my gut.

In starting a new life in Florida, I'd ditched my old one. A snake shedding its defunct skin, born again.

But that's as far as I'd gone to disappear.

Even with the accidental name switch at the office, I hadn't been trying to create a new identity.

These days, people leave paper trails wherever they go. If you look hard enough you can trace anything. Despite my adopted business persona, my social security number was unchanged. I still banked with State Savings in Manistique. O'Malley had found me, probably without a great deal of effort on his part.

I hadn't been trying to *hide*.

Now, knowing Murdoch was a free man, I was beginning to think I should have.

"Stop overthinking," I told myself. "There's probably a perfectly reasonable explanation."

Faulty wiring. A big bug sitting on the sensor.

I waited for the light to go out. It didn't.

"Damn it."

The question was: Would Murdoch come all the way down here just to tell me how pissed he was with my wrongful accusation?

The answer was: No. The Murdoch I knew wouldn't be satisfied with giving me a lecture. At some point, violence would take over the lesson.

Was he here now?

Heart thumping, I let go of the slats, and they whip-cracked back into place.

I didn't go to the closet and get a baseball bat, because I don't own one. Instead, I pulled on my sweatpants and a T-shirt and then picked up the nearest heavy object at hand—which turned out to be a porcelain phrenology bust from the dresser—and padded across the plush carpeting, out onto the landing, where I stopped at the top of the stairs to listen.

The house was in total darkness. Silent, aside from the distant murmur of chirping insects outside and the beating of my heart inside.

"This is ridiculous," I told myself as I peered down into the black stairwell. "That dream has got you seeing spooks in every shadow."

Then I thought I heard my name being called from outside, and the hot spike returned anew.

The door to Eve's bedroom was closed. At this hour, she'd be fast asleep.

I placed a cautious foot on the first carpeted step, just as my name came again, and a shiver ran through me.

I never believed in ghosts until Scarlett died. I don't mean those slack-jawed, hollow-eyed bedsheet types you see on TV. I mean the ghosts who haunt our minds.

I wrapped my fingers tighter around the neck of the bust and continued my slow descent of the stairs, into darkness.

I reached the foot of the stairs and crossed the tiled hall, feeling the cool floor suck heat from my bare soles.

The alien glow coming from the halogen lamp was cutting bright swaths out of the dark and lighting up a route to the back of the house, filled with sharp shadows and dancing dust motes. I picked up my cell phone from the hall table and tapped 9-1-1 onto the keypad, just in case.

Was I really expecting to find Zane Murdoch standing in the back-yard, shouting out my name, here to give payback for my testimony against him?

Would he be that reckless, that obvious?

Or, was it more likely my beer-soaked brain was blowing everything out of proportion?

A blood vessel started to twang in my neck.

In my house, the living room is situated at the back. Through a big glass wall, it overlooks the patio and the pool. There are vertical blinds to shield it from the rising sun, but I rarely have them drawn. So I hesitated before entering the room fully, poking my head around the doorway instead, trying to see if I could spot an intruder lurking on the lanai before he spotted me.

But there was nothing out of place.

Just the persistent light throwing shadows across the living room.

Avoiding furniture, I crept across the heavy shag pile, aiming for the sliding glass door, when the light went out, plunging the pool area and the living room into total blackness.

I stopped dead in my tracks, the breath snagged in my throat.

Ordinarily, I'm not easily frightened. It takes more than strange noises and impenetrable shadows to scare me. It's being disturbed from our sleep in the middle of the night that causes our minds to overthink. It harks back to our primal roots, when humans had to sleep with one eye open, ready to run for their lives the second the beast emerged from the dark.

Fireflies fluttered in my vision.

I breathed, and went to take a cautious step forward, intending to reach for the pool light switch, in the exact moment the halogen lamp lit up the night again.

And I found myself face to face with a ghostly apparition standing on the other side of the glass, facing me, his indistinct features blanched by the dazzling light.

A second later, the security lamp went out again, leaving me night-blind and with a pulse banging in my throat.

Then something brushed my arm and I almost jumped out of my skin. I spun around fast, to find Eve looking at me quizzically.

"What's wrong?" she asked sleepily.

"Someone's in the backyard. I didn't want to wake you."

She glanced at the darkened pool area. "Are you sure? I don't see anyone. What were you going to do—bash in their skull with a phrenology bust? How ironic."

Feeling foolish, I put down the porcelain head and went over to the sliding door, where I fumbled for the light switch and threw on the pool lights. The calm water brightened internally, turning turquoise.

"See," Eve said. "Not a soul."

"I'm not imagining things, Eve. He was standing right there."

I saw her nose wrinkle in the way Scarlett's nose had done whenever she'd thought I was mistaken about something, which had been disconcertingly often.

"Are you sure you weren't sleepwalking again?" she asked.

"Eve . . ."

"I'm just throwing it out there, Greg. It wouldn't be the first time I've found you wandering around the house in the middle of the night. You know alcohol makes you prowl in your sleep."

"Look at me. I'm wide awake. And I'm telling you, he was right there."

"Who?"

"I'm not sure."

I unlocked the door and slid it open. Warm, moist air rushed in, bringing with it the constant crackle of cicadas.

"This is pointless," Eve said, "and you're still tipsy. You need to sleep it off. Go back to bed."

"I need to make sure."

"It's after three. You have work in the morning. You need to sober up."

"I'll be okay."

"Famous last words."

I ventured outside, Eve in tow.

Although my screened pool area is one of the largest on the block, there aren't that many places to hide. A quick scan told me there was no one cowering behind the chiminea or crouched behind the outdoor grill. In fact, there were no signs that anyone had been there at all. Just a few inquisitive moths flapping against the screen.

"Be careful you don't bump into the Invisible Man," Eve whispered sarcastically.

"I'm not imagining this. He was out here."

"Well, there's no one here now. Except for us crazy wide-awake people."

"I wasn't sleepwalking."

"Okay. So tell me what you *think* you saw."

"*Did* see."

"Now you're being picky."

"I'm not sure, but I think it might have been Kyle."

It took her less than a second to make the connection. "Your childhood friend? The one you haven't seen since you were seventeen?" She saw my frown unfurl and added, "Stop looking so victimized. I'm just saying. Unless there's another Kyle you know?"

"Eve, I'm not making this up." I went over to the screen door leading out onto the grass. Automatically, the security light flooded the patio in sterile light. I checked the door. The inside latch was still in its place. I rattled the clasp, but the metal brace stayed put.

She joined me at the door. "A teenager?"

"No. He was older. My age. I know what I saw, Eve. It looked like Kyle." I squinted at the halogen lamp.

"I know it's the middle of the night. I know you've been working yourself too hard lately. I know you came home intoxicated. I know the mind can play tricks when you're drunk and half-asleep. All I'm saying is, is it possible it was just your reflection in the doorwall?"

I pulled away, suddenly on the defensive. "I wasn't seeing things, and I'm slightly offended by your assumption. I know what I saw. I'm not the one who sees things that aren't there, remember? I'm not the one who got hooked on hallucinogens."

Now it was her turn to pull away. Her whole frame seemed to curl in on itself, like the universe was trying to suck her out of this dimension. "Ouch," she whispered, giving me a wounded look. "That hurt. You went straight for the sucker punch there, big guy. Shame on you."

I reached out a hand. "Eve, I didn't mean to—"

"Please, don't." She twisted out of my reach, pulling farther away. "This isn't about me. I'm in full control of my senses. Those psychedelics had no long-term side effects. Besides, if I remember rightly, you were the one who told me about them."

"I made a mistake."

"So why throw it in my face? The dose I took wasn't harmful. It was inspirational. It gave me vision in a period of creative blindness. All the world's greatest writers do it."

She said it like it justified it, like it was the *thing to do*.

But I had only mentioned the drugs in passing—when reminiscing about Scarlett—never intending Eve to be seduced.

I took a step closer, but she backed around the edge of the pool.

"Oh, no you don't. You didn't think twice about using them yourself. What makes you better than me?"

And now it was my turn to take her sucker punch on the chin and absorb it like a man.

The pot calling the kettle black.

Taking drugs had never appealed to me. It wasn't even attractive to me when I was younger. I was an odd teenager, an exception in that I wasn't interested in experimenting. Not like Scarlett. Growing up, I had friends who smoked marijuana regularly. Forced into a corner by peer pressure, I'd tried it once, mainly to see what all the fuss was about, only to be put off by all the coughing and the distinct lack of positives.

Some people have a greater resistance to dependency.

Sitting in a cloud of thick smoke, one of my fellow drug users had told me, *High achievers need bigger scores, so stop wasting my weed, man.*

I'd never tried it again.

But it wasn't the last time I'd dirtied my hands with drugs.

In college, Scarlett had begun to experience cluster headaches and then migraines. They came from nowhere and lasted for days, often so bad that she could hardly get out of bed. She'd suffered from regular headaches since puberty, often accompanied by a nosebleed. But the intensity had amplified to the point where the headaches had become unbearable, not only inducing nosebleeds but also severe vomiting.

Concerned, I'd told her about a study I'd read, suggesting that psychedelics helped—not for one second thinking about the negatives, the far-reaching ripples. Not for one second *thinking*. Scarlett had never been one to shy away from experimentation, or to back down from a challenge. When the headaches started interfering with her studies, she remembered the article. She abandoned her ineffective prescription pills and sought out a local dealer to supply her with what she'd called Wonderland.

I hadn't found out about it until weeks later, by which time it was too late to talk her out of it.

Wonderland had come in the shape of small squares of blotter paper—the LSD having been premixed with a water-and-alcohol solution and then infused—each square bearing the image of a white rabbit printed in edible ink on the surface. All that was needed was a wet tongue to get the party started.

Being the protective brother that I was, I'd been against it from the moment I knew what she was doing. Okay, so I had planted the seed, but only in the hope that she'd see there were alternatives, that there were other avenues she could take. I hadn't liked the idea of my sister using drugs. Who would? No matter how small the dose was or how low the chance of the long-term health risks was, in my view, unsupervised drug-taking was dangerous, and I'd voiced my concerns, seeing it as my duty to talk her out of it, or at least try. But Scarlett was the most headstrong person I've ever known, and there was no changing her mind once it was made up.

She'd told me, *You can't get addicted to LSD.*

But she was hooked within days—not because the acid was physically addictive, but because it was psychologically habit-forming. To her, the pros outweighed the cons. Sometimes, I'd find her completely out of it, in her dorm room, or bubbling over with ideas for paintings or poems but hardly remembering even to eat. Months later, when the LSD had failed to keep her cluster headaches at bay, she still hadn't given up on it, claiming that the acid boosted her creativity and she'd be foolish to limit herself.

Scarlett had said, *You follow the White Rabbit into the hole, and Wonderland is right around the corner.*

And she had demonstrated, making appreciative noises as the blotter paper had dissolved in her mouth.

She'd smiled and said, *Now it's your turn, Greg. Come on. Hop to it. Don't be lame. It won't kill you. It'll liberate you.*

At first, I'd resisted Scarlett's urging to join her, to open up my own imagination in the same way the LSD had opened hers. I was studying psychology at the time, and to me the thought of rerouting logical pathways at the risk of losing focus had seemed counterintuitive to everything I was working hard toward.

But I had succumbed the day after our grandmother's funeral. Just one time, for Scarlett's sake, and never again while my sister was alive.

Eve clapped her hands together, and I resurfaced back in the present. "I need sleep," she said before I could conjure up an excuse and make myself look even more hypocritical. "Do me a favor and don't wake me in the morning." Then she turned on her bare heel and disappeared into the living room.

"That was a long time ago," I called after her. "We were kids. We didn't know any better."

But Eve was gone.

And I was talking to myself.

Chapter Seven

When I set out for the office later that morning—hungover and waxy-mouthed—I found a bright and breezy O'Malley leaning against the hood of his car at the foot of my driveway, eyes scrunched up against the light.

"Give you a ride?" he said as I approached.

"Why? You have a taxi license, too?"

"Very funny." He pointed at me with a finger. "You're a funny guy, Mr. Cole. As a matter of fact, I was just passing through, on my way home, and thought to myself: Hey, I bet that nice Mr. Cole needs a ride into work this morning, seeing that his car is still parked at the Irish pub." He pulled open the passenger door. "Come on. Let's drive and talk."

I cut behind his car and crossed the road. "No, thanks. I'm looking forward to the walk."

"Really? In this humidity and with a hangover? It must be going on two miles."

"Closer to three. And please don't worry about me. I'll pick up my car along the way."

"Good luck with that one, Mr. Cole. Donovan's only opens at midday."

"How would you even know that?"

"Because you don't need to be a detective to read the hours on a sign."

I grunted under my breath but didn't stop.

The truth is, I never walk to the office. It's more or less a straight line and otherwise a pleasant jogging route along the beach road, but I've never attempted it. A combination of cheap gasoline, heat, and laziness rules it out. It's a sad fact that most of us drive everywhere these days, even when our destination is easily walkable.

Annoyingly, O'Malley closed the car door and scurried after me.

"You do realize this constitutes stalking?" I told him as he caught up. "Don't you have anyone else you need to harass?"

"Not today I don't. Tomorrow's another story. How about you?"

Automatically, I glanced at my watch. "Busy with appointments, booked until five."

"You've got my sympathies there."

Regular as clockwork, Wednesdays and Thursdays win my busiest days of the week award. A while back, I'd come up with my own theory to explain it: subconsciously, we think of the weekend and in particular of Sunday as being devoted to family time and home life, and midweek is as far away as you can get from that kind of normalcy, which makes it the ideal time to let our demons run amok.

"Mr. Cole, will you please slow down a little? We need to talk."

We'd barely gone fifty yards, and already he was sounding a little breathy.

"So call the office and make an appointment."

My reply was curter than it should have been, basically because my dehydrated brain wasn't in any fit state to ward off another of O'Malley's inquisitions. Not today. A brisk walk along the beach road with my sunglasses on and my messenger bag swinging was just what the doctor ordered this morning. Absolutely no interrogations. Already, I'd consumed enough coffee to make my brain buzz, and the Tylenol had just about taken the edge off the dull ache behind my eyeballs. But the fresh air and the exercise were my way of fully detoxing.

"There's something you should know," O'Malley said.

"Maybe some other time."

"Trust me, Mr. Cole, you'll want to hear this. Something's raised its ugly head. Overnight as a matter of fact. Something of a very dark nature."

Again, superficially, I glanced at my watch. "My first client is in fifty-five minutes."

He fell into a jog. "You won't regret it. You'll thank me afterwards."

I doubted it. In fact, I doubted anything that O'Malley wanted to say was something I wanted to hear. Generally, people fall into one of two categories: reluctant or rambling. O'Malley was definitely in the latter.

Again, I increased my speed. I have long legs and therefore a long stride.

"Are you deliberately trying to give me a heart attack, Mr. Cole?" O'Malley did his best to keep up, but he was clearly unfamiliar with the concept of running. His heels clacked against the asphalt; his breathing was heavy and ragged.

"Mr. Cole! Please!"

I turned to see him at a standstill, struggling for breath, hands on hips.

"It's no good," he gasped. "I'm not cut out for power-walking. I think I've given myself a hernia."

"Have a nice day, O'Malley," I said, continuing on my way.

I hadn't gone three more yards when he called, "You should know this: Zane Murdoch is on his way here, to Florida."

And now it was my turn to come to a sudden stop.

"What did you just say?"

"Zane Murdoch. He's driving down here as we speak. He set off yesterday. Allowing for a stopover or two, he could be here by this time tomorrow. And I'm confident he's not looking for a vacation."

I turned to face him. "How could you know such a thing? Never mind—you're not going to say, are you? And anyway, why are you even telling me this?"

"Because, Mr. Cole, I read those court transcripts in detail. I know what a bad seed this Zane Murdoch is. It's my Christian duty to warn you that your life might be in danger." He mopped sweat from his brow. "Anyway, that's all I've got to say on the subject. I need a nap."

"Good-bye, O'Malley."

"Good luck, Mr. Cole."

I swiveled on my heels, leaving him behind. If O'Malley made another comment, I didn't hear it; my ears were whistling like a boiling kettle.

I walked the rest of the way to my office in a bit of a blur.

Cars whooshing by. Lights blinking at the crosswalks. The morning sun beating down and siphoning moisture from my skin.

The thought of Murdoch coming down here to confront me came with mixed feelings. Half of me wanted to barricade myself in my home and pull down the storm shutters, while the other half wanted to get my hands on Murdoch's throat and take up the judicial system's slack.

Who am I kidding?

I'm about as aggressive as a Seeing Eye dog on Valium. The second I muster up enough adrenaline to trigger my fight-or-flight reflex, I faint. I'm no hero. It's been this way for as long as I can remember, and it can be embarrassing.

In my youth, I would faint for the weakest of reasons: the sight of a spider on my pillow; a prick of blood on a finger; a mop falling unexpectedly out of a closet. I wasn't picky. If it even remotely warranted a faint, I had it covered. Sometimes, if I held my breath long enough, I could even black out at will, and would perform that trick in front of amazed onlookers at friends' parties.

I'm lucky I'm still alive.

But I'm not dying—they've run the tests to prove it. The doctors tell me I have something called vasovagal syncope, which roughly translates to "sissy syndrome." Essentially, it means that whenever my body is under extreme emotional duress, my blood pressure drops drastically, reducing blood flow to my brain. The end result is, I black out. And I am powerless to stop it.

My grandfather, who was always eager to try alternative therapies, had said, *You don't need to go down the medication route. What you need is to avoid stressful situations. Recognize the triggers and steer clear. No use polluting your system unnecessarily.*

Fortunately, I do get some warning signs, although I'm not always given enough time to act on them. Becoming light-headed is the main precursor. Impaired vision is an imminent indication. Ringing in the ears is a dead giveaway. My grandfather's advice was, *Sit down when those things happen, slow your breathing, breathe into a paper bag if you happen to have one on hand.*

He'd said, *Low blood pressure is a blessing from God.*

I wasn't so sure.

Growing up in Michigan, I lost count of how many times I fainted. I blacked out during horror movies, and one time at a friend's party when the hired clown pretended to drive a nail through his finger.

A weedy Greg Cole, toppling like a statue, while the rest of the kids laughed and played.

Duration time varies. I can be out of it for seconds or hours; there's no saying how long. It may not be fatal, but it is humiliating, and it can be a limiter.

Which was why, when I was old enough to drive and I went for my driving skills test, I never mentioned my blackouts to the tester.

I was determined not to let them get in the way and hold me back.

And I still felt the same about them, twenty years later.

By the time I arrived at the health center, I was hot and flustered. Several people were already seated inside the air-conditioned lobby, browsing magazines or texting on their cells.

Although small and unassuming, the beach road center is a fully functioning community medical facility, offering a wide range of treatments and diagnostic tests, plus a couple of offices rented out to add-on service providers, including a chiropractor, an acupuncturist, and me, with my talk therapy. Office hours are nine to five, and it was fourteen minutes until nine.

I'd made good time walking. But the price was a coating of sweat and achy feet.

I nodded a good morning to Glenda, the receptionist, who was on the phone behind the counter, and headed straight for the restroom in back. I didn't stop to catch up as I normally do. Glenda's eight-year-old granddaughter has acute lymphoblastic leukemia and is currently undergoing chemotherapy. The prognosis is good; they'd caught it early. Good news, but still Glenda was going through the wringer with worry, and a few minutes of my time each day to lend an understanding ear was the least I could do.

Maybe later, I thought.

I locked myself inside the restroom and guzzled water straight from the faucet, then splashed it over my sun-heated face. A combination of the hangover and the brisk walk had left me parched. I used paper towels to mop the moisture from my face and neck, then pulled out my shirt and dabbed my fiery armpits. In spite of my fuzzy brain, I'd had the foresight to bring deodorant with me. I took the can from the messenger bag and sprayed it over skin and clothes, indiscriminately. Then I left the restroom, smelling of bergamot and mandarin.

Glenda was still on the phone. *Maybe much later, then.* I headed down the hallway leading to my office, then slowed automatically when I saw a man leaning against the door at the far end. My door.

He looked sixty, give or take, with combed-back silver hair and a bushy gray handlebar mustache that would have brought a smile to Wyatt Earp's face. He wore a crumpled tan suit that looked like it had seen more time hanging around in airport lounges than in a closet.

He didn't look one bit like Doris Tucker, my first client of the day.

"Can I help you?" I asked as I approached.

He'd been looking down at his cell phone, scrolling with a thumb. Now he looked up, and I could see that his face was as tired as his department store clothes. His baggy eyes would have given Droopy the cartoon dog a run for his money. "Gregory Cole?" His voice was deep, smoky-rough.

"May I ask who's asking?"

In what seemed a well-practiced move, the man swapped the phone for a wallet and held it open so that I could see his ID. "Detective Sergeant Curtis Dunn, Michigan State Police," he said in a nasally accent. He pronounced his name Cur-dis-dunn, all as one word, like he was named after a country in central Asia.

"Michigan State Police?" I didn't sound nearly as surprised as I might have just a day before. "You're a long way from home, Detective Dunn."

"Makes two of us." He gestured toward the door. "What's with the name change? You trying to hide or something?"

"Or something, yes. And clearly not very effectively." I couldn't be bothered explaining the mix-up all over again.

"Wow, you're hostile."

"Hungover." I jangled the office keys. "May I?"

"Be my guest." He flattened himself against the wall, sucking in his paunch so that I could squeeze past.

I opened up, swinging the door wide, and breezed inside.

"You're the guy I saw marching along the street like the devil was snapping at his heels," he commented as he followed me in.

"I'm sorry?"

"Half an hour ago. I visited your home address right before driving over here. We must have missed each other by minutes."

More than once, my grandfather had warned me, *Unless you want to be mauled, never poke a sleeping bear with a sharp stick.*

So, as instructed, I'd left Eve undisturbed in bed. I'd tiptoed around the house, my hangover and cowardice keeping me quiet.

I wondered if she'd heard Dunn knocking.

He was inspecting my setup. "Nice office, by the way."

"Thanks." Systematically, I went around the room pulling open the window blinds, letting morning sunshine dissolve the shadows. "I'm presuming you're here to warn me about Zane Murdoch?"

"No flies on you, I see."

"I try my best. That's why you're here, isn't it?"

"Indirectly."

I went behind the desk and dumped my bag on the leather inlay. "I heard he was a free man. How does something like that happen?"

Dunn's hands were shoved in his pockets. He looked slovenly, his weary eyes scanning the office. "How much have you been told?"

"Not a great deal. Only that new and incontrovertible evidence has come to light." O'Malley's words, not mine.

I saw Dunn think about my choice of words. I imagined his lips stretching into a smile somewhere underneath his mustache.

"You're absolutely right on the button with that one," he said. "'New and incontrovertible evidence.' That's one way of phrasing it."

I unbuckled the messenger bag. "Do you know the specifics?"

"Murdoch confessed to another crime." He said it matter-of-factly, as though he recited the sentence on a daily basis.

"He . . . Wait, what?"

"He confessed to another crime."

"Yes, I heard that. I'm just a bit confused by it."

"Excessive alcohol does that to the brain."

I pulled my phone out and placed it on the desk. "Murdoch's a bad egg. During the trial, the jury got to hear all about his long history of petty theft. It doesn't surprise me one bit he's admitted to being bad."

Dunn glanced my way for the first time. "You're suspicious about them quashing his sentence?"

"I'm bound to be. He was convicted of my sister's murder by a unanimous jury. Now he's out and off the hook? Something like that doesn't happen every day of the week. You guys found a knife in Murdoch's trash with Scarlett's blood on it. The evidentiary discovery formed the backbone of the case. He was guilty. Releasing him has to be a mistake."

"I guess it would give me the heebie-jeebies, too, if I were in your shoes. Got to mess with a guy's head, knowing the person you thought killed your sister was wrongly convicted." He ambled up to the desk. "You think you've had justice and got everything figured out. You accept things and move on. Then something like this comes out of nowhere and pulls the rug from under your feet. It's got to affect you."

"That's an understatement."

Absently, he picked up a paperweight from the desk and began to examine the insects encased in the acrylic. "All the same, this particular crime—the one Murdoch recently confessed to—provided him with an airtight alibi for the night of your sister's murder."

Now I balked, blinking. "Hold on. That doesn't make any sense." It didn't—at least not to me. "Murdoch couldn't have been in two places at the same time."

"Exactly. Hence the pardon." He held the paperweight up to the light, squinting. "We're working on the theory it was planted."

"What?"

"The knife we found in his trash. We're working on the theory the real killer intended to frame Murdoch."

The breath snagged in my throat, like a ball of barbed wire.

Dunn nodded at the paperweight. "This thing in here has two heads. What the hell kind of creature is this?"

"Mated lovebugs. Florida's full of them."

"Jeez Louise." He returned the paperweight to the desk and wiped his hand against his crumpled jacket. "So, anyway, his alibi checked out, and the court had no choice but to overrule the conviction on the back of the appeal."

"But there was never any mention of Murdoch having an alibi. Why didn't it come up at trial?"

"Our assumption is he never told his lawyer, or if he did, he was advised not to use it."

My balk was back. "Really? I mean, *really?*"

Dunn shrugged inside his jacket. "What can I tell you? These things happen. People have their reasons to lie and to cover up the truth. Not everything's black and white. But then a man in your position doesn't need someone like me to tell him that. The point is, our forensics team was able to confirm that Murdoch did perpetrate a different crime in another town the night your sister died."

Behind my eyes, the throbbing had returned with renewed intensity; floaters pulsed in my vision. "What kind of crime?"

"Home invasion." Again, very matter-of-fact. "According to the original police report, that perpetrator—who we now know to be Murdoch—broke into a property in Ontonagon, where he assaulted the homeowners before locking them in the basement. This was around midnight, the night your sister disappeared. The homeowners say he left around five in the morning."

"What was he doing there all that time?"

"Aside from ransacking the place and torturing the homeowners? Apparently, helping himself to pizza."

"Holy crap."

"When he left, Murdoch took with him over a thousand dollars in cash, and jewelry worth ten times the amount."

"And you're sure it was him?"

"Absolutely."

"So why hasn't he been charged for that? Why's he a free man? More importantly, why did he wait ten years to use his alibi?"

Contemplatively, Dunn stroked his bushy mustache. "You can thank the statute of limitations on both counts. In itself, burglary is a class E felony, punishable with up to five years in prison. But Murdoch used a switchblade on those homeowners that night. And assault with a deadly weapon during the commission of a robbery is a class A felony, punishable with anywhere up to life in prison. But under Michigan law, both home invasion and assault with a deadly weapon fall under a ten-year statute of limitations. Once we passed that milestone, Murdoch knew even if he confessed he couldn't be prosecuted."

"He got out on a technicality?" I was dumbstruck.

Murdoch had made the law work in his favor, I realized. Had he admitted to the home invasion at trial and used it as an alibi he would have guaranteed himself a life sentence, then and there, no matter what the verdict of the murder trial. In holding his tongue and waiting for the golden ten-year limit to pass, he knew he could use the alibi and walk away from both life sentences with only a decade served, period.

I swallowed with a gulp. "And he was definitely in Ontonagon that night?"

"He was. So you can see how things don't add up here. Disregarding the evidence we found in his trash, both the timeline and the location make Murdoch being in two places at once an impossibility."

I blew out a hot breath.

I knew Ontonagon was a small town located northwest of Manistique, on the shores of Lake Superior. Easily two hundred miles away. Even at night and pushing the speed limit, it was a three-hour drive away. According to Claire Knapp—Scarlett's friend and the last person, other than the killer, to see her alive—my sister had left Claire's house at one in the morning to head home after an evening of pampering, popcorn, and *Pretty Woman* for the hundredth time.

Scarlett had waved her good-byes for the last time and set off on foot to walk the quiet quarter mile across town to our home on Elm Street. On any other night, it was a safe walk, and one she'd taken many times previously.

This time it wasn't and she hadn't.

Scarlett never came home.

All along, I'd convinced myself and others that Murdoch had intercepted her that night. But his alibi proved he was two hundred miles away until at least five in the morning.

"I know what you're thinking," Dunn continued, refocusing my attention. "Did these homeowners identify Murdoch this time around? The answer is, they didn't need to. Not that they could have done so in any case. The man who broke into their home wore a balaclava."

"How, then?" I was hooked.

"He directed my colleagues to where he'd stashed his spoils. And sure enough, they found the jewelry right where he said it would be. Buried under a tree at the edge of his parents' backyard in Manistique, together with loot from a handful of other burglaries. Everything untouched for over a decade. The Ontonagon homeowners and their insurance company both confirmed the jewelry was theirs."

I swallowed against the barbed wire. "This has to be some kind of trick. Murdoch is a born liar. He probably knew the real thief and got him to plant those items."

My outburst sounded desperate, unreasonable. The frantic grappling of a grieving brother. After all, what petty thief would sit on such a stash for over a decade, just in case he needed it to provide an alibi for someone else sometime down the line?

No honor among thieves.

I could see Dunn was thinking the exact same thing.

75

"Which is why we dusted the larger gems for prints," he said. "Murdoch's were all over them."

"He could have taken her afterward, when he got back to town." My desperation was on show.

"Well, it's doubtful," Dunn said. "According to the original investigation, Murdoch was at his father's lube shop the whole of that day from nine in the morning. Even if he'd headed straight back to Manistique after leaving Ontonagon, it would have been after eight before he'd arrived there. That would have left him with a small window of opportunity to find your sister, abduct her, kill her, and then dispose of her body, all before turning up at the shop."

"But—"

"You reported your sister missing at seven thirty-five, right?"

I nodded, knowing in my heart that she had disappeared much earlier than that.

On the day I'd learned my sister was dead, I'd risen at 6:30 on the dot, as usual, and fallen into the shower, numbly going through my daily routine in preparation for another long shift at the health food store.

The health food store was my grandfather's baby. He'd birthed it long before we were born, at a time when people thought smoking was good for you and whiskey warded off cancer. In those happy-go-lucky days of Cold War heat, people thought him mad.

There's no future in soybeans and superfoods, they'd said. *You'll go hungry and end up eating your own words.*

But he was stubborn. Tell him he couldn't do something and he did, just to prove he could. Scarlett all over.

Organics are the future, he'd argue. *One day, we'll all be eating Tofurkey.*

When I worked there, my grandfather's brick-fronted store was located in the middle of town, across the street from a bar that used to be a video rental outlet.

Help out in the store, he'd urged over the phone the week before I'd graduated from community college. *It'll give you something to do while you're waiting for the new academic year to start. Besides, it'll be nice having you under my feet.*

I'd never wanted to work in my grandfather's store—not permanently. The smells of malt and ginger made my stomach turn.

But I'd never told him.

A week later, age twenty, I had an associate's degree in abnormal psychology, and every intention of going on to Michigan State come fall, where I could work toward my PhD in clinical psychology. It was doable, too. My trust fund—created after the death of our parents—became accessible when I turned twenty-one. It would put me through grad school and then some, giving me a great head start. Scarlett too. If everything went smoothly, I could eventually open a practice "under the bridge," what Yoopers call everywhere south of the Mackinac Bridge, like Detroit and Grand Rapids.

But the best-laid plans have a habit of coming unstuck when we least expect it.

The week I'd graduated from community college, our grandfather had suffered a fatal stroke. He'd opened up the store as usual. He'd stacked the shelves and swept the floor. He'd put cash in the register. He'd gotten everything shipshape. Then he'd dropped dead, falling facedown into a bin of nut mix.

And my life had been put on hold.

We can't leave Grandma high and dry, Scarlett had warned me quietly when she'd found me checking out Michigan State University online. *She needs us now, more than ever.*

I'd argued my case. But Scarlett always got the last word.

So helping out at the store had been a short-term agreement, just until I could train a new manager. Just until I knew our grandmother was okay.

But that day had never come.

I've heard it said that people can give up when faced with overwhelming odds, lose the will to live when their soul mate is lost, die from a broken heart. I'd never believed any of it. Not until our grandmother had passed away in her sleep the week after her husband's funeral, leaving Scarlett and me in deep water.

Not surprisingly, I never went away to college.

Feeling obligated, I'd stayed at home, to take care of matters of the heart, choosing to look after the two things that provided safe harbor: my grandfather's store and my sister.

The first was straightforward, a matter of balancing books and basic stockkeeping. The second proved a little trickier—for soon after the funerals, Scarlett sank into a bottomless depression.

The crux of it was, she felt directionless.

With our anchor points gone and our lives capsized, she was adrift.

Her dependency on hallucinogens became a problem. Like a wounded creature, she curled up in a corner, not wanting to engage with the world or her feelings. I did my best to care for her, to encourage her to come out of her shell. But Scarlett always did her own thing, her way, and in her own time.

Eventually, when she did break free from her emotional cocoon, she was changed. A butterfly in reverse. Darker, somehow. Tougher, harder. More reckless than ever before. She drank. She partied. She gave the finger to the world, and me.

She fell into bed with Zane Murdoch.

For four years without a break, I bailed out the boat. I completed my bachelor's degree online, in the evenings, stooped over my computer while Scarlett played our grandmother's Barry Manilow records over and over upstairs, smoking pot and making out with Murdoch.

Managing the store—that's what I'd been getting ready for the morning I'd sensed that my sister was dead.

"Do you need a moment?" Dunn asked, dragging my cold thoughts kicking and screaming back into the present.

I shook my head. The office wobbled. "I'm okay."

"How about a glass of water?"

"No, thanks."

"Okay. So, as I was saying, you found out she was missing at seven thirty-five?"

"Her bed hadn't been slept in. One look and I knew she hadn't come home."

"Did she sleep out, ever?"

"Scarlett was a homebody. She never slept anywhere but in her own bed." That was a lie, and I didn't mention her bedroom also doubled as a drug den. It was none of his business, the same way she'd insisted it was none of mine. "When I saw everything was the way she'd left it the day before, I knew something was wrong."

"So you called the police."

Not at first. At first I'd called her cell phone, only to hear it go straight to voice mail. Then I'd called Claire, the friend she'd spent the previous evening with. Held my breath for the full minute it had taken her to pick up. When a sleepy Claire had told me Scarlett had left at around one in the morning, I knew something bad had happened.

"It was like someone ripped out my stomach," I said, feeling the makings of panic begin to stir deep down inside. An echo of the fear that had gripped me that morning. "I knew she was gone. Right there in that moment. I could . . . I could *sense* it."

As I'd hung up with Claire, I'd felt Scarlett's absence fold around me as if it were an icy cloak, smothering, mummifying, asphyxiating. My whole world crumbling to dust. Then darkness had rushed in and pressed me out of existence. A blessed blackout. But only temporarily.

I blinked at Dunn, my mouth dry. Cool sweat was pricking out on my hairline and under my collar. I pictured myself with the color completely drained from my face, my eyes like bullet holes in snow.

I saw his gaze harden. "You knew she was dead?"

"I guess I did. I knew right away something terrible had happened. The feeling of dread was immediate."

Like the adrenalized moment when you open up your wallet to discover you left your credit card back at the gas station—only a hundred times worse and a million times more intense.

"Hit you hard, huh?"

"Like a freight train."

"You *sensed* she was dead?"

I nodded quickly.

"I'll be damned. You and your sister were fraternal twins, right? There's a strong case for telepathy with twins, I've heard."

It's a universal observation, and one we'd heard all the time growing up: twins communicate telepathically.

"Scarlett would agree with you in a heartbeat. That's what she called it, too. She believed in telepathy and all that paranormal mumbo jumbo."

She'd believed we shared the same soul, halved at birth. She'd believed we were connected spiritually. She'd believed we were the opposite poles of the same magnet, passing invisible information between us. Forever coupled.

"But you don't believe it, do you?"

"I didn't. But my mind was changed that day."

Like our grandmother, I was trained in the sciences. Schooled to believe that everything is explainable through observation, prediction, and testing. And that anything presently unexplainable will one day be explained by the same scientific method. I was trained to separate fact from fantasy. I wasn't trained to believe in a spirit dimension.

"Back then, I put it down to sibling intuition," I said.

But the truth was, if it was anything at all, I'd believed it to be something called quantum entanglement. My godless twenty-five-year-old brain had had no other way to explain it. Throughout our lives, whenever something had happened to move me emotionally, Scarlett had always sensed it from afar. Never the other way around, though, as if the invisible information channel only worked one way.

The first and only time it had happened in reverse was the day she died.

"You guys were close," Dunn said.

"Thick as thieves." My breath was as dense as mustard gas.

"I'm sorry."

"It was the worst day of my life. No other has come close."

On that fateful morning, I'd called city hall, left a panicked message with a civilian administrator, and then had to wait through the torturous thirty minutes for a police officer to call me back.

My sister's missing, I'd told him. I couldn't say what I was thinking, what I *knew*, that she was *dead*. I couldn't say that word out loud for a long time after.

For the first time in my life I'd felt dislocated, *alone*.

"Forgive my brusqueness," Dunn said.

I flapped a shaky hand, wiping away acidic sweat before it ran into my eyes and mixed with the tears forming there. "It was a long time ago."

Scarlett's death had hit me hard enough to displace every one of my molecules all at the same time.

He nodded. "I can see why the news of Murdoch's release has you spooked. And I hate to be the bearer of bad tidings and darken your mood even further, but Murdoch isn't the whole reason I'm here."

"It isn't?"

"Unfortunately, no. You might want to sit down for this next bit."

"I'm good, thanks." Anything but, actually. The desk was propping me up and digging into my thighs.

"Suit yourself. I'll do my best to say this in the least painful way possible. Several days ago, we received an anonymous tip, pointing to the possible whereabouts of your sister."

I felt a knee wobble, then give a little. "You found her body?"

"Yes, sir, we did." He must have seen my aghast expression, because he added, "I'm ashamed to say it took us a few days to send someone out to the location. We receive plenty of false tips. And we work on a priority basis. No excuse, but that's the way it is. So it transpired that yesterday, our investigators began to exhume what we believe to be your sister's remains from a bog out by Crooked Lake, just off Ninety-Four, north of Manistique."

The other knee buckled, and I fell involuntarily into my leather chair with a thud.

"They found Scarlett?" Each word came out as a separate statement of disbelief, each one lacerating my larynx on the way out.

The intercom buzzed, and Glenda's voice could be heard: "Heads-up. Your first appointment is here."

Dunn glanced at his watch, then licked a thumb and used it to slide a business card from his wallet. "Look, I realize this is big news and you're going to need a little time to wrap your head around it. I also know you're a busy guy and you're probably up to your eyeballs in clients today, so let's continue this conversation later, after office hours. Hopefully by then your hangover will be cleared and you'll be ready to talk." He slid the card across the desk. "The US Marshals Service has kindly offered their assistance while I'm here in Florida. I'll be at the Federal Building in Fort Myers for the rest of the day. I'll expect to see you there at six thirty, for a formal interview."

Chapter Eight

The first move I made the minute Detective Sergeant Dunn left the office had been an impulsive one. I buzzed Glenda back and asked her to cancel and rearrange all of the morning's appointments. Selfishly, I didn't care when, or even how, so long as I didn't have to deal with other people's anxieties just then. My own were burning their way to the surface, melting flesh and sinew, and I needed breathing space, time to be alone when they burst through.

On the back of an anonymous tip, the police had recovered remains that they were confident were Scarlett's, and the implications were bouncing around in my head like popcorn in a microwavable bag.

Even so, the last thing I wanted was to fail my clients by being distracted, which I was, understandably—first by the news of Murdoch walking free, and now with the knowledge that the police had found Scarlett. That's if I could trust anything either O'Malley or Dunn had told me.

What I needed was confirmation, on both counts.

Did that include a visual identification of her body? I wondered with a start. Could I even do something like that? Was it even possible, after her being in the ground all this time?

If so, I needed to drop everything, run home, pack an overnight bag, and catch the next plane to Sawyer International.

What could stop me?

"But Doris is already here, and she's speaking to the empty chair next to her," Glenda protested in a whisper from the intercom's speaker, after listening to my harebrained plan. "You can't let her down. She's come all the way over from Punta Gorda, specifically, and in rush-hour traffic. She won't be a happy camper."

Obstacle number one.

Now in her seventies, Doris Tucker has been a widow since her husband suffered a fatal heart attack on their wedding night, some fifty years ago. Even so, Doris lives with him every day of the week. They share experiences. They hold full-blown conversations. They have a relationship. She isn't seeing ghosts. Doris has a condition called CVH, otherwise known as complex visual hallucinations. To her, he seems completely real and as solid as you or I, but her husband is imaginary, manufactured by trauma and a mind pushed to the brink. She and her husband turn up to her appointments together, but he prefers to remain in the waiting room, I'm told. I haven't pushed the point of his invisibility. Not yet. Not until Doris is absolutely ready to take the leap. But I will.

"Then there's Mr. Gunderson," Glenda was saying. "Your ten o'clock. He'll blow a gasket if you cancel."

Obstacle number two.

"You know how obsessive he is about his appointments. Every Thursday at ten o'clock on the dot. Sure, if I can get hold of him, I'll do my best to rearrange, but I have a feeling he'll suffer a nervous breakdown if I do. Then your next appointment is at eleven with—"

"Glenda?"

"Yes?"

"You know what? Forget it." I apologized for being short with her, explained I was hungover and grouchy, apologized some more, and then said, "Give me five minutes and then tell Doris she can come right in."

Chapter Nine

The morning dragged, and I dragged myself through it like an unwilling victim on his way to a grisly end. I forced myself to listen to one client after another, trying to remain conscientious and objective, all while fighting to keep my panic from messing with my face.

Finally, lunchtime came, and I made a visit to the restroom, splashed water over my horror-show face, and ran my fingers through my hair.

"You've got this," I told my Halloween reflection, which didn't seem particularly interested in anything I had to say. "Four more clients. That's all. Four hours. You can do this. Now pull yourself together. You don't have a choice."

My reflection had dark circles under its dead eyes.

You get out what you put in, it said.

After Eve had left me in the pool area, I'd spent an indecent amount of the night unable to sleep, hypnotized by the whirring of the overhead fan and haunted by the image of the man I'd seen in the backyard. Or thought I'd seen.

Could it have been Kyle, all grown up?

Eve had me questioning myself, leaving me torn between the possibility that it had been my own drunken reflection and the possibility that my old friend had been on my patio, here in Florida, which seemed less likely the more I gave it airtime.

I hadn't seen Kyle Sanders since we were seventeen, and infrequently before that. He was one of those impermanent friends who wanders in and out of your life at their own leisure. The reality was, I could go months without seeing him; once or twice a full year had passed between encounters. But it was never uncomfortable when we got together. It was always easy being around Kyle.

He was everything I wasn't. He fascinated me. If I was the proton, then Kyle was the electron. Caught in an eternal dance.

Undeniably, he was a bad seed, and I won't make excuses for his questionable behavior at times. Kyle could overstep the mark without hesitation, often taking me with him. But he wasn't like Murdoch. We were kids, and all of our transgressions were minor. Of course, I would resist, at first. I'd argue he was a bad influence on me, presenting all the valid reasons why I shouldn't go along with his mischief. Then I'd give in. Not because I was easily manipulated, but because Kyle offered the only alternative in what was an otherwise unremarkable life.

Each time we met, he was a little older, a little more the social rebel, and a little darker around the edges, like the sunlight itself was having a hard time defining his profile.

I hadn't laid eyes on him in eighteen years.

Part of Eve's escape plan had required keeping our final destination a secret to those we left behind, including friends and acquaintances. Home is where the heart lives, but for me, home was where the heart died. Persuading me to relocate was an easy sell.

No one had come looking.

Until now.

And the only person with a vested interest in tracking me down, to break into my home in the dead of night, was Zane Murdoch.

Not Kyle.

I was mindful of the conversation I'd had with O'Malley earlier, specifically the bit involving Murdoch coming to Florida.

Even if he was innocent—something I still couldn't wrap my head around—I knew he was trouble. And I knew he wouldn't let me get away with my damning testimony against him.

One night, the week before Scarlett had vanished, Murdoch had cornered me on my walk home from the store, hauling me into an alleyway and pushing me up against the rough brickwork, out of view of any onlookers from the street.

With venom, he'd spat, *Either stay out of my business or you're a dead man. You hear me? Keep your snotty nose out or you'll pay the price.*

To emphasize his seriousness, he'd punched me in the gut, hard enough to pancake my lungs and bring on an inevitable blackout.

When I'd come to, I'd found my wallet gone and my pants soaked with urine. Not mine.

Even to this day, the memory makes me shudder.

So last night, unsettled by what I'd seen on the patio, I'd snuck downstairs after Eve had gone back to sleep, leaving off the lights, creeping up to the sliding door, irrationally hopeful of spying someone lurking near the pool. Finding nothing, I'd gone outside, tried the screen door again, then opened it fully and ventured out onto the spongy Bahia grass that separates my home from its neighbors.

I'd checked out the house, padding through the rough lawn, looking for signs of trespassing, which had been wishful thinking given the lack of light.

I'd even wandered down to the river, out onto the creaking boat dock, comforted by the feel of the warm wood under my damp feet. I'd stood there for long, quiet minutes, listening to the chirping of the cicadas and the random splashing of nocturnal creatures out in Fish Trap Bay, scanning the sleeping houses and the black water, which seemed to reach all the way up into the inky sky.

And the more I'd replayed the split-second glimpse of the man in my backyard, the more he seemed to take on a ghostlike appearance, until I'd been left wondering if I'd imagined the whole darn thing.

Or dreamed it.

At the health center, I left the restroom, grabbed a coffee and a bag of chips from the vending machine on the way back to my office, and then sealed myself inside.

Eve always tells me I bottle things up, and that one day I'll blow my top.

I needed answers.

I had forty-five minutes until my one o'clock client.

I took a deep breath and hunched over my laptop, searching for news reports about the exhumation of the body of a murder victim in the Upper Peninsula. Unsurprisingly, there weren't any. Not yet.

It didn't stop my pulse from drumming away in my throat.

Rarely do you hear of someone being convicted of murder without a body to back it up. For that to happen it takes a rock-solid indictment, fortified with concrete evidence and the total elimination of reasonable doubt.

In Scarlett's case, the jury had been unanimous in finding Zane Murdoch guilty as charged, partly because of my testimony against him, but mostly because the bloodstained murder weapon and Scarlett's bloodied shirt had been found in his trash.

First-degree murder had locked him in a cage, but I was the one who had thrown away the key.

The twenty-five-year-old me, with my big mouth and my fiery rage. The empty me, banging a drum for my loss and beating out a funeral dirge. The vengeful me, saying everything I could to convince the world that Zane Murdoch had killed my lovely sister, callously and in cold blood, without a shred of remorse. The vulnerable me, with my visible pain and my inconsolable grief, reducing members of the jury to tears.

Thankfully, I am not that angry, resentful hater anymore.

But I have every reason to think that Murdoch is.

Zane Murdoch—Insane Murdoch, as I'd thought of him back then—with his shifty eyes and his even shiftier lifestyle, selling one-way tickets to dead-end trips.

If he had threatened to take my life then, just for supporting my sister's decision to ditch him, I could imagine what he had in mind for me now, after a decade of stewing, of seething, of scheming.

Jesus Christ. Do I need a bodyguard?

The thought made my head spin.

The state police were digging up my sister.

Damn!

All along, Murdoch had refused to say where he'd hidden Scarlett's body. The arresting officers had tried to squeeze it out of him. The investigators had tried to lever it out of him. The prosecutor had tried to trick it out of him. All this time, Murdoch's lips had remained tightly sealed, and Scarlett had never been found.

Until now.

Until an anonymous tipster had told the police exactly where to look, coincidentally mere days after Murdoch's full pardon.

What were the chances?

In my mind, it left two possibilities: Either Murdoch was the anonymous caller, which meant he had played a part in my sister's death despite his so-called alibi, and revealing her location was his sick way of him maintaining control. Or her true killer was the informant, and the disclosure of her whereabouts was his way to take back ownership now that Murdoch was off the hook.

So where did that leave me?

To begin the process of rewriting history, to change my mind about Murdoch's guilt, I'd need to be convinced of a substitute killer. A credible *someone else* who had taken her life that night. I'd need a name. More than that, I'd need a motive. I knew Murdoch had had one. But try as I might, I couldn't think of anyone else who had wished my sister harm.

Meanwhile, I believed Murdoch had been deadly serious when he'd made those death threats after they broke up.

Would he really come here seeking retribution?

Putting myself in his shoes, I suppose I, too, would come looking for closure, or answers, or to find a palatable excuse for why the brother of the woman who I hadn't murdered had insisted in open court and to the press that I had.

Of course, I was also acutely conscious of the very real possibility that Murdoch wouldn't ask any questions at all, but rather let his fists do the talking, or worse still, the sharp edge of a knife.

My grandmother used to say, *Knowledge is a blessing, but without wisdom it's a curse.*

So I searched online for the phone numbers of some of my Michigan contacts and experienced an unexpected bout of nostalgia as the familiar area code came up.

I found the number for the Schoolcraft County Prosecutor's Office and placed a call, asking for Bob Stanwick. I got put on hold for ten minutes before eventually being told he'd retired five years ago and his replacement was presently unavailable. Bob had been instrumental in the case against Zane Murdoch. Bob had taken me under his wing, coaching me on what to expect as a trial witness. He'd taught me how to overcome stage fright by using my hurt as fuel to power my voice, so that I could speak publicly without being a nervous wreck. Now, I learned, he was living on a golf course in Scottsdale, enjoying the Arizona sunshine. Good for Bob. Bad for me.

"Ted Loewe is the current prosecuting attorney," the clerk informed me crisply down a scratchy telephone line. "He's out of the office right now on official business. On a scale of one to ten, how urgent is your call?"

Even though I use this method myself, I always sigh at this kind of question. Given the choice, the overwhelming temptation is to say *ten*. It's human nature. If something is important enough to move us to action, then it's probably urgent and therefore ranks at the top of our list.

Instead, I said, "Can I leave a message?"

"Go ahead."

"Please tell him Gregory Cole called about the body they're digging up out by Crooked Lake on Ninety-Four, and we should talk as soon as he gets this." I gave her my numbers.

"I'll pass along your message," she told me and hung up.

I could sense from her disinterest that the likelihood of Loewe returning my call was minimal.

Next, I called Manistique City Hall, asked for the police department, and got patched through to a bored-sounding guy with a lisp. I could hear a TV in the background, turned low. People jeering and chanting. I pictured him sitting in a drab office, with his feet up on the desk and an old TV in the corner showing Jerry Springer, laughing as half-naked contestants on his tabloid talk show tried to bitch-slap the last shred of dignity out of each other.

"I'm sorry, sir," he told me after I told him the nature of my call. "I'm unable to comment on any current investigations being conducted through this office. We do accept written requests, but I'm unable to give you a time frame on a response. Of course, you're free to try the state police at their district headquarters in Marquette. Their number is—"

I thanked him and hung up.

I wasn't having much luck.

I studied O'Malley's business card. Against a dark background, his numbers and Jacksonville business address were printed in plain white. No e-mail or website.

Out of curiosity, I called his office number, letting it ring a couple of dozen times before hanging up.

Useless. That's how I felt, suddenly, from nowhere. Utterly useless.

Not quite as I had felt before coming to Florida, but close.

I drank the cool dregs of my coffee, then ran another search on my laptop. This time, I wanted to know more about Murdoch's alibi and how he'd used the law against itself.

Hand up, I am the first to admit I know nothing about the intricate mechanisms of the law. I ought to. The legal system has structure: cause and effect. It's an organized system of checks and balances. As someone who thinks of himself as being schooled in the sciences, I should find it familiar, even comforting. But I don't, and it doesn't interest me one bit.

After clicking through a dozen dead-end sites, I came across an archived news report dated over ten years ago. The article was from the *Daily Globe*, a newspaper with a six-day-a-week print run, serving the western end of the Upper Peninsula.

Homeowners Subjected to Terrifying Nighttime Ordeal, the headline read. Embedded in the small article was a video feed from the local TV station. I hunched over the laptop and clicked the "Play" icon.

A female reporter with impossibly straight blonde hair, and an even straighter face, addressed the camera from beneath a black umbrella. The tip of her narrow nose was reddened with cold, and dreary rain could be seen and heard falling all around her.

"Early this morning, Bryan and Margareta Jenkins endured what can only be described as a terrifying five-hour ordeal at the hands of a masked intruder. The attack took place in this regular family home on the shore of Lake Superior." Expertly, she swiveled to one side, so that the camera revealed a single-story house in the background, complete with rain-soaked police officers deep in conversation, several blue police cruisers, and lengths of yellow crime-scene tape strung limply between trees. "As you can see, it's a modest house, in an area that neighbors describe as a quiet part of town."

She turned back to face the camera. Collected rainwater sluiced off her umbrella.

"Around midnight, the couple say they were disturbed from their sleep by a scratching noise coming from the rear of the property. This is an area regularly frequented by coyotes, and homeowners around here have been advised to secure their garbage cans, especially at night. So when Mr. Jenkins went to investigate, he thought it was a coyote, and it was then that he was confronted by the masked man."

The point of view switched to a longer shot of the property as the camera panned down the length of the shore road, with police vehicles coming and going in a heavy downpour.

"What followed next was something the couple say they will never forget. They were bound and then beaten, over and over, and threatened at knifepoint by the masked intruder."

The camera cut back to the female reporter, her nose redder than Rudolph's, her whole demeanor one of wanting to be anywhere other than where she was.

"As you can imagine, police want to apprehend the man responsible as soon as possible. They describe him as about six feet tall, with a medium build, and say he may be driving a dark-colored pickup truck. Anyone with information is being asked to call—"

The recording came to an abrupt end, and I sat back with goose bumps effervescing on my arms.

The report hadn't revealed anything factually new about the home invasion, but it had brought it a little closer to home, making it more real and present to me. And I couldn't deny the fact that Murdoch fit the description perfectly. Back then, he'd had the kind of physique that some would call wiry, and the mentality of a terrier to go with it. I remember he'd owned a black Subaru pickup, the same truck I'd seen him filling with gas in the photo on O'Malley's phone, and maybe the same one the eyewitnesses had seen fleeing the Ontonagon crime scene.

Could Murdoch be innocent of killing Scarlett?

Could I have been wrong all this time?

The intercom bleeped on my desk.

I pressed the talk button. "Yes, Glenda?"

"Mrs. Sweeney, your one o'clock, is here, ten minutes early."

The time had flown, as it does when visiting cyberspace.

"Thanks, Glenda. Please tell her I'll be out in five."

I took one last look at the news report on the laptop, and then picked up my cell and called Ray Stitt.

Ray is a former client of mine who also happens to be one of Bonita Springs's more outspoken lawyers. Like many of the people you meet down here, he isn't a native. From top to toe, Ray is all Texan, right down to his Lone Star belt buckle.

When I first met Ray six years ago, he was a semiretired trial lawyer specializing in major cases. He'd moved to Florida after suffering a heart attack and on the advice of his doctors to take things easy. He'd come here to pursue a less hectic lifestyle. Ray was used to inhaling the fumes of his high-octane murder trials and not Bonita Springs's relatively low crime rate and cleaner air. It was good for his health but not his career, so after the first year here, he'd had to rethink, to come up with a work-around that kept his hand in the legal process while freeing up time to kick back and play golf.

A lack of meaty cases and the growing sue-me society meant that these days most of his business was personal injury claims. *The way of the world,* he'd told me. *Got to go where the work is.*

"Ray, can I get your advice on something?" I asked him now, after swapping pleasantries. "I'll pay the going rate."

"Sure thing, buddy," he answered cheerily. "But don't insult me by offering money. That's like a dagger in the chest. We're pals, okay? As far as I'm concerned, pals work for each other free of charge and will do so until the cows come home—unless, that is, you've committed a felony, in which case, I ask a hundred-buck retainer."

I surprised myself and laughed for the first time today. The first time in a while, according to the stiffness of my smile muscles.

"So, what can I do you for?" he continued in his deep voice with a Texas twang. "Not like you to call in the middle of a workday. Have you been injured and it's someone else's fault? Have you been hit by an uninsured driver? Have you taken a tumble on a broken sidewalk?" He paused to hear my reaction. Varying only slightly, these were the same questions he asked every time I called. It was an old joke that never wore thin, at least for him.

When I failed to respond, he chuckled. "Shoot," he said. "I'm just messing with you, buddy. It's the spiel. I live, eat, and breathe the spiel. God bless litigation. Sure, let's talk. It's been ages, anyways. And it's always a pleasure. But, hey, I'm a little busy right now. I'm caught up on the fairway on the run up to the ninth. Why don't you swing by the club later—say, after five? I should be done here by then."

Chapter Ten

Unless you're a monster, dealing with the loss of a loved one affects each of us differently but equally. Some people explode, shattering into a million bloody pieces, never to pull themselves together again, while others parcel up the pain and post it to the darkest recess of their mind, pretending it never happened, or if it did, that it was to somebody else. Then there are those who soldier on, battle-scarred but brave-faced, mostly for the sake of their sanity and the comfort of others. For a few, their grief is a vicious dog, chained at the bottom of the yard, snarling and howling, desperate to break free.

The day it does, it will go straight for the throat.

At 5:11 p.m., after closing the office at lightning speed, I collected my car keys from the bartender at Donovan's and then drove a mile north along the Tamiami Trail to Highland Woods Golf and Country Club, with the air-conditioning on full blast.

I was hot and sticky and breathless after speed-walking to the Irish pub. The sky was bruised with rain clouds, and the humidity was cloying. Torrential rain was imminent.

An image of Scarlett had plagued my thoughts all afternoon thanks to Dunn—a nauseating picture festering away in my mind's eye. It wasn't the image of my sister I'd cherished these last ten years—the portrait of a flame-haired girl with sparkling eyes and more energy than a nuclear reactor. That image had been burned to a crisp. Dunn's words had taken her Polaroid snapshot and dropped it in a fire, where it had bubbled and blistered, melting into a monstrosity.

Dunn hadn't been overflowing with details—but they weren't necessary for my imagination to ignite. I'd tried really hard not to get hung up on the little he had told me, and failed.

Ten years is a long time to be buried in the soil without a casket—to protect, to prevent decomposition, to stop the maggots from feasting.

I didn't want to think about what little remained of my sister, her fragile corpse enduring a decade of winters, freezing and thawing, with ultimately everything breaking down.

I didn't want to think about her snow-white skin bruising, blackening, crumbling.

I didn't want to think about her fiery hair turning to ash.

I didn't want to think about any of it.

But I did.

Dunn's words had provided me with a new image of Scarlett, and it was all picked bone.

I drew a shaky breath and pushed the sepia picture to the back of my mind.

How had she ended up at Crooked Lake?

I knew the area well. In our youth, Scarlett and I had explored every twist, turn, and body of water within a thirty-mile radius of home, including just about every accessible puddle in the southeast corner of Hiawatha National Forest. Crooked Lake could be found on a federal fire road just off 94 on the way to Shingleton. You couldn't see it from the roadway. It was secluded, surrounded by trees. Seen from the air, the lake resembled an embryo. One summer, we'd camped there for almost a week, while navigating Stutts Creek. It was one of the shallower tracts in the area, with a smattering of summer cottages smooching the muddy shoreline.

I like it here, Scarlett had said. *It's peaceful. When we're older and we have enough money, we should think about buying one of these quaint little cottages. This is the kind of place I'd like to grow old in, die in. Do you think it will ever happen?*

It seemed unreal, as if it were a dream.

Rain began to pepper the windshield as I turned off the highway. I followed the tree-lined road as it wound through carefully tended flora toward Ray's golf club.

Although I've played a few holes here over the years, always as Ray's guest, no one considers me a regular. I'm one of those hapless golfers with a handicap that rarely gets me out of the rough.

Silently tut-tutting, I went through the laborious guest-sign-in process and was asked to tuck in my shirt and smooth out the creases. I performed a pirouette, much to the consternation of the receptionist, and then made my way to the Grille Room.

The restaurant was busy, clogged with happy silver-haired patrons enjoying a beverage or two with their sandwich selections, replacing precious lost calories after a hard afternoon of putting, or splashing water in aqua-fitness classes. Here in Florida, this is how the other half lives, albeit those with shrewd fund managers and nothing but time on their liver-spotted hands. Tanned senior citizens in slacks and pastels.

I found Ray seated alone at a window table overlooking the eighteenth green, hunched over a half-eaten club sandwich and two glasses of dark beer, one only half-full. When he saw me, he extended a telescopic arm and waved me over.

The blond-haired and suntanned Ray Stitt is six five in his bare feet, with the fatless physique of a dieting scarecrow. Everything about him looks longer than it should, even his face, like he's been stretched out.

A red paper napkin was tucked into the neck of his white golf shirt, giving the impression that his throat had been slit.

As I approached, he got to his feet, yanked the napkin from his neckline, and wiped crumbs from his slash of a mouth, then stuck out a bony hand. "How's it going, buddy?" he said. "You look like a man with the weight of the world on his shoulders. Pretty much the same face I wore the first time we met, if I remember rightly."

Ray Stitt had first sought out my services after the sudden death of his wife, Anita.

Professionally, Anita had worked as an administrator at the city clerk's office in Fort Myers. According to Ray, she was his high school sweetheart and the love of his life, and I believed him; it was evident in the tone of his voice whenever he spoke of her—the same breathless, giddy sound I made whenever I spoke about Scarlett.

Socially, Anita ran marathons, which had meant a strict daily work-out regime, including gym time and the adherence to a special diet. Most evenings, come rain or shine, she could be seen running up and down Bonita Beach Road, from I-75 to Barefoot Beach. She always ran with her headphones on, listening to her favorite ladies of country. And she always ran with a smile on her face.

On a gloomy December evening, she'd kissed Ray good-bye and set out on her daily jog.

Fifty minutes later, Ray had received a personal phone call from the Lee County sheriff, informing him that Anita had been involved in a hit-and-run incident and that she was on her way to the hospital. Ray had dropped everything and rushed over, but Anita was gone by the time he got there. Later, he'd learned that the driver was a thirteen-year-old boy who had been on his way to pick up his sick mother's medicine from a nearby pharmacy. The boy told the police he'd taken her car because it was an emergency, he hadn't seen the stoplight or Anita until it was too late, and he was sorry.

Ray had been a wreck. I'd helped hammer out his dents, applying the same techniques I'd used on myself.

Over the past few years, Ray and I had grown into good friends, happy to poke fun at each other while draining beers and complaining about recessions—both economic and hairline.

Every now and then, when the conditions were right, we'd take my Yellowfin out onto the brackish waters of Estero Bay and spend long, lazy hours fishing for snook, occasionally hooking a tarpon, and snapping plenty of posed photos for Ray's Facebook wall.

"So, what's got you looking like there's a hellhound nipping at your heels?" he asked as we seated ourselves.

I told him all I knew about O'Malley, Detective Sergeant Dunn, and the probability of Zane Murdoch and his brass knuckles paying me an unexpected midnight visit. I told him about Murdoch's overturned conviction for the murder of my sister and the basics of the case against him. I told him I was understandably nervous about Murdoch doing something stupid, in particular, mashing me to a pulp. I told him I needed to know where I stood, legally speaking, if he did show up.

Now it was Ray's turn to prove to me just how paranoid I was being.

"First things first, buddy. I'm sorry to hear about your sister. All this time, you kept it under wraps."

"It's not something you talk about."

"I'm your friend. You could have told me."

"It was a long time ago."

"So was Anita's death, but I think about that last kiss we had every single day." He made a steeple out of his fingers and studied me over their manicured tips, his gold rings standing proud, like the pope in prayer. It was a posture I'd seen before, and I knew what was coming.

"Can I be frank?" he asked.

"Sure."

"Do you own a gun?"

"You know the answer to that."

"I do? I've never asked it before. Humor me." He licked his teeth. It's a habit of his. Randomly, sometimes midsentence, Ray will rub his tongue over his front teeth and suck at them. At first, I'd ascribed it to dry mouth and nerves; he'd done it repeatedly when under my care. Later, I'd learned that he suffered from what he called sticky-lip syndrome. It could be distracting, if you let it. I didn't.

Quietly, I answered. "No, Ray, I don't own a gun. I've never owned a gun, and I don't believe I will ever own a gun."

"Your answer worries me."

"If it's any consolation, it worries me, too. I think I'd feel a whole lot safer if I had one."

"Bad mistake."

"Why?"

"Because most suburbanites can't even piss straight, let alone shoot straight. Not to be insulting here, buddy, but you give some stringy suburbanite like you a handgun and the first thing they do is shoot themselves in the foot. And that's a mess, believe me—I've seen it happen. Bone and ligaments everywhere." Ray flapped a bony hand toward me. "Look at your hands. Go ahead. Take a look at them."

Mindlessly, I did.

"Tell me what you see?"

I turned them over, as though I'd see something that shouldn't be there, like scales or vampire claws. Or blood.

"See those slender fingers, those small knuckles? At best, you have the hands of a woman right there. Now there's nothing wrong with that. I'm no sexist. Women's hands are, on the whole, much nicer to look at than a man's. Softer too. But stick those lady hands on a man and, well, they're as good as useless. Put you in a hand-to-hand-combat situation with those and you'll go down under the first blow."

"Thanks for the vote of confidence."

"You're welcome. Honesty can be a lifesaver. Without question, your best bet would be to learn how to protect yourself properly. And that's with a gun. It's your constitutional right."

"Ray, you just said—"

"I'm not going to beat around the bush here. You want this Murdoch character breaking into your home and sodomizing you in your sleep?"

"No, but I don't think he would—"

"There you go."

"Do I?" I let my confusion show.

He leaned his bony elbows on the table. "First, you need to learn how to shoot, and then you need to arm up. Owning and being trained to use a gun responsibly doesn't make you a criminal or a danger to your neighbors. In fact, it makes you the exact opposite. You become an asset to your community. Look at me. Heck, I practically grew up with a gun in my hand. I could shoot before I could walk. Look how I turned out."

I shook my head at his everybody-loves-a-gun-in-Texas routine and let out a sigh.

"Ray, thanks for the advice, but I don't think—"

"I could teach you."

"You could?"

"Be my pleasure. We're buddies. You trust me, right?"

"Right."

"So I'll teach you. Show you how to handle an Uzi, too, if that's something you fancy. Only trouble is, you'll need at least a dozen lessons to be anywhere close to battlefield-competent, and a whole bucketful of time you don't have right now. If you're right about this Murdoch character being on his way here, we're already too late to talk defensive tactics. Either way, I'm worried about your suburbanite ass."

I closed my mouth, opened it, and repeated the action a few times, my only objection being "I don't live in the suburbs."

Ray leaned forward, glanced around us, and whispered, "Come here."

I pushed my beer aside and leaned on the table.

"Let's look at this from a criminal's perspective. You live on the waterfront in a three-bed, two-bath home worth in the region of half a million. Am I right?"

I nodded.

"You've got a swanky Yellowfin boat and a state-of-the-art aluminum lift out back, with exclusive Gulf access through the idle zone. Am I right?"

Again, I nodded.

"Add that to your income and you're an easy target for the criminally insane among us."

"I am?"

"Sure you are. And on a side note, you're a well-respected member of the community with friends in high places. People don't like people like you."

I pulled my neck in. "People don't like people like me?"

"Not specifically you. The *idea* of you." He breathed out onion breath. "Look, buddy, this isn't a popularity contest. It's a well-known and widely accepted fact that some folks without wealth resent those folks with it. They see someone like you—a singleton sitting comfortably and with what they think is a cushy job—and they have hard feelings."

"They do?"

"Heck, yes. They resent me all the time."

I leaned back. "Which has nothing to do with you being larger than life in any shape or form?"

I didn't say *in-your-face* and *the center of attention*—even though Ray could be and often was.

An offended frown broke out on his forehead. "Buddy, are you saying I'm loud?"

"No noisier than a jumbo jet."

He nodded, sucking at his teeth again. "You know, I was pretty sure you owned a gun."

"Sorry to disappoint. I don't even own a box cutter."

"For a grown man, that's sinful." He sat back in his chair. "Joviality aside, here's what you need to do. The moment this Murdoch character shows his face, you need to call the cops. You don't play the hero and try reasoning with him or try talking him off the bridge. I know you, buddy. I know you'll think you can talk him out of going postal. But, trust me, it's a mistake. Words can get you killed. And you certainly don't want to take the law into your own hands. You don't buy a baseball bat and try knocking his head out of the park. You call the cops. Do you hear me, Greg?"

"Me and half the people here."

He smiled at our silver-haired onlookers, who promptly went back to their gin and tonics, one by one.

"Call the cops," Ray repeated. "Don't try anything with those lady hands. That way, you make it official and everything goes on the record. And then you keep calling the cops every time he makes an unwelcome appearance. Video him on your phone if you can. Show him trespassing on your property. That way, it'll make things a whole lot easier when we apply for a restraining order." He picked up his beer. "One more thing. It'll do you no harm to get yourself a *Canis familiaris.*"

"Wait, what?"

"A dog."

"I know what *Canis familiaris* is."

"So what's with the face?"

"It's just an odd suggestion, that's all."

"Objection. It's a great idea. Look, buddy, the fact is you need an early warning system. The Romans had their geese. NATO has its 'eye in the sky.' You don't own a gun. We've already established you'd fold like a bad hand of poker in a fistfight. So what you need is some other kind of deterrent. Something to make this Murdoch character think twice about invading your home in the middle of the night. Err on the side of caution, my friend. It may sound extreme, but you never know with these prison types. Do the dog thing."

"That's your best advice?"

He reached across the table and patted my arm. "It's golden. Better yet, it's free. Do yourself a favor. Visit the pound first thing tomorrow. Get yourself a furry friend. It doesn't need to be a rottweiler, so long as it goes ape at anything that moves. Now stop looking so put out and drink your beer."

I did, wondering if I had space in my life for a dog, wondering how Eve might react if I turned up with one.

"Besides which," Ray said after draining his own glass, "this Murdoch character is the least of your problems. The real threat to your continuing liberty is this Detective Dunn. State police, right?"

"Right."

"Way I see it, there's only one reason he's flown all the way down here at the taxpayers' expense, and that's because they think you're implicated."

Now I stared at Ray, my shocked expression saying more than I could ever vocalize. Of course, he was right; I hadn't thought it through. Why else would Dunn have traveled all the way down here from Michigan?

Implicated is a big word, and it's often followed with another one: *consequences.*

Suddenly, the beer tasted like vinegar.

"They think I had something to do with Scarlett's murder?"

"I believe they do."

"But Dunn said he just wanted to update me about the case."

"They have phones in Michigan. Right?"

I nodded.

"So the correct protocol here would be to give you a call. They didn't. Instead, they sent this Dunn guy down here on the first available flight. To the best of my knowledge, the only time things like that happen is when they're chasing a hot lead."

"They think I'm a suspect!"

Now, heads really turned our way. All of them, including the caterers behind the buffet counter.

Jesus Christ. They think I'm a suspect.

The thought stuck out in my brain like an ice pick.

Ray put on his crowd-dispersing smile again, sucked some teeth, and then turned back to me. "Buddy, it looks like you did the right thing seeking my advice. In my experience, they only think you're a suspect if they have evidence to back it up. You said this Dunn guy mentioned an interview?"

I snapped out of my shock and checked my watch. "In about forty-five minutes."

"Then you need to give me a buck."

"Why?"

"Just indulge me, buddy."

"I don't have one."

"You don't?"

"No."

"Prove it."

Sighing, I took out my wallet and showed him the empty cash compartments and the credit cards peeping out of their pockets.

He cocked an eyebrow. "What kind of guy doesn't carry cash around?"

"The kind who lives in the twenty-first century and uses cards." I put the wallet away.

Licking his teeth, Ray produced a bulging billfold, tweezed out a crisp dollar bill, and handed it over. "There's the buck I owe you. Now give it back."

I did.

He folded it in half and slipped it in the breast pocket of his polo shirt. "Okay. That's my retainer worked out, right there. Now smile for the camera, buddy. You just hired yourself a kick-ass attorney. Let's go."

Chapter Eleven

Get a dog. Ray's best advice. I imagined a big Saint Bernard crashing through my home, slobbering everywhere, and sending furniture flying.

Eve will never go along with the idea.

This was my predominant thought as I drove farther north on the Tamiami Trail with the wipers on and Ray sitting next to me, sucking at his teeth. Not the upcoming meeting with Detective Sergeant Dunn of the Michigan State Police. Not the possibility of him thinking I was a suspect in my own sister's murder.

I was talking myself out of getting a dog.

It was two hours before sunset, and yet the sky was battleship gray, pocked with powder burns. Vehicles with their lights on dazzled against the gunmetal clouds storming in from the Gulf.

Ray said the obvious: "Thunderstorms tonight."

They were needed. So far, the May temperatures had been a consistent ten degrees higher than the seasonal average. You could feel the change in the air pressure, as though gravity had less of a pull. The hot air vacuuming up water vapor in the Gulf.

"Love a good T-storm." Ray chuckled.

One of the many things I have learned about living in Florida is that the next storm is always just over the horizon.

"Ray, you don't need to do this," I told him as brake lights lit up ahead. "I can handle Dunn."

Ray made a snickering sound. "What are pals for? You'd do the same for me, in a heartbeat. Besides, I've been dying to get my teeth into something juicy for years."

Despite the rapidly blackening sky, Ray wore mirrored sunglasses. I was undecided if it was in protest against the invading clouds or as a defiant fashion statement. I could see the rain-pebbled glass and wind-blown palm trees reflected in the lenses.

Rain slows everything down, and the rush-hour traffic was bad, jammed with an equal number of workers headed home for the day and vacationers looking for somewhere to eat dinner, preferably under cover.

So it took us longer than expected to reach the Federal Building in Fort Myers. I parked on the street, and we skipped over rain puddles until we were inside and dripping on the tiled floor. We took the elevator to the desired floor, and I asked a pleasant-looking admin for Dunn's whereabouts.

"Interview Two," she informed us cheerily. "Right down the hall, second door on the left."

The office space smelled of ink toner and computer heat.

We found him seated at a metal table, working on a laptop. There was an inch-thick file folder on one side of the laptop and a foam cup on the other. He got to his feet as we shuffled in.

"You made it," he observed. "I was beginning to think you got lost."

"Thunderstorm," I said.

He reached out and shook my hand. "Well, I appreciate you making the extra effort, Greg. Who's your chaperone?"

Ray stepped up and took over the handshaking. "Howdy. The name's Raymond Stitt. I'm his lawyer."

Dunn looked at me. "You brought legal representation?"

"Don't give the guy a hard time," Ray said. "It was my idea."

"All the same, you do know this is an informal interview? No one's under arrest here."

"It's okay," I said. "Ray's got my best interests at heart."

"Plus," Ray added, "it's his right to have his attorney present."

Dunn nodded in the way that someone nods when they're not completely sure they like what they're nodding at. "I see. In that case, I'll do my best to watch my p's and q's. You guys have obviously got the jump on me." He motioned with a hand. "Please take a seat."

We did. The metal chairs screaked against the poured cement. Ray leaned a bony elbow on the table and licked his teeth.

Dunn seated himself opposite us. "First things first," he said as he closed the laptop lid. "I appreciate your cooperation in coming down here. As I said this morning, I know you're a busy man, with commitments, and I'm mindful of your situation. I know this isn't easy for you. Our conversation must have brought it all back. How are you holding up?"

In general, people don't ask. We see some stranger shaken by grief and white as a sheet, and we don't ask. It's not because we're disinterested or we don't care. It's not because we're being polite or we don't want to pry. It's because, deep down on a basic level, we fear the grim reaper might notice us showing an interest and take one of our own as payment.

Before I could answer, Ray said, "My client isn't sure why he's here."

Dunn looked at me. "You're not?"

"No," I said. I didn't want to put the word *suspect* in his mind if he wasn't already thinking it.

"Okay. We can fix that soon enough. You do know it's about your sister, though?"

"I do."

"Okay." He didn't appear happy with my answers. "Then let's hope all will become crystal clear as we proceed. Meanwhile, can I get either of you two a coffee or a water?"

I shook my head. "No, thanks."

"Mr. Stick?"

"Stitt," Ray said quietly. "The name's Stitt. And I'm good."

"Okay." Dunn's baggy eyes found me again. "Right, Greg. Then let's get started."

Ray held up a hand. "Objection."

Dunn frowned. "Mr. Stitt, this isn't a court hearing. There's no need to behave like it is."

"You haven't read my client his rights, which is in itself a clear violation of . . . his rights."

I saw Dunn's handlebar mustache twitch. It was hard to tell if it was the result of a pout or a smirk.

"That's because he's not under arrest."

"And what I meant to say was you haven't *advised* him of his rights. As an officer of the—"

"I get it, Mr. Stitt. Thank you." Dunn made a low rumbling noise in the back of his throat and swung his gaze back to me. "Greg, do I need to advise you that you are here of your own free will and that you can leave at any given time?"

"No."

"Do I need to tell you that at this time you are not under arrest and that you are here to assist in the reopened investigation into your sister's homicide?"

My stomach clenched. "No."

"Very well. I'm glad we cleared that up without anarchy breaking out." He took a small silver Dictaphone from his jacket pocket, placed it on the table between us, and pressed a button to start recording. "Interview with Gregory Cole. Fort Myers. Florida. May nineteenth. Mr. Cole's counsel is in attendance."

Ray leaned into me and whispered, "Buddy, if there's anything you're unsure about, anything you feel could adversely affect your good standing, say nothing. You hear me?"

I nodded, not wholly confident I could perform as directed.

Although I spend most of my waking hours listening to others, my one failing is that I am still a man, and men like to hear the sound of their own voice, especially when they feel cornered.

Dunn slid the file folder across the table until it was in front of him. "Okay. Let's get this show on the road. The purpose of this interview is to bring you up to speed on the latest developments in your sister's homicide, and to clarify one or two historical points."

"Exactly what do you mean by historical points?" Ray asked.

"We'll get to those in a moment. Meanwhile"—Dunn placed a hand palm-down on the manila folder and held my gaze—"I must warn you, Greg, this is going to be unpleasant. But I ask that you bear with me. Deal?"

I forced my rigid neck muscles to perform a nod. But if someone had hollered, *Fire!* I would have been the first one blazing his way out into the parking lot.

Dunn opened the folder, and I caught a glimpse of color photographs interleaved within computer-printed notes. I imagined the file was filled with all the original case notes plus those created in the last few days. The overall impression was dark and well thumbed.

I knew what was coming. I'd known it all day.

The back of my tongue tasted like copper.

"I think I already mentioned this: last week, we received an anonymous tip regarding the location of your sister's body."

"You said it was Crooked Lake."

"Correct."

"Did you trace the call?" Ray said.

Dunn all but rolled his eyes. "We're not Homeland Security, Mr. Stitt. We don't have those kinds of resources at our immediate disposal. As far as I know, the call was placed from a disposable prepaid cell phone somewhere in Schoolcraft County." His gaze returned to me. "Two days ago, our crime-scene response team out of Marquette used ground-penetrating radar at the indicated location. Yesterday morning, following positive imaging results, they conducted a dig, about a quarter mile southeast of the Colwell Lake Campground, between Clear Lake Road and Crooked Lake." He licked his thumb and then used it to slide one of the 8 × 10 photos out of the stack, then turned it around and slid it across the table.

Automatically, both Ray and I leaned over.

It was a photograph of an area of marshland under a cloudy sky, with tall birch trees in the background and spring leaves unfurled. There was a speckling of blackflies across the scene, with a gray splinter of lake water visible through silvery tree trunks. Nearer to the camera, a large white tent had been erected on the spongy green marsh. It had no canvas sides, just a peaked roof supported by four metal poles. Beneath this canopy, red-and-white tape marked out a grid pattern on the moss. There were buckets and garden spades on one side, and a trestle table with plastic containers stacked on the top. Three people, each wearing white hooded coveralls, their mouths concealed by surgeon masks and their feet wrapped in black plastic bags, were in the process of conducting the dig. I could see mud on their knees and more of it discoloring their blue rubber gloves. At the edge of the shot was a small mound of freshly turned soil, with leaves and sphagnum moss in the mix, and directly under the center of the canopy was an excavated depression.

A shallow grave.

I felt my windpipe constrict.

"Do you know the area, Greg?" Dunn asked.

"Yes. We camped there." I paused, acting on Ray's interruption, which had come in the form of his foot poking at mine. "I'm familiar with all the lakes in the region."

"Okay, good." Dunn slid another full-page photograph across the table. "Do you recognize this?"

Now, my windpipe wasn't just constricted; it was closed altogether.

"Take a moment," he said. "No rush."

The picture was of a small wristwatch. It looked like a child's wrist-watch. It had been laid out in what looked like a Tupperware container, the kind that usually plays host to packed lunches or baked cookies. Normally innocuous. Not here. A metal ruler lay beside it, used to denote dimensions.

I hunched a little closer, which was the exact opposite of what I wanted to do.

My ears were listening out for the *Fire!* announcement, but all I could hear was static hissing in my head.

The watch had a broken brown leather strap that had at one time been cream in color. Dark soil was clogged in the clasp, and the crystal was cracked, with a bit of it missing, so that it exposed the number 2. The remainder of the glass was scuffed, but on the face I could see Mickey Mouse smiling manically next to the dial. His kid-gloved hands were fixed at the 1 and the 9 positions, indicating that the watch had stopped ticking at 1:45—possibly the same time Scarlett's heart had stopped beating, I realized with a jolt.

Something like prickly heat burst out on my chest and flushed up my neck. The room swayed a little, and I had to grab at the table to steady it.

Distantly, I heard Dunn ask, "You need a glass of water, Greg?"

I shook my head, eyes pinned to the photograph.

The watch looked like it had been in the earth for a long time.

"Whose watch is this?" Ray asked.

"Scarlett's," I sputtered. The word was a razor blade in my mouth. "It's Scarlett's watch. It was a gift, from me."

One of her prized possessions, she'd said. I never knew if she was being genuine or just gracious, but she'd only ever taken it off to bathe, and she'd never left home without it.

It had gone with her to the grave.

The heat in my neck plumed into my face.

"I appreciate your cooperation," Dunn said. "I realize this is difficult for you, each and every way."

It was an understatement. My fingers were white against the metal table. My sweat was giving off a sour scent of zinc and something else. Something that broadcast fear on the pheromone frequency.

"Ready for the next?"

"Is this absolutely necessary?" Ray interjected. "This is tantamount to cruelty."

I sensed that Ray was already becoming irritated with the interview. Ray has a short attention span. It isn't ideal for a lawyer, but he is what he is, and I know he tries his best to hold on to his patience. He'd tell me later that his shutting Dunn down was his way of protecting my interests, his way to make sure I said nothing—especially nothing incriminating. But I knew from his curt tone that he found Dunn's slow and methodical approach tiresome. Ray was all about the big guns. The blaze and the glory.

"It's his sister, Mr. Stitt," Dunn said dismissively. "Let the man speak for himself. I believe he wants to know the truth. Isn't that right, Greg?" His voice sounded like he was speaking in an adjacent room.

Ray leaned into me again. "Buddy, you don't owe these guys a dime. Let me be your eyes and ears on this. I can go through it and give you the gist of things later. You don't need to put yourself through this."

But I did.

And it wasn't for the sake of closure. I know the grave difference in definition between the terms *missing* and *dead*. I know that in cases where a loved one goes missing, with no dead body ever found, it's human nature to hold a candle for them, to hope that they are still alive and will one day come home. I have counseled such people—those who stumble across the rocky terrain between hope and grief, searching for proof of *missing* or *dead*. But in this respect, I imagine I was the atypical griever. The one-percenter who didn't need physical confirmation to know it had happened.

Dunn placed another 8 × 10 in front of me, and I swear my heart stopped beating for at least two seconds, allowing gravity to pull precious blood from my brain.

In vivid color, it showed the open grave in its entirety.

I could see the spade impressions where the dark, fibrous soil had been scraped back, scooped out to a depth of a couple of feet to reveal what looked like a ragged red woolen blanket lying at the bottom. The slight undulations of its surface hinted at the horror that lay beneath. A white-suited technician was kneeling at the side, leaning over, with a paintbrush in his gloved hand. It looked like a regular paintbrush, bought from any hardware store. The camera had caught him in the act of sweeping soil from the stained wool, which he was getting ready to put in an evidence bag.

"As you can see," Dunn said softly, "her killer didn't just dump her at the lakeside, Greg. He rolled back the sphagnum moss and laid her to rest. He took care here. He took his time. In our experience, a killer only ever covers his victim's face like this for one of two reasons: either remorse or affection." He slid another photograph over the top of the last. "Sometimes both."

Hornets were humming in my ears.

This one was a close-up of something unrecognizable.

At first, I didn't know what to make of it, not sure I wanted to. There is a condition known as pareidolia. It's an offshoot of apophenia, which is when our minds assign patterns to otherwise meaningless or random things. It's pareidolia that prompts people to report seeing a face on Mars or a religious figure in a piece of toast. But for the life of me, I couldn't see anything remotely familiar in the photograph.

Look closer, whispered a voice inside my head.

The picture was of a twisted lump of *something* against the dark-soil background.

It resembled part of an old leather purse, dropped by accident on a camping trip and lost in the woods, then slowly absorbed into the marsh soil. It was brownish in color, with blacker creases where the leather had folded over on itself and fused. A ring of darker mottles crossed it on the diagonal, like ink soaked in blotter paper.

Look closer, whispered the voice. *What do you see?*

And suddenly my brain worked it out.

It was a human neck, slightly bent to one side, compressed, with a soft curve of shoulder running into it. The flattened, angular impression of a jawline disappeared out of the top of the picture. There was no way of telling if it was a woman's neck. But I knew that it was. The conditions had dyed her snow-white skin into a darker pigment. Hardened her soft flesh into waxy leather. There was the sawtooth ridge of a collarbone and the squashed dip of a suprasternal notch.

Scarlett's neck.

I swallowed in vain at the vomit welling in my throat.

Through the ringing in my ears, I heard Ray asking questions a mile away: *Why does it look the way it does? Why isn't it just bone by now? How can there be anything left after ten years in the ground?*

And just as distantly, I heard Dunn's responses: *These particular soil conditions slow decomposition. There's less oxygen for bacteria to break down matter. Peat bogs partially preserve, because the humic acid acts like vinegar, effectively pickling the body. In other words, the cadaver was naturally mummified.*

All the while, my brain was superimposing a memory of Scarlett's living neck on the photograph, futilely attempting to discredit it as a fake. But the closer I looked, the more the unalterable truth squeezed at my heart.

My sister had become a fossil.

Half a minute passed before I realized Dunn was speaking my name.

"See those black patches, the ring of stars? Greg?"

I blinked. "Excuse me?"

"The black freckling." He pointed at the inkblots circling her throat. "Our forensics people believe this is traumatic bruising, likely caused at the time of death. Added to the fact that her killer covered her face, we're looking at what could be a crime of passion."

"Whoa," Ray said. "Slow down there, partner. It's my understanding she was stabbed to death. It formed the bulk of the case against Murdoch. The police recovered the murder weapon together with a blood-soaked blouse in his trash, right? Now you're saying she was strangled?"

"I'm saying, until the full pathology results come back, we won't know for sure if manual strangulation was the cause of death or if the bruises you see here were inflicted antemortem. But it's certainly on the table. As for the stabbing theory, initial indications show a lack of visible knife wounds on the body."

"In other words, you believe the murder weapon was a fake?"

"We're not ruling anything out. Until the body is examined in its entirety, we won't be able to say for sure what role, if any, the knife played in her death."

I had lava in my throat.

"How sure are you it's her?" Ray asked.

"Pretty sure. We found a wallet in the grave. Inside, among other things, was Scarlett Cole's driver's license. Of course, at some point we'll need a visual identification to confirm things." His eyes came back to me. "You good with that, Greg? Maybe next week sometime, when everything's sunk in—you come up to Marquette and do the deed? The department will cover your expenses."

I blinked. The lava was scalding the back of my nose.

"We'll see," Ray said.

Dunn shrugged an okay, and then he placed another photo over the last. It was the close-up of a hand. A crooked witch's hand with brown batwing skin. With twig fingers terminating in yellowed talons.

In my stomach, something was trying to claw its way out.

"Within the last hour," Dunn said, "I received word that our forensics team has found what they believe to be epithelial cells under those nails."

"Someone else's skin?" Ray said.

"It's unlikely they belong to the victim."

"So," Ray said, "you're saying she scratched her killer?"

Dunn's eyes were aimed at me, locked and loaded. "Given the preserved nature of the corpse, they're confident viable DNA can be recovered from under those nails. And if that's the case, they have orders to fast-track the testing. We'll know within the next seventy-two hours, either way."

Ray blew out an expletive under his breath. "And if you find a match to someone on record, you find her killer." He turned to me. "This is great news, buddy."

Dunn was staring at me with sharklike intensity.

"It'll come back with a match to Murdoch," I said confidently. "He was physical with Scarlett toward the end."

And occasionally before that, too, I knew. One of the reasons Murdoch and I had come to verbal blows so many times.

Dunn's expression was set in stone. "I'm sorry, Greg. Each and every way, Zane Murdoch did not kill your sister."

"He had a motive," Ray said.

"Yes, he did. But he also had an alibi."

Ray sucked his teeth, then said, "We all know alibis can be fabricated."

"Not this one," Dunn said. "Where were you that night, Greg?"

"You've read my statement."

"It says you also failed to provide an alibi."

"That's because I didn't need one." Roughly, I shoved the photographs back across the table. "You're wrong," I said.

"About what?"

"About me killing my sister."

"What makes you think that's my endgame?"

"I'm a psychotherapist. Reading people's minds is what I do. That's the real reason why you came down here. Not to tell me you found my sister. You're following the path of least resistance. Blindly taking a cheap swing at the piñata, hoping I spill the goodies. You think I killed my sister."

"Did you?"

I slammed a hand against the table, hard enough to make Dunn blink. "How dare you!" Suddenly, my skin was aflame, my blood boiling. I am not a violent man, but something animalistic inside of me, the creature clawing away in my belly, wanted to reach out and grab Dunn's throat. "She was my sister. My twin. I would never hurt her. Who do you think you are, coming here accusing me? I'm the last person in the world you should be looking at!"

Ray reached out a cautioning hand. "Buddy, that's enough. Don't say another word."

I shrugged him off. "This isn't about finding her real killer. This is about your department saving face. I imagine everyone back home is walking on broken glass after Murdoch's release, and you've been sent here to apply a Band-Aid. A quick fix." I slammed my hand down again. "For the record, I loved my sister. I loved every atom of her being. I loved her more than life itself. I protected her. She was all I had. I would have died that day in her place rather than cause her any harm."

Dunn didn't look fazed by my emotional outburst. He stroked his thick mustache, like he had all the time in the world. "And yet you frequently supplied her with psilocybin, a powerful hallucinogenic. Do you call that the act of a responsible brother looking out for his sister's well-being?"

All at once, the ceiling seemed a foot lower than it had been moments earlier, the walls a few feet closer in, the air a little thicker.

"Detective," Ray said, "if this line of questioning is in any way designed to entrap my client, there will be legal ramifications. We're here in good faith. I'm advising my client not to answer any questions which might incriminate him. So unless you plan on arresting him, please back off."

"Mr. Stitt, I'm just trying to clarify a few points here. To establish your client's whereabouts that night, for the record, and to get to the bottom of any drug use that may have played a crucial part in the victim's mental state at the time."

"Scarlett's mental health is none of your business," I said.

Dunn looked at me. "Except, you do want to get to the truth, don't you, Greg?"

I had fire in my lungs. I was on the edge of my seat. I wanted to get up and run, slam a few doors on the way out, make a big deal out of feeling victimized. But I stayed seated, simply because I wasn't the victim here. Scarlett had been strangled and dumped in a shallow grave. And the lure of wanting to know what had happened to her was stronger than my own cowardice.

"The original police investigation exposed you as a small-time drug dealer, did it not?"

"No, not exactly."

"The way I hear it, if anyone in Manistique wanted to trip the light fantastic, you were their first port of call."

"That's not true."

"And yet your own statement says otherwise."

He slid a sheet of paper across the table. On it was a detailed laboratory report, complete with hexagonal formula diagrams.

"The toxicology screen for the blood found on the knife and the shirt recovered from Murdoch's garbage can showed traces of psilocin. Do you know what that is, Greg?" He didn't wait for me to answer. "It's a mind-altering drug. It says right here"—he glanced down at another document in the folder—"that psilocin is produced in the body as a by-product after a person ingests psilocybin, a substance found in psychedelic mushrooms." He looked up again. "Is this right, Greg?"

"I guess."

"And under questioning, didn't you admit to selling magic mushrooms right out of your grandfather's store?"

Now I felt Ray's curious eyes on me. I imagined he was asking himself exactly what he'd gotten himself into. I know I was.

"As I said in my statement, I didn't sell them directly."

"Indirectly, then. But you still supplied them. Says right here they're an illegal substance regulated by the Psychotropic Substances Act."

"It was a harmless extract, in powdered form. My grandfather had it shipped in from China. He'd stocked it for years. No one regarded him as a drug dealer. Besides, it satisfied all the customs checks. It wasn't in its pure form. It came combined with several other herbal extracts. You mixed the powder with water and drank it, like a tea. It was a customer favorite. I even drank it myself."

"But this isn't just trace amounts we're talking about, Greg."

"That's because Scarlett consumed it in the powdered form."

"She exceeded the recommended dose."

I nodded. "For medical reasons."

It had been another one of my bright ideas, to help lighten her depression following the death of our grandparents. Like telling her about LSD in college and its power to ward off headaches. The psilocybin had helped Scarlett shake off her depression and her LSD dependency. It was switching one addiction for another, but a lesser of two evils, and one we thought we could both live with.

I heard Ray lick at his teeth. It sounded like a barber's cutthroat razor being sharpened against leather.

"It was never brought up in court," Dunn said, "you being the town's go-to guy, because by that point you weren't a prime suspect."

I leaned close to the Dictaphone. "For the record, I was never a prime suspect."

"And the only reason drug-dealing charges weren't pressed at the time was because of the extenuating circumstances."

And my solemn promise to discontinue retailing the potion.

"Puts a whole new complexion on the case, don't it?" Dunn said.

He had a good way of making me sound bad.

Ray pushed his chair back noisily. "Okay, I think we've heard enough here. It seems to me you brought my client here under false pretenses. Shame on you, Detective. At no point were you one bit interested in giving my client solace. Instead, you wanted to walk him into a confession. And that's leading a material witness."

Dunn's mustache twitched. "No, it isn't."

"Either way, the long and the short of it is, we're done here." Ray got to his feet, hooked his skeletal fingers under my arm, and hoisted me up. I stood, heavily but willingly, with dots in my vision and gasoline in my veins. "Come on, buddy," he said. "This interview's just about burned itself out. Let's go someplace that doesn't smell so much of manure."

We were at the door when Dunn called, "I will need that visual ID. Plus, I have a feeling we'll be talking again when those DNA results come back."

Ray paused in the doorway. "Take my advice, Detective. Next time you're down here on a deep-water fishing trip, I suggest you bring your long waders."

Chapter Twelve

A flat disk of platinum sunshine hung in a cobalt sky, creating ghostly reflections on the lake. Blurry watercolor renditions of trees and marsh grasses on the periphery. Swarms of blackflies forming a visible wind, blowing and swirling over the mossy ground.

I knew I was dreaming, because Scarlett was alive and walking toward me.

I was standing on the muddy shoreline at Crooked Lake, with its soft silt oozing between my toes and the warm spring sun warming my back, giddied by the sight of my sister as she emerged from the silvery water without causing a single ripple. Her skin was completely dry, her red hair afire, as though she were surfacing from a lake of liquid mercury.

"I'm dead because of you," she said as she joined me on the narrow beach, sparks crackling from her scalp. Her eyes were bottomless holes.

I tried to speak, but no sound came out.

"You killed me, Greg."

As if to confirm her words, a reddened noose developed on the skin around her neck. Starfish imprints of fingers and thumbs.

I tried to reach out, but my arms remained limp at my sides.

"I wouldn't be here if it weren't for you." Purposefully, she raised her hand, and in it I saw the curved blade of a chef's knife glinting in the sunlight. Then she let loose a high-pitched scream and lunged.

I stumbled backward, heels catching on the sphagnum moss. The world tipped up, and I fell into the ground, into her shallow grave, the breath knocked from my lungs.

Then we were teleported to my darkened bedroom in Bonita Springs, with me sprawled helpless on the bed while a snarling Scarlett came at me with the chef's knife held high, her blue lips peeled back and her banshee scream shredding air molecules.

Instinctively, I tried to scrabble away from her, across the bed, but I couldn't move even a fraction of an inch. Fear had me paralyzed, I realized. Every atom fixed in place.

Her arm swung higher; her scream intensified. She reached the edge of the bed, looming over me.

Scarlett was going to gut me like a fish.

The makings of my own terrified scream gargled in my throat. I tried with all my might to roll aside, but I was trapped in an unresponsive body. All I could do was watch, horrified, as her hand plunged in a smooth arc, slicing through the remnants of the air.

The blade buried itself in the soft dough of my chest.

And I burst back into consciousness with a jolt, vibrating like a tuning fork, Scarlett's chilling scream still ringing in my ears.

For a second or two, I still couldn't move, pinned to the mattress like a bug, naked and spread-eagled, while my heart flapped around in my chest like a caged bird. Then my muscles sputtered out of their paralytic state, and cool air rushed into my lungs.

The ceiling fan revolved slowly above the bed, its broad blades churning up starry motes in my night vision.

And I realized with relief that the nightmare was over.

It had started shortly after Scarlett's death, the sleep paralysis. My physician had told me it was stress-induced, which wasn't the least bit surprising, given that I was a complete mess. He said I had a nervous energy, and that it needed burning off at regular intervals. He compared it to a heating system with no release valve; the pressure builds up until something gives. He told me to join a gym. I told him exercise wouldn't cut it. So I'd tried conventional medication, exhausting all of the over-the-counter remedies, but my sleep problems had persisted. I'd moved on to meditation, humming *om* until I gave myself a migraine. Still, with no positive effect. I'd even tried holistic treatments and burning incense. Nothing had worked. Nothing except psilocin, in its undiluted powdered form.

Taking psilocin had completely broken the sleep paralysis spell. But the reprieve wasn't without its side effects, the principal one being an occasional disposition toward drug-induced hallucination.

For months I was caught between a rock and a hard place. Go cold turkey and when I woke I'd do so stuck inside a nightmare, my skin hardened into a sarcophagus with me trapped inside. Take the psilocin and the sleep paralysis was gone, but I'd see ghosts everywhere I looked, sometimes following me home.

With Eve's help, I'd weaned myself off. But there were still moments when I thought I saw things that weren't real, worried that my brain chemistry was permanently altered.

The nightmare had ended, but the echo of Scarlett's bloodcurdling scream still clawed at the insides of my skull.

I tilted my head on the pillow and listened.

Not Scarlett's howl, I realized. A night creature caterwauling outside. Either a raccoon or a neighbor's house cat, complaining about an invaded territory or a locked garbage can.

Something else, too. Rain. I could hear its steady rhythm as it drummed against the backyard. When it rains in Florida, it's often torrential. I looked toward the window just as lightning strobed through the closed blinds, and then I waited, holding my breath and listening, to hear a crash of resonant thunder a second or two later.

Bones creaking, I rolled out of bed and padded over to the window, parted the blinds, and peeped out.

My bedroom faces the river. In daylight, it's a picturesque scene, split equally between vivid green and serene blue. The window overlooks the top of the screened pool area, past the creeping river, and on to the tangled mangrove forest beyond. It's a great place to spot osprey on still days or watch neighbors tinker with their pleasure craft. At night, aside from a few lights denoting the locations of the boat docks, everything is pitch-black.

And that's why the new light caught my attention right away.

It was a small white disk, playing over the grassy backyard and out across the rain-beaten water. A flashlight, sweeping back and forth, turning the downpour into iron bars. I watched it for a second, wondering who was down by the river at this hour in the middle of a thunderstorm. Then I saw the beam pick out the wooden skeleton of my boat dock, and my curious thoughts were immediately upgraded to a panic station.

Somebody was messing around near my boat!

Know this: to a boy brought up on Michigan's lakes, interfering in any way with his boat is comparable to a rustler stealing a pioneer's horse in the days of the Wild West.

It's not just bad manners; it's unforgivable.

I let the blinds snap closed, fumbled around at the foot of the bed for my sweatpants, hopped clumsily into them, and then headed downstairs, pulling on a T-shirt as I went.

Another burst of brilliant lightning lit up the house as I hurried to the kitchen. Without slowing, I slid a chef's knife out of the block on the countertop.

Then I caught myself short, staring at the silvery blade in my hand, suddenly catapulted back into the nightmare, with my heart banging and bright blood dripping from the razor edge.

Scarlett's death knell rising inside of me.

Who was I kidding? As Ray had rightly pointed out, I knew less than nothing about self-defense. The only hand-to-hand combat I was familiar with was a fist bump. Under threat of violence, I couldn't tell the difference between kung fu and egg foo yong.

I looked at the knife, remembering Ray's advice. If pushed, could I actually use this thing? Did I even want to?

Recent events had made me paranoid. There was probably a perfectly reasonable explanation for someone skulking around on the dock at three in the morning. Maybe it was Phil Duffy, my next-door neighbor, looking for his cat. It wouldn't be the first time I'd woken in the night to find him fishing his cat out of the water. Maybe I was just overreacting.

"And if it's not Phil, you're just going to scare them off," I said out loud, as though hearing the words would embolden me.

But I was unsure exactly who would be the most scared when it came down to it—me or the trespasser. You hear about the citizen vigilantes and the woefully inexperienced knife-wielders who think they're up to the challenge but end up dead.

Paranoia gets people killed. And I know from experience that the simplest answer is usually the right one. Unless I wanted to wake the neighborhood and cause a scene, there was no need for me to go rushing out there like a crazy fool and scare the living daylights out of a neighbor rescuing his beloved feline.

I slid the knife back in its slot.

But what if it wasn't Phil? What if somebody was trying to steal my boat?

What if it was Murdoch?

A voice in my head said, *Call the police.*

It was the sane and responsible thing to do.

Even so, I picked up the knife again. "You're just going to warn them off," I repeated, this time less shakily. "If it turns out to be trouble, you run."

Besides, I'd made the drive from Manistique to Bonita Springs myself almost ten years ago; I knew that unless Murdoch had driven the sixteen hundred miles south without a break, there was no way he'd be here now.

In the dark, I backtracked and made my way through the shadowy living room, deactivating the security light before opening the doors and stepping outside.

The downpour was deafening.

The thunderstorm had reduced the nighttime heat and transformed everything beyond the mesh into a chaotic fuzz. Noisy raindrops battered the screens, dripping through the mesh and into the pool, puddling on the lawn chairs. I reached for the flashlight hooked on the wall, then frowned when I saw it wasn't there. I contemplated returning inside and searching for the spare, but decided it would waste too much time.

Somebody was on my dock.

Barefooted, I crossed the wet patio and slipped silently through the screen door. The full force of the rain drenched me within seconds, my hair plastered to my scalp and my clothes clinging. The only saving grace about Florida rain is it's rarely cool. I kept the knife pointed down at my feet and ventured out onto the rain-slicked grass. Wet blades sliced between my toes.

Down by the river, the disk of light was still roving around on the boat dock, offering brief flashes of wet planking and the ribbed underbelly of the vinyl canopy. Rain hammering on the roof sounded like a never-ending drumroll.

Just a neighbor, I told myself.

I slithered down to the dock, blinking away raindrops.

"Hey there," I called. "That you, Phil? Your cat gone in the river again?"

The flashlight stopped its dance, then rotated like the beam from a lighthouse until it struck me in the face and stayed there for a couple of seconds without the owner answering, which suggested I was wrong about the identity.

I squinted from behind a raised hand. "This is private property. This is my dock. You shouldn't be down here."

From behind the glare, I heard a man's voice shout, "Just admiring your boat, is all."

"In the middle of the night?" It came out a scoff, and I immediately regretted it. I had no idea who I was dealing with.

Okay, so I was armed, but I wasn't dangerous. Far from it. Ask me to dice an onion and I've got that covered. Expect me to stab through flesh, maybe scuff bone, causing mortal injury, and you and I are going to lock horns. The knife was more for show than anything else, a deterrent. Hopefully, the intruder wouldn't know the difference.

"I see she's got twin Mercury Verados," he called from behind the glare, completely ignoring my comment. "What's her maximum speed—forty-five?"

"Fifty."

"Nice."

I couldn't see his face, or anything else for that matter; everything behind the flashlight was totally black, and my vision was blurred by rainwater sluicing into my eyes.

I curled my fingers tighter around the knife handle and blew a drip from the tip of my nose. "Why don't you come out of there?"

"Sure. No problem." I heard him clambering around—*in my boat*—wet soles squeaking against the smooth hull, then heavy footfalls splashing on the planks, coming my way.

The flashlight stayed in my eyes the entire time, jiggling as its owner stepped down onto the grass.

I motioned with a hand. "You shouldn't be here. This side of the river is all private property. My neighbor's a paranoid insomniac. He sees you skulking around, he'll call the police, the National Guard, and CNN."

Bad humor. It's a knee-jerk reaction of mine, my way of displacing negativity. It's not always appreciated, and it's not always appropriate. Worse still, it isn't always funny. Even so, it helped me handle the fact that I was talking to someone who, seconds earlier, had been messing around in my boat.

I nodded at the glare. "Do you mind?"

"Oh, excuse me."

The beam fell, leaving white-hot brands on my vision.

"I'm not looking for trouble," he called.

The heavens lit up, momentarily illuminating the waterfront and the man facing me, but it was too quick to reveal his features. All I caught was the outline of his plastic rain poncho—the kind tourists pick up at theme parks for a couple of bucks—and a ball cap pulled tight on his head.

"Do I know you?"

"Sure you do." He raised the flashlight and shone it over his own face. "It's me."

Thunder exploded across the sky, and a hot spike of adrenaline pierced my chest. I willed my legs to run, but they refused.

Murdoch!

"How'd you get here?" I heard myself say pathetically.

"On gasoline and caffeine." He smiled. "Long time no see."

Now my mouth flapped wordlessly.

He was older than the last time we'd stood face to face. He was heavier, and unshaven, with his blond hair stuffed under his cap. Even so, he was unmistakably recognizable as the man I'd seen in the photograph on O'Malley's phone.

Anger surged, and every one of my muscles tensed.

Instinctively, I brought the knife to bear and held it between us, hand shaking, with warm rain running down my arm.

Murdoch didn't flinch one bit.

Run! the voice in my head screamed. But my legs weren't listening.

A couple of long seconds stretched past, while the buckshot rain crackled against his poncho.

"Back off, Murdoch!" I shouted at last, in a voice at least two octaves higher than normal. "I don't know what you're hoping to achieve by coming here. But you're not welcome."

Nevertheless, he took a step forward. "Come on, Greg. What's with the knife? This is no way to greet an old friend."

"We were never friends."

"You're right. All the same, I've come a long way to see you. The least you can do is invite me in and let me dry out. Lord knows, we have a bunch of catching up to do."

I hoisted the blade. "We have nothing to talk about."

He tilted the flashlight so that it lit the nylon strands of rain between us. "Don't turn me away. Not like this. Where's your charity? I used up the last of my gas money on the ride down." He took another step toward me.

"I mean it, Murdoch. You shouldn't be here."

"Last time I looked it was a free country."

"Not on my property."

"I just want to talk. I hear that's what you do these days."

"We have nothing to talk about."

"Sure we do. For starters, my innocence."

I flicked the knife. "I said, back off!"

He didn't. He took another cocky step forward. "Will you stop with the hostility already? You owe me, Greg. All I want is for you and me to have a conversation. A few minutes of your time, face to face and man to man. Is that too much to ask after what you did?"

Now I was shuffling in reverse, bare feet sloshing through the water-logged grass, with both hands held out defensively. I snatched a glance left and right, hoping that one of my neighbors had heard us shouting. But the din of the downpour drowned everything.

Thunder growled down the street like a defensive dog.

I felt the wet mesh of the lanai push against my shoulders, and realized I'd backed up as far as I could go.

Murdoch pressed on, slowly, assuredly, like a leopard cornering a gazelle, blinding me with the light.

He stopped within inches of the blade and held the flashlight pointed upward, so that it illuminated our faces. "I'm not here to fight with you, Greg. I'm over all that. Sure, I was angry in the early days. Maybe for a long time. But I found God inside. I learned the power of absolution. It was the best thing ever to happen to me. It changed me. I'm born again."

The knife was wavering. "Good for you. So, what do you want with me?"

It was an unexceptional question in exceptional circumstances, and it didn't need to be said. I was too scared to come up with anything more original. The last thing I expected him to say was:

"I'm here to tell you I forgive you, Greg."

"Forgive me?"

"For all those nasty and untrue things you said about me. I know they came out of your darkness. I know you didn't mean any of it. I forgive you."

"I don't want your forgiveness."

"Yeah, well, sometimes we get what we need instead." He motioned with the flashlight. "So come on, will you? Let's cut through this bullshit. Let's be real about this. We both know I didn't kill Scarlett. Heck, I loved the girl, just like you did."

"You turned her into a monster!"

I'd always thought it, always sickened myself with it, but it was the first time I'd said it out loud, and it shocked me to hear the words take a life of their own.

All Murdoch could say was "Wow." Then: "Scarlett was a free spirit. You of all people know that. I never forced her to do anything she didn't want to do."

"You supplied her with drugs."

"We both did. Okay, so my decision-making capacity back then wasn't great. I was in a weird place. We all make mistakes, Greg. None of us are saints. Don't be angry with me for my past sins. If anyone has any cause to be pissed, it's me. I'm the one who lost the last ten years of his life."

Before I could respond, his free hand swooped in and plucked the blade right out of my grasp. And suddenly it was pointed at my chin.

I flattened myself against the mesh, cowering. My stomach was all over the place, my windpipe tightening into knots. I blinked at the rain running down my face. Somewhere in the back of my head I could feel the pressure changing as gravity drained the blood from my brain.

My precious vasovagal syncope was going to steal me away, rob me of any chance to talk my way out of the jam I was in.

I was going to faint, and there was nothing I could do to stop it.

"In spite of what you think, Greg, I did love her. Maybe not the same way you did, but she meant a lot to me. Her death didn't just affect *you*. I lost her as well, and much more." He brought the tip of the blade to my jaw. "I've done a lot of thinking in the last ten years. Trying to figure out who really killed her. Funny thing was, I could never get past you." He stroked the tip against the stubble on my chin. "Was it you, Greg? Were you the one?"

When there is no way out, a cornered rat will fight to the death, even one with little expectation of surviving the fight.

I don't know what came over me, other than some prehistoric rush of hormones and any number of emotions, all slamming into my hypothalamus at the same time: fear, anger, shame. Foremost, a frantic will to live.

My arm came up and batted his hand aside. Then I was throwing my weight into him, knocking the flashlight from his other hand and forcing him back on his heels.

But Murdoch had had ten years of warding off such attacks, and with little effort on his part, he turned aside and used my own momentum to sling me to the rain-soaked grass.

I hit the ground hard enough to send me sliding a few feet through the surface water, coughing and spluttering as I went. I came to a stop with cymbals clashing in my ears and rolled onto my back, rain bombarding my face.

Murdoch's silhouette loomed over me, a shawl of rain wrapping itself around him.

Lightning flickered, and in its harsh freeze-frame glare I caught a glimpse of the knife in Murdoch's hand and the makings of a cruel laugh beginning to divide his face.

"It's time to face your demons!" he shouted.

I blinked against the rain pathetically, too frozen by fear to even lift a finger in my own defense.

"You're going to confess before God even if it kills you!"

Then thunder bellowed, and the scene went black.

For a second or two, my only sensation was my hearing, and it was filled with the high-pitched scream of my brain as it cried out for oxygenated blood.

Then, even the screech of approaching death was sucked away into the interminable darkness, and I fell helplessly into a bottomless pit.

Chapter Thirteen

One summer, in an effort to be different, Scarlett had assigned Native American names to both of us.

Being someone other than ourselves is a universal fantasy. What child doesn't pretend to be a Disney princess or a Marvel superhero? To kids, playing make-believe is a natural part of social development. It helps overcome fears and fuels imagination. And the costume manufacturers are making a killing off it.

Scarlett never admitted to it, but Kevin Costner was her first Hollywood crush, even though he was a little before her time, and too old for her by twenty years. The movie that got her smitten was *Dances with Wolves*. I remember our grandmother grudgingly buying it on video, just to keep Scarlett quiet, and Scarlett watching it obsessively, over and over, until she could recite the script by heart.

My Native American nickname was Costner's fault. For the remainder of her time on Earth, Scarlett had called me Fainting Goat.

Hey there, how's my favorite fainting goat doing today? Why is Fainting Goat looking so down in the dumps again? Does Fainting Goat want to go for a paddle in a puddle?

Looking back, I'm sure she meant it as a term of endearment. Let's face it—it could have been much worse; until my head grew into my features, I'd had sticky-out ears and legs as thin as string, with knots for knees. Couple those with my carrot-top, and is it any wonder I ended up interested in therapy?

I suppose, even though Fainting Goat was nowhere nearly as cool as Superboy or Batkid, it was preferable to Jumbo or Jughead, and I'd lived with the nickname without complaint.

But there is no dignity when it comes to vasovagal syncope. Not then and not now.

As consciousness knocked me back into reality with a wet slap, I opened my eyes to find I was draped over a pool chair on my patio like a discarded beach towel.

Groggily, I pushed myself into a seated position and let out a quivering breath.

I had no idea how long I'd been out of it. It was still dark, but the storm had passed, leaving behind it a moonlit sky and a symphony of dripping sounds.

I rubbed my hands through my damp hair, then slapped my cheeks. Definitely awake.

The question of how I'd ended up on a pool chair on the screened lanai didn't raise itself right away. It was only as I got to my feet and looked down at the mud on my sweatpants that I began to wonder, to remember.

Murdoch!

I scanned the pool area, thinking I'd find him lurking in a shadow, preparing to come at me again with the knife, to finish the job. It didn't occur to me that he'd already attacked me and I was still alive.

I had no memory of what had happened.

"Greg?"

It was Eve's voice, coming from inside.

I turned and went into the house.

She was floating down the stairs, her hair all mussed up, one of my old T-shirts hanging to midthigh.

"What the hell is going on down there?" she demanded.

I paused, with my foot on the first tread, then backed up as she breezed the rest of the way down.

"Was somebody out by the pool again? The security light didn't come on." She peered over my shoulder, as though she had X-ray vision and could see through the walls.

"I switched it off."

She noticed the damp patches on my pants, and her disgust was evident. "You look like you've been crawling through a storm drain."

"I was out in the rain." It was less than a decent explanation, but I didn't have anything else to offer; there was a gap in my timeline and a turn of events I couldn't explain.

Eve leaned in and sniffed. "Jeez, you reek. What happened?"

"I fainted."

"You fainted? Again? Where? In the river?"

"You'd think so."

She didn't look happy. "Were you sleepwalking?"

I drew a big breath.

The truth is, face to face, I find it impossible to lie to Eve. Sure, I can obfuscate. I'm a man; avoidance is inbred. But like all women, Eve comes equipped with a sixth sense. It doesn't mean she can see dead people. It means she has a nose for emotional changes, and one that can sniff out dishonesty better than any polygraph machine.

"There's something you need to hear," I said, then took her gently by the shoulders and steered her into the living room.

She didn't go willingly; I had to push a little, but eventually she let me guide her to the couch.

"Is this about Zoe? Because you were definitely upset with her yesterday."

"No, it's not Zoe."

"Have you heard from her since?"

"No. But this is something completely different. Unrelated."

I sat down and indicated that she should do the same.

"You'll get the fabric dirty," she said.

"It'll wash," I said.

She sighed her disapproval and dropped onto the seat.

In the moonlight, she looked ghostly, petite, her pale skin almost translucent, her big eyes and full lips black. The freckles spattering her face were dark, and her hair was the color of blood. The Corpse Bride, hanging on my every word.

"I'm not sure where to start," I said.

"How about why this is the second time in as many nights you've gotten me out of bed?"

"I'm sorry. You'll understand why when I tell you."

She didn't look convinced.

Even so, I told her all about my visits from O'Malley, about Murdoch's release and how he'd turned up here tonight, about Dunn's insinuation, and finally about the discovery at Crooked Lake. I didn't leave anything out.

"Holy shit," Eve said when I was finished. "They think it's really her? I mean, people go missing all the time."

"In Manistique?"

"I'm just saying. And, yes, they probably do. Just because we don't hear about it doesn't mean it never happens."

"Eve, you watch too many movies."

"That's strange, because I only watch the same movies you do. So I guess that makes two of us. All I'm saying is, what if they're wrong? I know we never discuss this, but what if Scarlett is still alive?"

At no point in the past ten years had I doubted that Scarlett was dead. I mean, stone-cold dead. I'd *felt* her absence the day she'd died, as conspicuous as an amputated limb. My right arm, gone. I'd experienced half of me dying. How many people feel something like that?

No, I'd never questioned it . . . until recently, stupidly.

To be honest, the very first thought that had entered my head when Dunn showed me the photographs was one of denial. A natural reaction, I know, even though I knew the truth. For a moment, I'd told myself it wasn't her. It couldn't be Scarlett lying there in that makeshift grave. It didn't even resemble her! And if it wasn't my sister, then that meant she was elsewhere, and maybe still alive. As irrational as it was, for those few seconds my brain had entertained the notion of her being alive, right before reality had punched me in the gut, reminding me that she was dead, dead, dead and the proof was staring me in the face.

"It was Scarlett," I said slowly.

"You're sure? One hundred percent?"

I nodded.

"Well, that is a shocker. Greg, I'm sorry."

"Me too."

"So, what are we going to do about Zane Murdoch?"

"I don't know. I have no idea where he went or why he left me the way he did."

"And he was definitely here tonight?"

"Let's not get into the whole sleepwalking thing again. He was in the backyard. I thought he was going to kill me."

"Do you think he'll come back?"

I sensed her stiffening.

At first, before coming to Florida, Eve's agoraphobia hadn't been a problem. She'd come and gone without restriction. In fact, I don't think it played any significant part in her life back then whatsoever. But moving to another state, to a land of strangers and strangeness, had awakened the beast, and now she was as good as housebound. So the idea that someone could intrude into her domain, into her safe harbor, and threaten the security of her surroundings was disturbing.

"I have this under control," I said.

I expected her to be mollified, but she surprised me by saying, "Seriously, Greg, you don't have this. I don't think you even know what *this* is. Look how quickly the situation has escalated out of control. Two days ago, you were fine. You hadn't had one of your blackouts in years. Now you're a murder suspect and, thanks to Zane Murdoch, your life is in mortal danger. Trust me, this is as bad as it gets."

"I'll sort it out," I said, but there was lead in my belly. "First thing in the morning, I'll talk to Ray about getting that restraining order."

But I knew it would take more than a piece of paper to make Eve feel safe. And I knew a dog wasn't the answer.

Chapter Fourteen

Incredibly, I overslept and got up late, around eight thirty, at first feeling fuzzy-headed, with no recollection of my nighttime activities or of my conversation with Eve. But as I rolled out of bed, it all came rushing back, seeding my stomach with dread.

On autopilot, I shaved, showered, and got dressed, all the while unable to explain how I'd ended up sprawled in the pool chair or what had happened with Murdoch after I'd blacked out.

Luckily, my first client of the day wasn't due until eleven o'clock, giving me plenty of time to dissect the night's events, to try to make some sense of them. I had a feeling it wouldn't be that easy, though.

Heavyhearted, I headed downstairs.

Eve's bedroom door was shut, with no sounds coming from within. A good indicator that she didn't want to be disturbed.

I picked up my cell and made my way outside.

The overnight thunderstorm had blown over, giving way to atom-bomb sunshine and a humidity that varnished my skin in seconds. Steam hung over the grass, with more misty tendrils rising from the screens.

I called Ray and told him about Murdoch. He told me he'd speak with a judge friend of his and get back to me on the restraining order as soon as he heard anything. He reminded me to visit the pound. I joked him off the phone.

I spotted one of my neighbors down on his dock, preparing for a leisurely day of fishing the flats, and felt a twinge of envy. Once a boater, always a boater. These days, I don't get to go out as often as I'd like. Back in the UP, I made a point of spending most of my free time on the water, usually with Scarlett, until things changed and her depression took away her interest.

The neighbor glanced my way and waved a friendly hand. Hesitantly, I waved back.

Mist curled on the water. Mullet jumped, splashed. The shrill call of an osprey pierced the air as it floated over the gumbo-limbo trees.

Daylight makes everything look ordinary, harmless, as though bad things only come out after dark. Of course, it's anything but true.

I circled around behind the house, looking for evidence of a struggle.

Eve hadn't made a big deal out of it. All the same, I'd returned to bed with the feeling she hadn't fully believed I'd come face to face with Murdoch out here. I couldn't blame her. It wasn't as though sleepwalking and I were strangers. In my own persnickety way, I wanted to find something to confirm that my memory was real, that the stress of recent days wasn't blurring the lines between fiction and fact.

The damp grass behind the screened lanai looked no different than the rest of the lawn. No flattened blades. No heel gouges in the turf. Certainly, no scuffs of the mud that had stained my sweatpants.

If I had tussled with Murdoch out here, the rain had washed away any trace of it.

If?

Eve had me doubting myself, I realized. Eve has an inimitable ability to do this, mostly because she's able to look at my life from outside the fishbowl.

Smiling, I made my way down to the dock.

To protect the Yellowfin from the elements, I stow it underneath a vinyl canopy supported on four metal piles, the same stanchions that hold the boat lift. It doesn't stop the wind from scouring the hull, but it does protect it from torrential rain and the punishing heat of the sun.

I was beaded in sweat before I reached the dock, and then more so when I saw the big empty space normally occupied by my boat.

The Yellowfin was gone!

Someone had lowered the lift and taken the boat, and I had a pretty good suspicion who that someone was.

"Hey, Greg, dude. How's it going, man? Great day to be out on the water. That your brother who took her out this morning?"

I swiveled to see Phil Duffy, from next door, lingering on the grass behind me.

"What?"

"Your boat, man. I'm talking about your boat."

Phil is a wiry middle-aged guy with a perpetual three-day stubble and the ability to make everything he wears look sloppy. You've heard of the relaxed look? Well, Phil Duffy has the I'm-in-a-coma look. Today he had on a pair of plaid pajama pants and an extra-large Darth Vader character T with "Join Me on the Dark Side—Bring Beer" printed across the chest. Up until the recession had hit, Phil was in retail management, but now he was a stay-at-home husband, between jobs, while Katherine, his pediatrician wife, kept him stocked up with beer and idling in the lap of laziness.

In fact, he had a bottle of Coors in each hand right now, and he tipped one to his lips before saying, "What gives, dude? You look kinda pissed. My cat keep you awake last night? Because he can be a real pain in the butt with that howling of his."

"Someone stole my boat."

It took a few seconds to penetrate, and ever so slowly Phil's expression went from chill to mystified-chill.

"Phil, you're up at all hours. Did you see anything?"

His puzzled gaze was roaming the empty mooring behind me, and up and down the river. "Well, sure I did. Like I said, I saw your brother take her out just before sunrise. Oh, jeez. You think he stole it? Why'd he go and do a thing like that? I thought he was family."

"Phil, I don't have a brother."

His bewildered gaze stumbled back to me. "You don't? That sucks, dude. You sure about that?"

"I think I'd know."

"You definitely do not have a brother?"

"No."

"Since when?"

"Since always."

I'd never told Phil about my past life in Michigan, and I was sure Eve had remained equally tight-lipped. Perhaps this was his way of filling in the blanks.

"So who was he, then? I mean, tough break, man. You know me—I would've raised the alarm if I thought anything uncool was going on out here. I just assumed he was your brother, seeing as he looked so much like you from a distance and all."

He neglected to add, *In the dark and through the bottom of a beer bottle.*

Phil sauntered over, holding out the other Coors. "Consolation beer? Go for it, dude. Straight from the cooler."

"No, thanks, Phil. It's a bit too early in the day for me."

"Are you kidding? There's never a bad time for a beer." He angled the neck of the bottle at me. "Don't go all teetotal on me, Greg. Go ahead. It'll take the edge off."

I took the beer and popped off the cap.

"There you go." He guzzled his own, then smacked his lips and said, "So, do you have any idea who this thief is, the one masquerading as your brother?"

I began to give a nod, then forced it into a shake of the head. Phil didn't need to know about Murdoch, and certainly not his motive for stealing my boat.

"I mean, how'd he get the keys? I don't know how easy it is to hot-wire a boat, but I'm betting you need to know a thing or two about electrical systems."

He saw my wilting expression and nodded sagaciously. "Ouch. He had the keys, didn't he? That's a real bummer, dude."

Moronically, I leave the lift remote in the boat and stow the boat keys on a hook next to the flashlight in the pool area. They're not instantly visible, unless you know where to look.

Last night, I'd found the flashlight missing, but I hadn't noticed if the keys were missing, too.

"The insurance company will eat you up and spit you out," Phil was saying with a shake of his head. "What you need to do is notify Naval Intelligence, my friend. Get ahead of the curve."

I gave him back the beer. "Listen, Phil, thanks for this, but I have to go."

"Oh, okay."

"I don't mean to be rude."

"No, sure. It's cool. We're cool. You've got someplace else to go and I don't. That's cool. Hey, you want me to ask around, about the boat? See if anyone saw anything?"

"If you feel you need to." I started back toward the house, in a sudden rush to confirm that the boat keys were missing.

"I have this buddy who works for the Coast Guard. Maybe they can keep a lookout."

I flourished a hand over my head as I went. "Whatever you think, Phil."

"Okay. No problem, man. I've got this," he called as I slipped through the screen door.

Even before I got there, I could see that the flashlight was back in its holster. But the hook next to it was empty.

Murdoch had been on my lanai.

I went through to the kitchen, dialing the sheriff's office at Springs Plaza. The phone rang, then clicked, and an automated voice advised me to call 911 for all emergency situations. Although the theft of my boat was an emergency to me, it wouldn't be viewed as such by the authorities. Boat crime isn't a high priority. Not like murder.

I ground some teeth, feeling irritable. I couldn't believe Murdoch had stolen my Yellowfin! The voice on the recording began running through the nonemergency options. "Come on, come on," I said under my breath.

Out of habit, I flicked on the TV at the corner of the kitchen counter, then fished around in a cupboard for some food.

The automated voice told me I was number two in line.

I dropped a pair of Pop-Tarts into the toaster and filled the coffeemaker.

From an early age, our grandfather had instilled in us the value of eating a good breakfast. He was big on nutrition and healthy eating, probably because it was his business to be. *Always make time for the most important meal of the day,* he'd say as our grandmother conjured up homemade hash, thickly cut bacon, and eggs any way we liked. *No matter how busy you are, feed the brain, and everything else falls into line.* He would repeat the same to everyone he met, fat or thin. *Inner happiness begins with a balanced diet,* he'd say.

I'm not sure he'd approve of my Pop-Tarts any more than Eve does. Eve says they taste like hot cardboard, which is contradictory, considering she eats them, too. It's a pity most of the things we like are bad for us.

I couldn't believe Murdoch had had the nerve to steal my boat.

For a moment, I was tempted to cancel my afternoon clients in favor of tracking him down. But where would I even begin to start? The Gulf was a matter of minutes away. Murdoch had taken the Yellowfin during the night. Hours had passed since then. For all I knew he could be in Sarasota by now or even the Keys. My best chance would be to inform the sheriff's office and let them do the legwork.

From the TV, a female news anchor with nightclub eyes said:

"But first, breaking news this hour: the discovery of a body washed up at the Imperial Boat Club in Bonita Springs."

I tuned every sense into the report.

Washed-up bodies isn't something you hear about too often on a sunny Friday morning in Bonita Springs, or any other day for that matter. I knew of the boat club. It was a quarter mile down the beach road from my home. On any given day, the news of a body found there would spike my interest, but today it gripped it.

In my ear, a voice said, "Lee County Sheriff's Office. Thank you for holding. How can we be of service?"

The anchor with the nightclub eyes had been replaced with footage showing morning traffic creeping along the beach road. Sunlight glinting off windshields. Drivers slowing to take a look at the TV news crew and maybe catch a glimpse of what they were reporting on. As the camera panned, it brought into frame the driveway entrance to the aforementioned boat club, which was blocked by a white sheriff's cruiser and a deputy waving vehicles by.

A banner running along the bottom of the screen read:

BREAKING NEWS: BODY FOUND AT BOAT CLUB.

There was an unpleasant taste on the back of my tongue.

"Hello? You're through to the sheriff's office. How can I direct your call?"

I hung up, grabbed the TV remote, and upped the volume, suddenly all concerns about my missing boat evaporating.

"We now go live to our reporter at the scene, Carlos Diaz, who is keeping a close eye on the story."

The image switched to a young man standing on the sidewalk in bright sunshine. He wore a blue shirt and a yellow necktie, with clean poster-child looks and the makings of sweat patches under his armpits. He had his back to a wire-fenced compound, where white boats on trailers and snippets of the blue Imperial River could be seen through the mesh.

"The first anyone knew something was wrong was at seven thirty this morning when the boatyard manager, Mike Harvey, opened up for business. The last thing he expected to find was a dead body by the boat ramp, but that's exactly what was waiting for him. He says the body of a man was snagged on the ramp and partly submerged in the water. He attempted to perform CPR, but quickly came to realize that the man's condition was beyond recovery. It was then that he alerted the authorities."

I leaned a few inches closer to the TV.

The scene switched to a zoomed-in sweep of the boatyard, shot from over the perimeter fence. In among the trailered boats and the palm trees were a number of emergency vehicles with their red-and-blues flashing.

The field reporter kept speaking as the video rolled. "This is a popular spot for boat enthusiasts and fishermen alike, with good access to the river and the Gulf, so at first the man's death was believed to be a typical drowning. Tourists are known to rent boats around here and, on occasion, inexperienced people find themselves in difficulty, sometimes with tragic consequences."

The video ended, revealing the reporter with a finger pressed to his earpiece. "However," he said, "we've now learned that the Lee County Sheriff's Office is treating the death as a homicide. Back to you in the studio, Gretchen."

"Carlos," the anchor said, "do you have any idea why police think this is a homicide?"

The reporter nodded. "The sheriff's office hasn't officially confirmed this yet, but my sources tell me the man was found with what appears to be a fatal laceration to the throat."

Automatically, I glanced at the knife block on the counter, then felt a twinge of panic when I saw the chef's knife missing.

"So it's possible he died before going in the water?" the anchor said.

"That seems to be the consensus. Detectives are now on the scene, so we expect to have more information soon."

My mouth was open, but no air moved in or out. All I could think about was my clash with Murdoch, grappling for the knife with my life in the balance, and my unaccountable missing time.

"Carlos, at this point, do investigators have any clues about where the body came from?"

"Well, Gretchen, I spoke with some of the people who live nearby, and they told me there's been a significant influx of rainwater in the river due to the recent storms. One resident, a retired marine expert, told me that in his opinion the body could have entered the swollen river from as far east as the Old Forty-One Road and could have been carried this far west within just a few hours."

I imagined the body caught up in the swell, moving steadily toward the Gulf, rolling around in the black water like a bag of garbage. Occasionally, rebounding off a sandy bank or the wooden pile of a boat dock, silently passing by sleeping homes as the current pulled it along to its final resting place.

"That's quite a distance. One more thing, Carlos, the all-important question: Have the police had any luck identifying this man?"

My heart was in my mouth, my eyelids pinned open.

"As of this moment, it's something they're still trying to determine. There was no ID on the body itself. But crime-scene technicians will be conducting a thorough search of the area as the day goes on. I'll be back with the very latest details on the news at noon."

I stared at the TV, every sense still on high alert.

The Pop-Tarts popped, and I almost jumped out of my skin.

Chapter Fifteen

Half an hour later, I was in my car, waiting at a red light at the intersection with the beach road, having spent the preceding time combing the backyard again looking for the chef's knife, without success.

I had no evidence that the body at the boatyard was Murdoch's. But the more my search proved fruitless, the more I began to imagine the worse: somehow, during my lost time, Murdoch had ended up dead and in the river, taking my kitchen knife and my fingerprints with him.

And I had no memory of it.

I looked at the drivers filling up their tanks at the 7-Eleven on the corner, my palms slicked with sweat despite the frigid air-conditioning.

Everywhere in sight, the world looked normal, the way it should, with no hint that something very bad had happened nearby. People were going about their everyday business, most of whom would be oblivious to the top local news story unfolding in their own backyard.

Turn right and the boat club was less than thirty seconds down the road. I'd driven by it countless times on my way to the beach, and sailed past it on the river, following the channel as it curled south into Little Hickory Bay. I knew the slipway where they'd found the body; I'd used it. I imagined turning right instead of left, passing the small marina after a quarter mile, and looking over the hive of activity. Sheriff's cruisers with roof lights flashing, forensics technicians cataloguing the scene, detectives taking notes, Carlos and the TV news crew topping up their footage and beaming updates back to the studio for Gretchen's eloquent dissection. And in the middle of all the hubbub, at the focus of all the commotion, a medical examiner's assistant would be standing by, a black body bag at the ready.

By default, death is attractive, and not just to worms. It can't be seen, but it has a pull. Death has gravity. We call it morbid fascination. It's the one mystery that no one can solve, and that's what makes for compulsive viewing.

The red changed to green, and I pulled out onto the beach road, going slow, turning in the direction of my office, away from the scene of the crime. As the car straightened out, I glanced in the rearview mirror, thinking I might see the spectral lights of EMS vehicles in the distance, but I saw no sign.

Did I kill Murdoch?

The thought was unthinkable.

And yet there was a hole in my timeline that I couldn't account for. A hole that had ended with me draped across the pool chair, muddied and exhausted.

A car horn sounded, and a silver sedan accelerated past. I caught a glimpse of someone giving me the finger as the car sped away.

I wasn't aware of it, but I had been driving at half the speed limit, causing impatient rush-hour drivers to honk and yell: "Learn to drive, buddy!" "Get off the damn road!" "Move over, Grandpa!"

Even laid-back Florida has its fair share of fast-lane lunatics.

But I was distracted.

In fact, distracted doesn't even come close to describing it. I was on the edge of delirium.

I leaned on the gas, and the jeers fell away.

Right now, I imagined the detectives would be doing everything in their power to find the victim's ID and the answers to their questions: Who was he? What did he do? Where was he from? Why was he here? Why was he dead? Who might have killed him?

Soon, they would learn he was an ex-con pardoned after serving a ten-year sentence for killing my sister, and as soon as they started digging, they would unearth the reason why he was in Bonita Springs.

Me.

Add that to the fact he was found dead not quite on my property but within walking distance, and I would become the prime suspect in yet another murder.

Connection made, they would come knocking on my door, asking awkward questions:

When was the last time you saw Mr. Murdoch?

What did the two of you discuss?

Did you have an argument?

Where were you last night?

Can you explain why your fingerprints are on the murder weapon?

A pang of dread blossomed through my chest, and the car swerved as a result.

The knife.

Murdoch's presence in Bonita Springs connected him to me, but my missing chef's knife could connect me to his murder.

And I had no idea of its whereabouts.

I slowed for the intersection with 41, of two minds: Should I turn myself in or bury my head in the sand and hope for a miracle?

I pulled down the sun visor so that I could see my eyes in the vanity mirror, see the bloodless whites and the sweat dribbling down my temples.

I looked like a fugitive, and I was thinking like one.

"You know this is insane, right?" I told myself. "It's probably not even Murdoch back there."

The light changed, and vehicles started moving. I was through the intersection and accelerating when a double blast of a police siren sounded from behind. I glanced at the rearview mirror, expecting to see an EMS vehicle eager to pass, but instead saw an unmarked car with red and blue lights blinking behind its radiator grille.

My gut dropped.

The siren sounded again, and I pulled into a small strip mall, slowing to a stop. The unmarked car came to a standstill a few yards behind.

Relax. Breathe. Stop looking like you have something to hide.

I cuffed sweat from my face.

Through the side mirror, I saw a woman climb out of the car. She looked to be in her midthirties, with short dark hair and even darker sunglasses. She wore a burgundy shirt and gray dress pants. Sunlight sparkled from a gold shield hooked on at her waistline.

I rolled the window down.

"Sir, please step out of the vehicle," she called as she approached.

Another check in the mirror told me she had one hand resting on the handle of her gun.

I did as I was told.

"Keep your hands where I can see them," she directed. "Turn around and place your hands palms-down on the roof."

Again, I complied.

She tapped my feet apart with the side of her foot. Then I felt her hands pat me down, quick, hard, expertly, as if she'd performed this task a hundred times previously.

"Where are you headed?" she asked.

"The office."

"You're running late."

An observation, not a question.

"Slow morning. First client is in at eleven. Look, is this leading somewhere?"

As though to answer, her exploring hand moved to my crotch, where it stayed. I didn't flinch.

"What's this? Are you packing?" she asked.

I turned around and pulled her into me. "I think you know the answer to that, Zoe."

Then I kissed her, passionately, longingly, and with relief.

Chapter Sixteen

Zoe has been a homicide detective with the Lee County Sheriff's Office for three years now. From the wider angle of her comments, I gather that being a member of the Major Crimes Unit was emotionally demanding and draining, but ultimately satisfying. We never discuss details, but the overwhelming impression I get from the little snippets she feeds me is that she loves her job and wouldn't change it for the world.

Not even for me. Not that I'd ever expect her to, in the same way she would never put conditional demands on my career.

"I heard about the dead body washed up at the boat club," I said tentatively as we uncoupled. I couldn't help myself. It was my intention to sound conversational, but it immediately came across as probing, and I sensed Zoe thought so, too.

I smiled lamely, which only worked to emphasize the awkwardness.

This isn't something I do, we do. Even in an attempt to make small talk, I never delve into Zoe's casework, and she extends the same courtesy to me. We have an understanding, in place since day one: we never talk shop. Our jobs deal with sensitive stuff, matters of a personal nature. Unless there's a relevant crossover or a risk to human life, we're smart enough to leave our work at the office, which was why I was surprised she'd pulled me over.

She pushed her sunglasses onto the bridge of her nose. "You know about that?"

"Sure. It's been the hot topic on the TV news all morning. I guess because things like this don't happen every day around here."

Better. More relaxed. Good.

"Let's try this again," she said, sliding a hand behind my neck and pulling me close.

"You're on duty." A weak protest, and one I hoped wouldn't deter her.

"Let's just say I'm feeling bad about canceling our date. So forgive me if I bend the rules a little, just this once."

I didn't object. Kissing Zoe is one of my favorite pastimes.

"Bad news travels fast," she said afterward.

"The reporters are sure making a big deal out of it. Any idea what happened to this guy? It's definitely a murder, right? Do you have a lead on the killer?" I loosened up my shoulders, trying to hide my stiffness. But I was only fooling myself if I thought for one second that Zoe couldn't read me like a police report.

"Doc, what's going on here? Are you okay?"

"Never better. Why'd you ask?"

"Because you seem a little—I don't know—off somehow."

I let out a sigh. "Tired. It's been a weird kind of week."

I have a confession to make: I'm hopeless at lying and, if enough pressure is exerted in the right place, I crumple. Fancifully, like most of my gender, I like to think I'm a man of steel, able to withstand the harshest of onslaughts, but that would be untrue. Society expects men to wear emotional armor, to repel adversity with a lantern-jawed grin, when the reality is, men are hands-down the weakest sex. For all our grandstanding, for all the bullish masquerading, we are as transparent as glass, even the bulletproof type. Had modern man not become so adept at taming danger, natural selection would have weeded out my kind long ago.

"Did last night's storm keep you awake?" she said.

"Something like that."

"Are you sure it's nothing else?"

"Yeah, absolutely." I winced as a bead of sweat dipped into my eye.

"You know, if something's happened, you can tell me."

My evasiveness had triggered Zoe's sixth sense. She couldn't quite put a finger on what had alerted it—other than my obvious skittishness—but I knew she wouldn't sit easy until she'd figured it out. But how could I tell her I knew more about the murder without implicating myself?

"No, nothing. Nothing's wrong. Same old, same old." I forced a grin. It came out clownish, I was sure.

She studied me from behind her sunglasses.

The truth is, I didn't want to play this kind of game with Zoe. We were more than this. We were grown-ups with serious professions. Although we led separate lives most of the time, we were never evasive about what went on when we weren't together. We never intentionally hid things from one another. We never deliberately lied, and we certainly didn't interrogate, no matter how much we might want to try.

Zoe was looking at me with her head cocked slightly to one side. "What is this, Doc? Level with me. What's going on here?"

"I don't know." I shrugged a pathetic shrug. "Maybe it's too close for comfort, this dead body. I live a stone's throw from a murder scene. Call it a healthy interest. Self-preservation. It's got me on edge."

Then I played the emotional card by saying I was missing her, and it seemed to work, or at least redirect for a moment, until she said:

"Oh, I know what it is."

"You do?"

"Sure. You're still angry with me."

"No."

"What, then?"

Theatrically, I performed the same wretched shrug, hands turned out, smiling the downturned smile of a wannabe actor in his first week at stage school.

Zoe made one of those unhappy back-of-the-throat rumbles that women make when they refuse to swallow the line you're feeding them.

"Doc, please don't fall into a bottomless depression. I know you've been patient. I have as well, remember? We're still good for later, if that's what you're worried about."

In all the excitement, I had completely forgotten that it was Friday and we had agreed to meet.

I perked up a little. "Even with this body at the boat club?"

"Even if there were ten dead bodies at the boat club. John's overseeing things there while I have the weekend off. It's booked. And I'm spending it with you, starting tonight at my place."

Immediately, my whole mood brightened. "Your place?" My astonishment was visible and real. "We never do your place."

"Well, it's time we started."

She gave me a smile, pulling one from my own lips.

A police siren squawked.

We both looked around at her car, to see a man's head leaning out of the passenger window. It was Detective John Thompson, Zoe's partner, as unsmiling as usual.

"We need to go." He sounded bored.

"Be right there," Zoe called. She glanced at her wristwatch. "Look, Doc, I can't get into all the details right now, but the gist of it is, Troy and I have been talking. We've decided it's time he moved out. He's away on business through the weekend—some power-shake convention in Sarasota—but after that, he's moving into his own place."

"With his girlfriend?"

"I couldn't care less."

I was genuinely surprised; I couldn't contain it. "Zoe, this is fantastic news," I said, pulling her in to me again. "I mean, absolutely, this is the right decision. For both of you. It's been in the cards for a long time. You need this. You both do. This is great!"

Now her smile was back, with no hint of her earlier suspicion. "I appreciate the marital advice, Doc." She leaned in and pecked me on the mouth. "My shift ends at three. I'll be home around four."

I went to say I wouldn't be out of the office until at least five, but she silenced me with a finger against my lips.

"I promise your wait will be worthwhile."

Then she gave me a teasing smile before turning toward the unmarked police car and walking away, swinging her hips as she went.

Chapter Seventeen

S tress is a killer, and to underline this point to my patients, I refer them to a flip chart set up in my office.

Modern science has proven that visual memory is retained more efficiently than auditory memory. In other words, images are easier to remember than spoken words. I use this visual learning aid to help get across the danger of leading a high-stress lifestyle.

The hand-drawn diagrams may be cartoonish—just lines, loops, and arrows in heavy black marker—but they get my point across at a glance.

It shows frost action on exposed stone: how moisture invades cracks; how this water freezes in winter; how the ice expands, forcing the crack apart; how, over time and continuous pressure, even the mightiest boulders can be fractured and split by the smallest infiltration.

My patients are amazed, and not just by my simplistic artwork.

Emotional stress is mechanical weathering on the mind. It shatters lives and levers relationships apart.

It kills.

Right here in this office, I have seen crags of men reduced to rubble.

I like to think, in some ways, the naive chart has proven preventive in that respect.

Recent events had ramped up my own mental pressure. Fear and uncertainty fingering their way into the contours of my brain. I knew if I didn't calm down, if I remained in a permanent state of simmering panic, I'd break down and confess to everything.

Then where would that leave me?

Zoe was law enforcement. We were an item. She hadn't confirmed her involvement in the case, but she had said that her partner would be overseeing the boat club homicide. Come Monday, there was a good chance she'd be working it, too.

Half of me wanted to tell her the truth, to get in front of this misunderstanding while I still had a semblance of control, of face. Better to explain it on my terms and not as a reaction to the evidence their investigation would eventually piece together. Right? Let's face it, sooner rather than later, Zoe would learn of my connection with Murdoch, and in an instant she would link the location of his body to the same stretch of water that ran in back of my property. At first it would be unthinkable to her that I might be involved in the homicide. But it wouldn't stop her from pursuing the truth and exerting the right amount of pressure.

And I had no defense, principally because I had no memory of what had happened after my scuffle with Murdoch.

How had he ended up dead instead of me?

For the sake of our relationship, I had to level with Zoe, come clean about what I knew, hope she could see beyond the obvious, right before she recused herself from the case.

And yet the other half of me, the cowardly side, wanted to do nothing except run and stay running until I was back in Manistique, far away from Murdoch's waterlogged body.

I needed a distraction to keep me from going insane.

I still had an hour to kill before my eleven o'clock appointment. Instead of sitting in my office chewing my nails and worrying myself into a heart attack, I decided to put the time to good use.

A dark thought had been lingering in the back of my mind since I'd learned of Murdoch's apparent innocence:

If he didn't kill Scarlett, who did?

Manistique is a small town, and was even smaller when I last lived there. Not everyone knows everybody's business, but it does have the feel of a close-knit community about it. Sure, the town has its fair share of criminals. What place doesn't? Generally, people know who these questionable characters are and steer clear. But how many murderers does it harbor?

If I'd been asked that question eleven years ago, I would have answered with absolute confidence: *None.*

Yet there was at least one. Scarlett's killer.

So now, I spent some time racking my brain. Trying to recall old names, old faces. Trying to think of someone other than Murdoch, someone with a history of violence, of questionable ethics, someone who was diabolical enough to take her life. And trying to figure out why in the world someone would.

From the bruising on Scarlett's throat, Dunn had suggested her murder could have been a crime of passion. During the years preceding her death, Scarlett had had several boyfriends. But they amounted to a handful of brief encounters, none lasting more than a few weeks at a time, and none seemingly with any intensity—not until Murdoch had come onto the scene.

Even so, I drew up a list. Then, one by one, I ruled people out. There weren't very many to begin with. No one with any grudge against my sister that I knew of. No one with any reason to do her mortal harm. No one with any motive, except for Murdoch. Certainly, no one the investigators hadn't quizzed at the time.

If her murder was indeed the work of a rejected lover, then I had no idea who that might be.

Frustrated, I called Ted Loewe at the Schoolcraft County Prosecutor's Office, and was surprised to get through to him on the first try.

"Mr. Cole," he said as the clerk connected us. "I must apologize for not returning your call." He sounded like he was in the middle of several somethings and struggling to multitask. "It was late when I got back into town, and I'm snowed under this morning. I have exactly two minutes before I need to be elsewhere. So, please, let's make this quick. I understand you want to talk about the exhumation at Crooked Lake?"

Not even matter-of-fact. Less than that. Loewe spoke the words like he was referring to a parking ticket or some other petty misdemeanor. My hackles stirred.

Nevertheless, I kept my cool. "Do you know who I am?"

"I do."

"So you're familiar with my sister's murder case?"

"No. Not the original investigation, at any rate. Just the bare essentials. I do know all about Zane Murdoch's recent appeal, though, and his subsequent release."

"The state police paid me a visit. They believe it's my sister up there at the lake."

"I know. It was my idea to have Detective Dunn reach out to you."

I flinched. "*You* think I killed my sister?"

"Don't put words in my mouth, Mr. Cole." His answer was suddenly brusque, irritable. "Both this department and the state police will pursue all leads we deem worthy of interest to get to the truth. The brother of the deceased included."

"I didn't kill my sister."

"And I hope for your sake the new investigation proves you right. So, what's on your mind, Mr. Cole?"

I held back an impulse to growl. "Dunn said his people found the killer's DNA on her body."

"*Potentially* the killer's DNA," he said. "The cadaver has been taken back to Marquette for analysis."

More infuriating trivialization. This is what can happen with people on the front line: they become desensitized.

"He seemed pretty sure it's the killer's DNA and that his people will be able to process it."

I heard Loewe sigh. "I'm sorry to rush you, Mr. Cole, but do you have a particular question for me?"

I bit my tongue, then released my breath. "Yes, I do. Two, in fact. Other than me, is your department looking at a new suspect, and if so, who?"

Loewe hesitated, presumably choosing his words before answering. "Mr. Cole, please listen to me very carefully: I'm sympathetic to your situation. Really, I am. But you must know I can't discuss ongoing cases with you or anyone else outside of this office."

"But—"

"No, I'm sorry, Mr. Cole. We shouldn't even be having this conversation. If you have any further questions, please direct them to Detective Dunn. He's the one supervising this case. Now, I have to go. I hope everything turns out well for you." He said his good-byes and hung up.

I stared at my phone, then slammed a hand against my desk, making pencils jump.

Perhaps I was expecting too much. Eve says I can be demanding, but the truth is I just don't like being given the brush-off.

Bob Stanwick, the original prosecuting attorney, had had a soft spot for me and, foolishly, I'd thought his replacement might have an equally compassionate disposition. Apparently not.

Undeterred, I dialed O'Malley's office number in Jacksonville, trying a different tack.

This time what I wanted to know was, if Murdoch wasn't O'Malley's client, then who was? Who, other than Murdoch, would have an interest in tracking me down?

A woman answered after five rings, introducing herself as the agency's secretary. I asked to speak with O'Malley. She told me he was out of the office but she could take a message and have him call me back. I was about to say *never mind* when another thought occurred. So I said,

"Your boss did a great job for me this week, down in Bonita Springs," and left the statement hanging, holding my breath, hoping she would take the bait.

"Thank you," she said. "We do try our best to provide a five-star service. Is there something I can do for you, Mr. Hendrickson?"

Adrenaline flashed in my chest.

Hendrickson!

Who on earth was Hendrickson? For the life of me, I couldn't recall knowing anyone with that name.

"Mr. Hendrickson?" the secretary said in my ear.

"No, no," I replied, trying to contain my blossoming excitement. "And there's no need to trouble O'Malley either. I'll call back later. Thanks."

I hung up quickly, with my heart pounding.

Did I know any Hendricksons back in Manistique?

I opened my laptop, brought up a search engine, and typed in *Hendrickson Manistique*, to be instantly presented with more than ten thousand results.

Mostly, they were linked to Hendrickson Road in Hiawatha—a twenty-minute drive north from my hometown, along 94. There was a smattering of hits for the name Hendrickson, too, in various locations across the Upper Peninsula and beyond, but no one sounded remotely familiar. Out of the first dozen pages of hits, I managed to pinpoint only one Hendrickson family living in the town of Manistique, on Mackinac Avenue.

Eve tells me I have a naturally curious mind, hence my chosen career. It amazes me that not everyone has the same thirst for knowledge.

So I did some more digging. With just a few choice clicks on the Internet, it's surprising what you can find out about people. It's all there: contact details, genealogy records, census logs, social media posts.

The Hendricksons were a middle-aged couple with two daughters currently attending Manistique High. Nora, the mother, had a smallish online presence, primarily acting as a venue to showcase her amateurish photographs of Lake Michigan and the Beaver Island archipelago. Prints you could order online. Her Facebook page revealed the given names of her family members, plus pictures taken at birthday parties and outside in the summer sunshine.

They looked ordinary.

Nothing about them rang any bells.

I didn't recognize her face, or her husband's.

According to his wife's Facebook account, Melvin Hendrickson was the manager of a discount store in town. One of those where everything's a dollar. I checked out his employee photograph, magnifying it on the screen, trying to visualize him at least ten years younger, but I still didn't recognize him.

The dollar store hadn't existed in Manistique a decade ago. Judging from its Google Street View image, it occupied a building I knew used to be a car dealership. Sign of the times. It was possible the Hendricksons hadn't even lived in Manistique when I did.

But someone with their last name had enlisted O'Malley's services. Someone who knew me. And for a reason linked to Scarlett's murder.

I needed to know why, and if that meant taking chances . . .

I found the store's phone number and dialed it. A clerk who sounded about fifteen answered tersely. I asked to speak with the manager. He asked why. I told him to put me through. He said he was qualified to handle any inquiry. I told him I worked with the police—a little fib I'd learned from O'Malley—and to get me the manager. He muttered something unintelligible and put me on hold.

A minute later, a man's voice said, "This is Mr. Hendrickson, the store manager. How can I help you?"

I didn't recognize the voice. Not a great start.

"I'm calling on behalf of O'Malley."

There was a moment of silence, in which I began to get my hopes up, my pulse tapping in my neck. I figured if this particular

Hendrickson was O'Malley's client and I could fool him into speaking freely, he might reveal his reason for looking me up.

"O'Malley?" he said.

"That's right. From Jacksonville."

"Who is this?"

"A colleague of his. He asked me to give you a courtesy call."

"This is my workplace. Are you sure you've got the right person?"

"I am speaking with Melvin Hendrickson?"

"Yes. But I don't know any O'Malley."

"He's a private investigator."

There was a pause. Then, "Did my wife put you up to this?"

"What? No."

"Has she been spying on me?"

"Mr. Hendrickson, I'm not—"

"Damn it. I told her I'd put a stop to the affair. Why doesn't she believe me? How much has she been paying you? What have you told her?"

I hung up, feeling stupid and hot under the collar, mentally crossing Melvin Hendrickson off my list.

Eleven o'clock came sooner than expected, and with it my first client of the day.

Unexpectedly, listening was a good distraction, and as the hour wore on I was able to detach completely from my own insecurities and lose myself in my client's.

Talk therapy isn't just a job for me; it's a calling. And there's no bigger pick-me-up than immersing yourself in something that fulfills.

Lunchtime arrived, and with it a noticeable exodus of patients from the health center. My stomach had been vocalizing its displeasure all morning, ever since I'd dumped the Pop-Tarts in the trash at home, but I wasn't in the least bit interested in food. I got myself a bottled water from the vending machine and headed outside.

Glenda caught my attention as I passed the reception desk. She told me my final client of the day, Gus Toomey, had canceled.

Somehow, I'd been expecting it. You can never rely on people like Toomey.

I continued out into the emptying parking lot, eager to burn off stress.

Several years ago, I'd taken a beginner's class in tai chi, run by a fellow practitioner at the health center. By chance, I'd read in a medical journal about its health benefits, in particular its ability to destress. I was curious. So I had taken the class, learned the basic techniques, and gotten respectably good at it. I'd even passed my knowledge on to Eve, despite her being the least stressed person I know. For someone like me—someone who falls asleep when they meditate—tai chi had turned out to be an efficient way to open the valves.

And so at the back of the parking lot, I spent fifteen minutes out of the lunch hour performing a combination of slow-motion and high-speed exercises, my eyelids half-closed against the intense sunlight. Vehicles came and went, but no one paid much attention. Compared with the sights of today, seeing a grown man doing ballerina-like poses in a public place isn't newsworthy.

Done, I leaned against a palm tree and guzzled the water, letting my sweat evaporate in the shade, feeling less edgy.

Then I gave in and called Zoe on her cell.

There were two reasons I'd been itching to call her during the last two hours—itching, resisting, pushing, and pulling.

First off, and hopefully without rousing her suspicion any more than I had done already, I wanted to know if investigators were any closer to identifying the boat club body.

Desperate times make desperate people do desperate things.

We've all seen the TV shows: the police procedurals and the Lifetime movies. They're fictional, but sometimes they're based on factual events.

What viewer doesn't know that those who involve themselves up front in a murder investigation often have something to hide?

And secondly, my frisking had gotten me frisky. When you're in a healthy sexual relationship, ten days is a long time to abstain. My hormones were calling out Zoe's name, more so after our earlier encounter.

Her phone rang, then went to voice mail.

Even though Zoe and I are committed, it hasn't always been the case.

"Regular sex and good conversation," she'd told me on our second date, which was actually our first official date. "This is how it's going to be from here on out. No strings we can't snip at a moment's notice. No long-term plans and no meeting each other's parents. If you want to buy me a ring, then it's been nice knowing you, Doc."

But as the months passed, our union had grown way beyond F-buddy status. This can happen when two people enjoy each other's company, both socially and intimately. You could say we'd fallen in a kind of love. But so far, we hadn't used the L-word. We hadn't needed to, not yet. Actions speak louder, right?

For the next several minutes, I sat on the curb at the side of the health center, watching the traffic on the beach road, enjoying the light while thinking dark thoughts, thinking about the pathologists prodding and poking at my sister's exhumed corpse.

My grandmother used to say, *We are trillions of atoms defying gravity, held together by the weakest of forces. It takes little effort to topple us, to send our skyscrapers of cells crashing earthward.*

All the king's horses and all the king's men.

Before Scarlett died—before I was cast out from being the hard-as-diamond and carved-in-stone scientist that I was—I saw death as a transition, a recycling of matter. From ashes to ashes. I didn't believe in a soul or an afterlife, at least not in any conventional or spiritual sense.

The demolition of Scarlett's skyscraping cells hadn't changed me. Her vanished spirit had.

With half my lunchtime left, I went back inside and psyched myself up for the remaining three clients of the day: one with disabling anxiety, one in need of bereavement counseling, and one with self-esteem issues. Business as usual, but not necessarily in that order.

I could do this. Like riding a bike.

But the body at the boat club was back hounding my thoughts, like a dog harassing a sheep.

Out of habit, I hunched over my laptop and accessed Eve's blog. This is what I do, most lunch breaks: I tweak. Eve doesn't mind. She welcomes my input, my opinions, my two cents. The popular blog focuses mainly on self-help techniques and positive-thinking practices, which happens to be a specialty of mine. For me, it's a good way to distract myself from worrisome thoughts.

I began to edit an entry, then a new thought occurred, and I picked up my phone, scrolled through the contacts list to the entry for the sheriff's office at Springs Plaza, and dialed it.

"Hello," I said when the receptionist picked up. "I write a popular local blog, and I'm putting together a story on this morning's murder at the Imperial Boat Club." My earlier masquerade with O'Malley's secretary had given me both the idea and a smidgen of courage. Otherwise, this just wasn't me. "Do you have any information I can share with my readers, such as an identity of the man found or any persons of interest the sheriff's office would like to interview?"

"Who did you say you were?"

"I write a blog." Evasive, but not entirely untrue.

"One moment. Let me put you through to someone who can better deal with your request."

For the next couple of minutes, I listened to a muffled recording of "Africa" by Toto, my eyes closed as I nodded along to the seductive beat. Then:

"This is Detective Zoe Pinkerton. How may I help you?"

And I sat upright with a jolt, eyes springing wide. Fumbling, I canceled the call and dropped the phone on the desk, my stomach twisting into a knot.

Then I sat there, staring at the cell, wondering if Zoe would call back and what I would say if she realized it was my number.

A minute passed. I remembered to breathe.

The intercom buzzed, and Glenda announced that my one o'clock was on his way in.

I put my phone on silent and stuffed it in my messenger bag.

I figured if I didn't get a visit from police before it was time to go home, I would bring up the subject of Murdoch's murder with Zoe later, preferably after we had made love in her bed.

One way or the other, I needed to know whether the nerves clawing away in my belly were justified.

Making the decision seemed to lighten my load a little, and I tackled the afternoon appointments without falling to pieces.

At four o'clock, as my last client closed the office door behind her, I took out my phone and checked for missed calls.

There weren't any. But at 3:55 p.m., I'd received a text from Zoe: `I'm waiting for you, Greg`, followed by a pair of red lips.

I didn't need a second invitation.

Chapter Eighteen

E ven though I had never set foot across the threshold, I knew where Zoe lived.

Call it creepy, but I had cruised down her street once or twice in the early days, mainly out of curiosity. Each trip, a nighttime drive-by with the headlights off, was filled with unanswered questions about what was going on behind those stucco walls.

I never told her. That would have made me sound like a weirdo. I didn't consider it spying. More like getting the lay of the land. I knew Zoe was married. I considered it an intelligence-gathering exercise, a means to find out what I was measuring up against. It didn't work; I never saw anyone coming or going. Knowing Zoe, she probably did the same thing but in reverse.

From Terry Street, I turned onto Harbor Drive and slowed the car to a more reasonable rate for a residential neighborhood, then swiftly maneuvered out of the way of an approaching white sedan, traveling fast and taking up more than its fair share of the narrow road.

The bottle of merlot I'd picked up at the last minute from 7-Eleven rolled on the passenger seat.

I glanced in the rearview mirror, to see the car skid out onto Terry Street and disappear.

When Zoe and I first started dating, the unspoken rule between us was that we'd avoid being seen at each other's homes. Not because we were doing anything underhanded—we weren't sneaking around and having an illicit affair behind our partners' backs—but because there were other people's personal spaces to take into consideration. Zoe lived with an estranged husband, and the woman I lived with was my best friend. It would have been selfish and dismissive of us to disregard their feelings.

So right from the start, Zoe and I were up front about our budding relationship. I'd sat Eve down and effervesced about Zoe, knowing in advance she'd be okay with it, which she was.

Whatever makes me happy makes Eve happy.

Other than what Zoe had told me—that her husband was cool with the arrangement—I had no idea what he genuinely felt about us. Men protect their interests. They don't yield without resistance. I knew he had a similar setup with a girl he'd met at the gym. A girl barely in her twenties. Someone, according to Zoe, he could control, manipulate. That was in his nature, she said. He'd found himself a malleable mind, someone that Zoe wasn't and had never been.

It baffles me. I've been doing talk therapy for most of my adult life, and still I have no idea why couples remain living together while their lives run separate courses.

Some clients claim it's a matter of convenience. Some admit they have an aversion to change. Mostly, I think people have a hard time letting go.

Of course, her husband's suffocating control issues were none of my business. But Zoe had wanted me to know, from the beginning. She hadn't been seeking my advice. She'd wanted me to understand the breakdown of their marriage. Just the basics. Not the finer details, about explosive fights or awkward silences.

It had made no difference to me; I was already smitten. Verbally explaining the whys had helped Zoe work through things. And we were closer for it.

She'd said her husband couldn't care less about me.

Even so, I'd dealt with enough men with similar control problems to know he wouldn't be thrilled with his wife sleeping with another man, no matter how separated they were.

When colorful emotions are involved, not everything is black and white.

Zoe's house is situated at the end of a lane in a quiet subdivision of parallel streets with manmade canals in back of the dwellings. The ubiquitous leafy palms and white sandy driveways that make Florida neighborhoods so uniquely Floridian.

I did a U-turn at the end of the cul-de-sac and parked opposite Zoe's house, looking at it before climbing out.

The house was an understated beige-painted villa-style building, with arched windows and an American flag hanging limply from a pole in the front lawn. A tall fan palm to one side dwarfed everything. It could be anyone's home.

I opened the driver's door, then paused, momentarily taken aback by the strangeness of the situation.

This was weird. We didn't do *this*.

Despite Zoe's assurance that her husband was away on business, with plans to move out after the weekend, I couldn't help feeling unsettled about being here. Until Monday, this was another man's house. His domain, filled with his personal stuff: a den where he drank beer and watched games; a garage stocked with tools and fishing gear; a room where he slept. Previously, Zoe had stressed they hadn't had a physical relationship in years, that they bedded down in separate rooms. Everything platonic. Just like me and Eve. But men are territorial. And I was trespassing.

Could I be equally cool with the idea of some strange guy coming into my home and snuggling up to Eve on my couch?

"You're not doing anything wrong," I told myself. "Zoe wouldn't invite you if it wasn't a done deal."

I scooped up the wine bottle and experienced a sudden gush of indecision. What if Zoe was expecting flowers, or even chocolates? Would she approve of my last-minute wine choice suggested by the clerk at the gas station?

This was ridiculous.

This wasn't our first date.

We were good here.

I bit the bullet and got out, smoothing down my shirt as I walked up the drive. The late afternoon sun was a branding iron on the back of my neck, searing out sweat.

A guy fixing a sprinkler system in the neighboring yard glanced up. I waved a hand. He nodded an acknowledgment but didn't wave back.

Under my breath, I told myself, "Get a grip. You're not breaking and entering. You're here bearing gifts."

It didn't stop me from feeling uncharacteristically nervous.

On my part, my attendance came with an ulterior motive. And I berated myself for having one.

Sure, I wanted to spend quality time with my lover, to sate a physical need or two, but that wasn't the whole of it. I wanted to know all she knew about Murdoch, without giving the game away. I wasn't sure I could pull it off.

I went to the front door and filled my lungs.

Flowers. That's what I should have brought. Flowers were a given. I was at my girlfriend's house for the first time, with a cheap bottle of wine.

I looked at the merlot and scowled.

Zoe had left the front door slightly open. Through the inch-wide gap, I could see a slice of a white tiled floor.

Come on in, it beckoned. *She's waiting for you.*

I guessed Zoe was busy, cooking up whatever surprise she had in store for me. Goofily, I was hoping for something tastier than dinner. Then the wine would turn out to be immaterial.

I put hesitant fingertips against the painted wood and called out her name. When she didn't answer, I pushed the door and stepped inside.

"Zoe, it's me. Don't shoot. I'm coming in."

It was cool indoors, nice. Paradoxically, the house seemed bigger inside than out. It was open-plan, as most homes in Florida are, with white walls supporting a vaulted ceiling, giving the illusion of space. Bedroom doors, left and right, all closed. The tiled hallway opening out into a large L-shaped living area of rugs and dark wood furniture.

"Zoe?"

No signs of her.

No cooking smells either.

I ventured a little deeper inside.

"Zoe? My last client canceled. I got out early. Zoe?"

I scanned the living room, letting my gaze coast over the comfy-looking furniture, the tasteful trimmings, the metal floor lamps with their big colorful shades.

The first impression was good.

Zoe's home looked, in a word, homey. Lived-in. Ordinary. What had I expected—police paraphernalia and framed paper targets with grouped bullet holes in the silhouette? There was a jumble of hardback books on shelves, plumped cushions on the upholstery, strategically placed knickknacks that spoke of a homeowner with an eye for classy modern. I spotted a collection of photographs lined up on an accent cabinet and was about to investigate further when I heard a noise coming from the kitchen.

It sounded like a fish flopping around on a dock.

"Zoe?"

Still no reply.

"I brought wine. I hope you can stomach a 7-Eleven special?"

My thinking was, get the bad news out of the way first. Everything after that would be a positive.

The kitchen was tucked away in the smaller limb of the L-shape. I threaded my way through the living room, padding across the thick rug, homing in on the wet slapping sound.

"You know me. I'm more of a Guinness guy than a—"

I stopped dead in my tracks, the rest of my sentence backing up in my throat and causing an obstruction.

All I could see was red.

It was everywhere. Splashed on the kitchen cabinets and sprayed across the appliances. But mostly it was pooled on the white tiled floor, where it had run along the joints in all directions to form a bright-red grid pattern.

My knees buckled, and the wine bottle slipped from my grasp, bouncing on the rug at my feet.

There were no words to describe what my eyes were seeing.

If you're the hardened type unmoved by tragedy, if you're a paramedic desensitized to trauma, if you're a battlefield soldier living with death on a daily basis, then the sight of so much blood wouldn't necessarily cause your windpipe to close.

But it did have that effect on me.

A large puddle of glistening blood, with a naked Zoe flat on her back in the middle, one hand flapping uselessly at her side, splashing. Her pink flesh freckled red.

"Zoe?"

More blood than anyone could lose and survive.

Gravity pressed down, and I fell to my knees, sloshing and slithering through the crimson liquid until I had one hand cupped under her head, my fingers in her blood-matted hair, the other hand turning her bloodied face to mine.

In my emotional core, radioactive panic and terror were causing a nuclear meltdown.

"Zoe!"

I couldn't believe it, couldn't get past all the blood, couldn't . . .

"Zoe!"

Her face was blanched with fright, her eyes round, staring up at me, demanding me to do something, anything, to stem the blood loss and the inevitable.

Not dead. Not yet. But so close, so terribly close. A heartbeat away. I could sense her slipping, fading.

So much blood!

Cymbals crashed in my ears, and the cataclysmic reaction in my belly went supernova.

The handle of a chef's knife jutted out of her chest, just beneath her left breast. Blood pumped around the hilt, a steady stream of it running down her side. I was about to grab it, to pull it out from between her ribs. But I caught myself, knowing that if I disturbed it even in the slightest, it would accelerate her internal bleeding and I'd be as good as killing her myself.

"Oh my God! Zoe!"

A bubble of blood bulged over her lips and ran down her cheek. I wiped it from around her mouth, but it was immediately replaced. I was trying to figure out if she was trying to speak, to tell me something.

She was drowning in her own blood, and I was terrified. It was a terror unlike anything I'd experienced before. Burning up my insides and setting off a fire alarm in my head. But I was nowhere nearly as scared as she was, I knew. Not even in the same hemisphere.

Her gaze drifted. I yelped her name again, and her eyes homed back in on me. But her pupils were enlarging, her eyes maybe even unseeing.

She was on the brink of dying, and I should have been able to summon enough strength for the both of us, at least enough to keep her holding on until I called for help and the paramedics arrived. But in my uniquely weak and pitiful way, all I felt was faint.

In the distance, I could hear the scream of sirens.

I felt Zoe shudder in my arms, a soft rippling, as though a breeze had blown through her. I saw her eyeballs roll back in their sockets, heard the blood bubble in her throat as she struggled to breathe her last breath.

"No, no, no!" My lips were an inch from hers. "Stay with me! You're going to be okay! Just hang on! You're going to be okay!"

But she was already gone, face slackening, muscles relaxing, as her diaphragm gave up the battle to expel blood from her lungs. One final twitch of her hand in the bloody pool, then it too went limp.

And in my very unmanly way, I burst into tears.

Chapter Nineteen

I didn't black out. It was the only time in my life when I wanted to, desperately. I wanted a void to open up and suck me into oblivion. But, cruelly, I remained painfully conscious, with Zoe's warm blood seeping into my clothes.

The tears bloated into big sorry-for-myself sobs, coming thick and fast, quaking, blurring, a guttural howl resonating in my throat. I cradled Zoe's head in my lap, salty tears splashing her face, mixing with the blood.

In fact, I was so consumed by the emotional tsunami, so zoned-out, that it took me several moments to realize somebody outside of my torment was calling my name.

"Greg! Snap out of it, man! I don't wanna rush you here, but we've gotta go!"

Blearily, I raised my heavy head, blinking at the red mist veiling my eyes.

Blood everywhere. So much blood.

My stomach lurched. But my sobs had ceased.

The shape of a man resolved out of the red mist. A rough-cut lug of a man, oddly familiar, smiling lopsidedly from a mouth of crooked teeth, some missing. He was hunkered down on his haunches at the edge of the living room rug, occupying the exact same spot where I had stood moments before red had become my least favorite color.

"Kyle?" I rasped. It sounded like paper tearing.

"Hey, man," he acknowledged. "Stupid question, but how are ya?"

He was older than I remembered. My age, but much worse for wear. He had the sunken-eyed, cheeks-sucked-in, unshaven look of someone who had been sleeping on the streets for years. Given his coarse appearance, his voice was strangely soft, hushed, and as friendly as our favorite TV theme song from childhood.

"I don't understand."

"No time for explanations. They're on their way. Listen." Theatrically, he cupped a hand to his ear and mimed the act of listening.

I could hear sirens growing louder.

"Greg, we've gotta go, before they get here."

"Go where?"

"Anywhere but here. Listen to me. You're in shock. Your brain is out of whack. You're not thinking straight. The cops are on their way. And this doesn't look good for you, man. They'll think you did this. We need to leave, put some distance between us and here. Take a second. But make it quick."

"This can't be real. I must be hallucinating."

"No, you're not. Look, man, I know you're probably wondering how I can be here, just at the right moment. I admit it's pretty wacky, but there's no mystery. I'll tell you everything. But first we need to get you to safety."

He reached out a hand. I didn't take up the offer.

"Greg, I'm not joking. You need to snap out of this, right now."

"You're right." I slapped my cheek wetly, smearing blood. My skin stung, but Kyle's apparition didn't vanish in a puff of smoke. He just looked at me, slightly amused.

"We need to go," he said.

"I can't leave her."

"They'll think you did this."

"I don't care." My voice was monotone, robotic. I had external feeling—Zoe's hot blood on my hands, with more of it soaking through my chinos—but I was numb inside, in my brain, as though I'd been tranquilized. Shock is like hypothermia: you don't feel it coming on until you can't feel anything at all.

"Greg, I know you don't wanna hear this right now, but if you stay here they'll pin this whole thing on you."

Numbly, I stared down at Zoe's lifeless face, at the stillness in the turmoil, suddenly picturing all the happy years we'd had in front of us, now erased.

"They won't look for her real killer. All they'll see is you, sitting here red-handed, and it'll be game over."

I brushed matted hair from her brow, then sniffed up snot and swallowed it down.

"She's a cop, man. Cop killers get the chair down here. Is that what she'd want, you playing the martyr, while her real killer walks free?" He stuck out his hand again. "Come with me. I saw who did this. We can get her justice, but only if you leave. Now."

I took one last heartbreaking look at Zoe's unmoving body, at the chaos of red and the tranquility of death, and felt a wave of disbelief quake through me. Then, gently, I laid down her head and wobbled to unsteady feet.

No matter which way I hung my head, the world was on a tilt.

"Get the gun."

I glanced around. "What?"

He motioned, fingers wiggling, to the granite countertop, to Zoe's holstered handgun placed there. "The gun, man. It's right there. Take it."

"Why?"

"Just do it, man." He flapped an impatient hand. "Hurry—they're almost here!"

Sirens were rushing toward us.

I picked it up, holding it with bloodied fingertips, as though it were a dead rat I was removing from the house. As Ray had rightly pointed out, I didn't know how to use it. I'd probably kill myself if I had to try.

Kyle was at the French doors leading to the backyard, urging me to follow.

Insanely, I did. I stepped out of the blood pool and didn't look back. I knew that if I stopped to survey the scene, I would be frozen, hypnotized by the madness. I followed him outside, leaving red footprints behind, stepping out into daylight that seemed strangely color-drained, cool-toned, as though the world had shifted off its axis.

Kyle pulled at my bloodied shirt. "C'mon, man. We've got to get you to a safe distance."

I retched, spewing stomach acid.

Kyle yelped, leaping aside. "Watch the shoes!"

Then, blindly, I followed him across the balding backyard, floating along like a tethered balloon, my feet seemingly moving of their own volition.

To one side was a sizable mound of freshly chipped wood, where somebody had been tidying up the periphery of the yard. A dense, overgrown stand of trees lay beyond.

We went in that direction.

Sirens were ripping up the street behind us.

I imagined the sheriff's cruisers screeching to a halt at the end of the quiet lane, neighbors peering through windows as the patrol cars pulled up outside Zoe's house. Adrenaline-fed deputies leaping out, running up the driveway, rushing inside. Guns being drawn when they saw the bloodbath. Radio chatter as they reported the slaying of their fellow officer back to base. More deputies arriving, the street choking up with squad cars, an ambulance, a coroner's van. The whole area being cordoned off, the local TV news turning up, and a sniffer dog brought in to track the bloody footprints trailing out of the rear of the house.

My footprints.

"Man, you're superlucky I turned up when I did," Kyle was saying as he held back a tangle of vines.

"Where are we going?"

"Right through here. She's waiting for us. You'll see."

He pushed his way into the leafy undergrowth, and I followed like a zombie, with Zoe's blood saturating my clothes and tribal death drums beating in my ears.

My heart was skipping beats, my stomach doing somersaults—but all for the wrong reason.

Zoe was dead. I couldn't process.

It was humid in the grove, and swarming insects were attracted by the sweet scent of death on my hands. I batted at the first few inquisitive biters, then gave up.

"We need to think you up an alibi," Kyle said. "An unshakable one as well. Because they will come asking."

I looked at the back of Kyle's head, at the kink in his crown where he'd cracked his skull when he was young, and said, "I left the wine bottle."

"So? Everyone drinks wine. Don't sweat it."

"It's covered in my fingerprints."

"Relax, man. They can't prove you didn't give it to her some other time."

"What about my car? It's on the street."

"She borrowed it."

"The keys are in my pocket."

Kyle glanced over his shoulder. "Greg, work with me here, will you? Stop rocking the boat. I'm thinking on my feet. Trying to get you off this hook. We'll iron out all the creases the second we're at a safe location. Now, stop stressing and move it!"

The grove ended abruptly at the river. An expanse of green water with big properties rising up on the opposite bank. Boats moored at wooden docks. White egrets wading the shallows. And a Yellowfin with Scarlett's Native American name stenciled on the hull.

"That's my boat."

Kyle looked at me like I was brain-dead. "How do you think I got here?"

I dug in my heels. "Wait. I have to go back." I realized it at the same time as I said it. "Something's wrong."

"You mean aside from the fact your girlfriend is lying in a pool of her own blood? Time to get real, Greg. The whole toilet has hit the fan."

Kyle would do well in community theater.

I dumped Zoe's gun in his hand, then turned around and returned the way we'd come.

"You're making a big mistake!" he called after me as I crashed through the undergrowth. "You're gonna fry, man!"

But I already was frying. Inside. I was burning up with a feverish impulsion to go back. Something had sprung to mind, finally breaking through the molasses of my thoughts. Something that made even less sense than finding Zoe dying on her kitchen floor.

Half running, I hurtled through the thicket, brushing fronds aside as I went. Sweat stung my eyes. Vines lashed at my face.

The sirens were tearing the neighborhood in two as I broke out into Zoe's backyard and fell into a sprint, breathing hard.

The edges of my vision were blurry, but I was focused on the open French doors, which I went through without slowing.

For a senseless second, I thought Zoe wouldn't be here, wrapped in her shroud of blood, but she was. I didn't look and I didn't slow at the sight of the red and blue flashing lights in the front window. I kept going, clattering across the living room until I reached the accent cabinet with the framed photographs on the top.

Then I scooped one up in my bloodied hands, staring with incredulity at the picture as the front door burst inward and a wave of armed deputies poured in.

Chapter Twenty

The room was basic, with fewer creature comforts than a prison cell. It was a drab pigeon-gray box with a metal table bolted to the poured-concrete floor, matching chairs, and a reinforced door to one side. Arguably, its finest feature was the big mirror in the middle of one wall. Even with the greasy fingerprints flowering around its borders, the one-way glass was an impressive element and clearly designed to dominate.

It spoke of ancient Rome, of cold-eyed emperors shielded from the arena as they watched their prized gladiators pull apart other powerless prey.

Zoe's death had hit me like a sledgehammer, and I was punch-drunk from the blow. Dazed. Unable to process anything involving more than a handful of words, and only then in single syllables.

I couldn't believe she was dead.

I'd seen it with my own eyes. I'd seen her bleed out all over her kitchen floor. I'd held her lifeless body in my arms. I'd felt her last breath drown in her blood-filled lungs.

And yet I was a unbeliever.

It's different when you see death and killing on the TV news. You know it's real because the trusted reporter says so. You know the corpses are real because they're as still as mannequins. You know the blood you're seeing isn't corn syrup and food dye. You know that someone

Keith Houghton

has tragically lost their life and the ripples will be far-reaching. Luckily, you are in a privileged position. From the comfort of your armchair, you are at best a voyeur and at worst indifferent, safely distanced from death. Depending on your sensitivity, you may be affected to a degree. You may swallow a lump in your throat. You may wipe at moisture in the corner of your eye. You may even switch channels, thanking God it isn't someone you know or happening in your sleepy neighborhood. It's almost never personal and therefore rarely remembered in all its gory detail.

But when you're the one riding the emotional ripple, there's no switching off.

In the back of the patrol car, on the drive to the sheriff's office, I'd half expected the deputy in the passenger seat—the one eyeing me through the repositioned rearview mirror—to turn around and blow the lid off the joke, to confess that Zoe had been setting me up, and that it was all just a silly prank, a belated April Fool's joke. *Gotcha!* But his stare had been that of a provoked cobra, waiting for any excuse to strike. And I'd ridden the entire trip north to Fort Myers with my head hung and my breathing shallow, absorbed in the blood clotting on my hands and the image in my mind of the framed photograph I'd let fall to the floor as the deputies had swarmed in and knocked me to the ground.

"His lawyer's here," someone said from the doorway.

For the past few minutes, my eyes had been tightly closed, sealed with dried tears, while I'd visualized what was in the photograph. Now, I peeled them open, blinking at the sterile glow coming from the room's single fluorescent light.

Those charged with putting on a show for the faceless observers behind the mirror were still in their places:

The simmering deputy from the passenger seat was now standing with his back to the wall, one hand resting on the butt of his holstered sidearm while the other hand rubbed continuously at the sandpaper coating his jawline.

188

His partner, the driver, was holding open the door a few inches, just enough to relay the message from his colleague outside. He hadn't locked eyes with me once. Not once, the whole journey here.

Facing me across the bare metal table was a square-faced man in his midfifties. Everything about him was gray: his suit; his hair; his hard, accusatory eyes; even his pallor. I knew him, and he knew me. Previously, we'd attended the same parties, the same family barbecues; participated in noisy beer rounds at Donovan's; laughed and joked like buddies. Not anymore. That had all ended with the death of his partner, Zoe.

"Last chance to do yourself a favor and confess," Detective John Thompson said through clenched teeth, and not for the first time.

Thompson had been coming out with similar phrases for the past twenty minutes. In fact, during the whole time I'd been sitting here with my own teeth clenched.

Just confess. We know you killed her. Why'd you do it? Was she ending your relationship? Is that it? You're smart, Doc, but what you've done is stupid. No way out of this for you. We caught you red-handed. This kind of thing comes with a mandatory death sentence. A smart guy like you needs to get in front of this. Just confess. Tell us why you did it.

My silence had wound Thompson up like a jack-in-the-box, and he was on the brink of popping his lid.

Everyone within earshot thought I was being deliberately uncooperative when the truth was, I had nothing to say. Other than asking for my lawyer and repeating a puny *I didn't do it* several times on the way into the sheriff's headquarters on Cypress Parkway, I hadn't spoken a single word in my defense.

How do you begin to defend against something like this?

An emotional tidal wave had swept me up, and I was doing all I could to tread water.

"Come clean," Thompson urged. "You owe her that much."

He was doing his best to rein in his emotions, and I had to hand it to him—he was doing a good job of it. But his eyes betrayed him. Those eyes said everything. They told me he wanted nothing more than to get me in a room alone, with no mirrored observation window and no cameras recording, where he could show me exactly what he thought should happen to cop killers.

Inwardly, I balked at those words: *cop killer*.

To everyone here at the sheriff's office, that's what I was. Scum of the earth. Gutter trash. The lowest of the low. A monster. And there was nothing I could say to convince them otherwise.

The door opened fully, and Ray Stitt marched in.

"Y'all give me the room," he commanded. "I need to talk with my client. Right now." A glance at the mirror. "And in private."

At first, Thompson didn't budge. He just continued to stare at me with cold, hateful eyes. Then someone rapped knuckles on the other side of the glass and, slowly, begrudgingly, noisily, he pushed himself to his feet and left the room, taking the other deputies with him.

The second the door had slammed closed, Ray perched himself on the corner of the table, his back to the one-way glass, and looked down at me through concerned eyes. "Jesus in a G-string, Greg. Please tell me you didn't buy a gun."

"Ray, I didn't even get a dog."

"What happened?"

I looked beyond him at the big mirror.

"Relax," he said. "I've spoken with Sheriff Torres. Although somewhat reluctant, she's given me her word they won't be eavesdropping. She's a friend, and she's extending a professional courtesy. We have five minutes, so start at the beginning and don't leave anything out."

Even so, I kept the volume of my voice low as I recounted everything I knew. I listened to my dull and reedy voice as I replayed the day's events, shuddering as it cracked when I relived the discovery of Zoe in a pool of her blood.

Ray didn't speak, but his face reflected the awfulness of it all. How could anyone begin to find the right words? He listened, intently, sucking at his teeth while I retraced my steps through the bloodbath.

When I was done and in need of a Kleenex, Ray leaned over and held my shoulder in his twiggy fingers. "Buddy, believe me, I am so sorry for your loss. Anything I can do, you know you've got it."

I nodded and swallowed dryly. "So, can you help me?"

"Is Willie Nelson a Texan? Sure, I can help you. This ain't my first rodeo. Between suing the city for sidewalk slips and puttering around at the nineteenth hole, I've been waiting for something like this to come along for a very long time. But backtrack for me a little here, will you? Who's this Kyle character again?"

"An old friend from Michigan."

"Who just happened to be at the crime scene, same time as you?"

In all the madness, in all the drama of being arrested, fingerprinted, processed, and hustled into custody, I hadn't given it any thought. I'd left Kyle holding Zoe's gun, and I hadn't thought about him since. My thoughts had been consumed with Zoe, dead in my arms. Everything else was unfocused, unimportant.

Now I realized I should have given Kyle's appearance at Zoe's more brain-processing time.

"The last time I saw Kyle was in Manistique," I said. "Eighteen years ago."

"So how did he know where to find you, and at just the right moment? That's some unbelievable coincidence right there."

"I have no idea. I do know he was using my boat."

"You let him?"

"He didn't have my permission."

"Did you report it?"

"I was going to, but then . . ." My words trailed off as I remembered the body at the boat club.

"Maybe we're missing the obvious here," Ray said. "This Kyle character was already in the house when you got there."

"What?"

"Just you and him, right? According to the first responders, no one else was on the property. That's as good as pointing the finger of blame at him, right? It raises reasonable doubt."

"You think Kyle killed Zoe?"

It was yet another group of words that made no sense whatsoever. Another meaningless ensemble tagging along after Thompson's unintelligible interrogation. For starters, Kyle didn't know Zoe, much less have any reason to do her harm. I wasn't even sure he had it in him to take another life. But then . . .

There was this one time. We were ten. A cool autumn day in the woods north of town. As many coppery leaves underfoot as there were tumbling from the trees. We'd caught sight of a young doe and chased her, brandishing our makeshift spears and whooping battle cries as we'd crashed through the leaves. The doe had attempted to leap over a gully but had misjudged its width, falling ten feet to its uneven floor. We'd arrived, breathless and all howled-out, to find her lying on her side, looking up at us with big brown eyes. One of her hind legs had twisted back on itself in an unnatural fashion, with a splinter of bone poking through the hide. I'd hesitated, suddenly filled with fright, knowing we had caused her awful injury. Kyle hadn't hesitated. He'd scrambled down into the gully, hefted a big rock, and smashed it down on her head before I'd had time to blink.

"Exactly how well do you know this guy?" Ray asked, pulling me back into the present.

I let out a long and contemplative breath.

The truth was, if I gave it enough thought, I didn't know Kyle at all. Not the adult version. He was a character from a favorite book, one I kept coming back to at different points in my life.

In my mind's eye, I had a layered image of him. A mental flipbook showing Kyle in various stages of development, from kindergarten to puberty to our recent encounter. Essentially, snapshots taken each time he'd wandered into my life, each subsequent picture plastered over the last until, when flicked through in sequence, they pulled together his scattered timeline to form a continuous growth pattern not dissimilar to my own.

But I didn't know him the way best friends do. Not the person deep inside, what made him tick. Not in the way I knew my friends here in Florida. Certainly not in the same way I knew Eve or . . . Zoe.

Thinking of Zoe made my chest hurt in a way that I'd only ever experienced once before, and I backed away from it.

Kyle was a timber wolf, living outside of the community, occasionally venturing inside when he thought he could steal the best cuts without anyone noticing.

It's impossible to form lasting relationships with itinerant animals.

We were seventeen when we parted ways for the last time—or so I'd thought. High school, girls, and messing around in boats had all played their part in keeping my brain occupied and Kyle away. Hectic teenage years, passing by in a flash.

On the rare occasion Kyle had popped up in my thoughts, I'd remembered him with fondness—the way we do when we reflect on our happier childhood memories. Two scrawny thirteen-year-olds, dragging blunt hunting knives across their palms and then clasping hands, declaring oaths and sharing blood, forever bonded. But in reality, I knew less about him than I did about Phil, my neighbor. Much less, considering I hadn't seen him in almost two decades.

Every way I looked at it, Kyle was an unknown quantity.

I felt Ray's scarecrow fingers shake me back into the moment.

"Greg, focus. Here's what we need to do. We need to tell the sheriff everything you know about this Kyle character. Start to build you a defense by way of giving them a better suspect than you. If we can convince them he did this, we can have you out of here by tonight."

"It wasn't Kyle," I said.

"You don't know that. You said yourself you don't even know what he could be capable of."

"It wasn't him."

"He was in the house before you got there. You said yourself Zoe's attack must have happened moments before you arrived. It's got to be him. Who else was there? So work with me here, buddy. I need to know where we can find this Kyle character."

"I have no idea. He lived in Naubinway, I think, a forty-five-minute drive from Manistique. But I can't say for sure. He was never a constant in my life."

Ray let out a shaky breath and licked his teeth. "Okay. No worries, buddy. I realize you've got your head up your ass right now, so I won't push it." He slid to his feet and shook out his pants. "I'll give the sheriff a heads-up on this Kyle character. See if we can place him on a flight down here. Meanwhile, just sit tight and don't say anything. You think you can do that?"

I nodded.

"Good. You'll see me again the minute I've convinced the powers that be that they've got the wrong guy."

I dropped my eyes to the dried blood under my nails. The processing officer had made me rinse my hands before and after taking fingerprints, but the blood had refused to budge.

"It wasn't Kyle," I said, with anger hardening in my belly.

"We'll let the sheriff worry about that."

"I know who it was."

Ray paused with his hand on the doorknob.

Aside from the horrific image of Zoe slain in her kitchen, the picture overshadowing my every thought was the one I'd found on her accent cabinet, immediately preceding my arrest.

It was a photograph of two newlyweds—Mr. and Mrs. Troy Pinkerton—taken on the beach at sunset, with gold-leaf waves and a sky of burnished bronze.

A photograph showing a younger version of Zoe in her figure-hugging wedding dress, breathtaking—full of life and looking like a princess—standing with her new husband on the golden sand, their arms wrapped lovingly around each other as the waves curled and crashed behind them.

A photograph showing her caught in a moment of pure bliss, years before everything soured, before her marriage fell apart, smiling up at her high school heartthrob, in his tan suit and sandals, with him smiling down at her.

A photograph showing Zoe with the man I knew as . . .

"Gus Toomey."

Chapter Twenty-One

Ray turned back to face me. "Now who the heck is Gus Toomey?"

"Apparently, Zoe's estranged husband."

"You mean Troy?"

"I do. Except, that's not the name I know him by." I lifted my eyes, feeling an odd sense of accomplishment. "He's the one who did this. He killed Zoe."

Ray returned to his perch on the table. "Zoe's husband?" He didn't look surprised, probably because he'd seen one too many murder trials involving killings undertaken by the significant other.

"Estranged," I said. "They've been having issues for years. Basically, living together but leading separate lives."

"That's where you come in."

I nodded.

"Shame when that happens. People need to work harder or choose better. Okay. For the record, she wasn't cheating on him with you?"

"Ray, it wasn't like that."

"As far as you know."

I let him see the full length of my frown.

"Sorry, buddy. I have to ask these difficult questions. So clarify something for me here. What's with this Toomey name? The husband's Troy, right?"

"Right. Troy Pinkerton. And here's the thing: he came into my office a couple of days ago, masquerading as a new client, this Gus Toomey person. He didn't use his real name, apparently. He told me he was experiencing marital problems. He was obsessing about his wife. Of course, I didn't know he was talking about Zoe at the time. He was fixated, wanting to know if—" Suddenly, my throat was choked. I couldn't believe the run of events and what I was saying.

"It's okay," Ray said. "Take a breather there, buddy."

I took several, then said, "He wanted to know if it was normal to fantasize about killing his wife."

"Sumbitch. And you didn't recognize him?"

I shook my head. "That's just it. We've never met. Zoe and I made a point of not letting our home lives get in the way. Today was the first time I've ever visited her at home, and that's when I saw them together, in a photograph: this Toomey person and Zoe."

"Somebody slap me."

"He was booked in for a second appointment this afternoon. My four o'clock. But he canceled, which meant I got to Zoe's earlier than planned. We'd texted each other about it. He must have known I was on my way." My belly felt full to the brim with acid, sloshing back and forth.

Ray was sucking his teeth. "The murder was premeditated. Son of a gun. Pinkerton set you up."

Other than madness, I had no idea why Pinkerton had wanted Zoe dead. According to her, he had no issue with us. According to him, he had been thinking about killing her for months.

I imagined him plotting and scheming, bottling up his jealousy, biding his time, waiting for the right moment to present itself, working it so that it would appear as though I had killed her.

"Did you by any chance tape Pinkerton's session?" Ray said. "Because if you've got him on record, confessing to wanting Zoe dead, I can use it to sweeten the DA. Buy us some leverage."

It's something I ask all my clients, at the top of each session: *Do you mind if I record this, purely for reference purposes?* Most balk at the idea of having their innermost thoughts taped. You can't blame them. Some of the things I hear are cringeworthy. Unsurprisingly, the man presenting himself as Gus Toomey said no.

"He declined," I said.

"Well, that's just great. What about eyewitnesses? Is there anyone else who can confirm he came to the clinic Wednesday?"

"I guess Glenda, the receptionist." All new patients were required to complete a health-and-lifestyle questionnaire. "I'm sure if you show her Pinkerton's photo, she'll identify him as Gus Toomey."

"Okay. Better. Plus, this Kyle character, right?"

"Kyle?"

"If he was at the house before you got there and he didn't kill Zoe, then it's possible he saw who did."

And now I remembered Kyle saying exactly that.

"So, what happens next?" I said.

"I need to have that conversation with the DA, see if I can show him probable cause, or at least raise some doubt where you're concerned. He owes me a favor or two."

I nodded.

In political circles, favors are a way of life. I had no idea what leverage Ray had over the district attorney, but I hoped it was good. Back in Texas, Ray had been something of a celebrity lawyer, taking on the highest-profile cases and blossoming in the media spotlight. The kind of behavior that can make enemies faster than friends. There will always be toes you tread on, egos you dent. It's hard getting influence on those terms. Coming to Florida had cooled Ray's engines, but he hadn't lost his drive, his competitiveness. I'd found him a likable person with a big heart and an impeccable moral compass. But what kind of sway did he have here?

"In the meantime," he said, "do you need me to let anyone know you're here?"

I thought about Eve, about panicking her with the idea of leaving the sanctuary of our home to come rushing all the way to Fort Myers at night, and I shook my head.

I wasn't worried about her missing me. She knew I had arranged to be with Zoe tonight—all night—and that it was Saturday tomorrow. She knew she could expect to see me in the morning or even later.

After that . . . well, I wasn't sure what would happen after that.

Chapter Twenty-Two

C op killers receive preferential treatment.

Above all else, this is what I learned as my arrest, processing, interrogation, and subsequent detention at the pleasure of the Lee County sheriff stretched into its fourth hour.

Where other, less undesirable offenders—the drunks, the dealers, the white-collar wife beaters—were corralled into the same cramped holding pen to sweat it out while their lawyers arranged bail or more comfortable accommodation, I was left alone in my interview room, manacled to the metal table, positioned so that I faced the big silvered screen, knowing that I was being observed but not knowing by whom.

My cop-killer status kept me separated from the rest of the rabble, and right now it came as a blessing.

I know my limitations. I'm not too macho to admit I'm not cut out for a life on the wrong side of the law. I'm generally a model citizen. Running the occasional red isn't in the same league as murder. For the most part, my everyday existence is predictable, mapped out with routine and dependability, my only interaction with the law through Zoe.

Zoe is dead!

Unrestrained, crushing emotions washed over me like white water, battering my brain against submerged rocks, and I gasped, clinging to the table, my bloodied nails leaving rusty prints.

Don't black out . . . Breathe . . . Slowly . . . Breathe.

The suffocating memory had been coming in waves for the past hour or two, all the time I'd sat here on my own, left to stew.

Here and now, I was treading water, doing my best to stay afloat in a whirlpool of emotion. But my life was wrecked, and I knew that sooner or later the full impact of Zoe's death would hit me like a flood.

The one-way mirror was looking down on me like the eye of God, judging and forcing reflection.

After Scarlett's murder trial, it had practically taken divine inter-vention to break me out of my yearlong funk. But I was stronger now, older and a little bit wiser, better equipped. I knew all the answers, or at least those that mattered. All I had to do was marry them up to the right questions.

What would Eve say if she were here?

She'd tell me to trust Ray, that he was a damn fine lawyer and my best chance of sorting out this whole mess. If anyone could throw me a lifeline, it was him.

Another unstoppable surge flowed through me, and I closed my eyes, sucking back the tears. The last thing I wanted was for those behind the screen to see me cry. To them, I was a pathetic excuse for a human being, I'd taken the life of one of their own, and I didn't deserve to breathe while she didn't. They wouldn't see my weeping as that of a man wrongly accused of his girlfriend's murder, genuinely sobbing for her loss, broken. Altruism had taken the weekend off. My emotional display would be viewed as a way to drum up support for a sympathy vote, a ploy to make them take pity and hence a softer line.

No one would offer me a Kleenex, let alone a plea deal.

So I held it in, quaking, tensing, letting the current take me where it chose.

My grandfather had said, *Tears make women look vulnerable, and all you want to do is protect them. But tears make men look weak, and all you want to do is tell them to toughen up.*

I never saw my grandfather cry, not ever. Unlike my grandmother, who had cried for them both.

I took a deep breath and pulled myself together, wiping snot from my nose with a blood-crusted sleeve.

Zoe was gone, and there was nothing I could do to change it. Sure, I could do the expected grieving-lover thing: sit around moping and feeling sorry for myself, revel in the pain. Or I could do the opposite, put my newfound knowledge to good use. Make sure Pinkerton paid for what he'd done.

A deputy came in and placed a bottled water on the table in front of me—I imagined, probably something to do with the Geneva convention and prisoners of war—and I guzzled it down as though I'd spent the day wandering a desert.

Then I turned my thoughts to Kyle.

First and foremost, I was at a loss to explain how or why he had shown up when he did. No doubt, the universe can be a strange place. Coincidences abound, and if Carl Jung would have it, these meaningful interactions can be attributed to what he called synchronicity. But I wasn't convinced of this being the case where Kyle was concerned.

Kyle never played by the universe's rules.

The earliest complete memory I have of him was from our first day of elementary school.

We were scrawny five-year-olds, and I was self-conscious and clumsy, blindly feeling my way through the bigger social mix for the first time. Scarlett was in front of me, ahead of me, as always, forming a bow wave as she plied uncharted waters.

Even at five, Scarlett had radiated confidence. It was something I sorely lacked back then. I remember she drew gazes as she floated through the room on that first day, like a ball of light attracting dusty moths. I was safe in her shadow, happy to remain relatively unseen, until a chubby kid with a bucktoothed grin—Goofy, we later came to think of him—had noticed my low profile and had started pushing me around, calling me Carrot-Top and other unimaginative names. Not just me. He'd already worked his charm on most of the other miserable-looking kids, leaving a trail of turned-out pockets and snotty sniffles behind him. Goofy was smart, but not in any upwardly mobile way.

You look like a girl, Goofy had said to me. *What's your name— Curly Sue?*

And Goofy had yanked on my hair, hard enough to ring a bell in my head.

You're mine now, he'd said.

I was five. I had no idea what he meant. But Kyle, on the other hand, did. Until this point I'd been only vaguely aware of Kyle loitering in the background. Kyle: the brooding type. Kyle: the impulsive type. Kyle: the-never-needing-two-invites-to-a-party type.

Kyle had stepped in and assumed control. This was Kyle to a T. Before anyone could stop him, he was on top of Goofy, pinning him down with his knees, fist balled and raised to strike. Goofy was stunned. Kyle was smaller but faster. His fist had struck Goofy on the mouth, hitting harder than any five-year-old should have been able to hit, his knuckles coming away with red goo on them.

Goofy wasn't the only one in shock.

The whole class was speechless, even our teacher.

Foolishly, I decided then and there that Kyle was the best thing ever to happen to me.

But it turned out to be the last I saw of him for a while. My next distinct memory was made a couple of years later, which was when I learned that his mom had elected to homeschool him after the incident in kindergarten, to move back to her parents' place in Naubinway, returning only occasionally to see friends. After that, whenever Kyle came visiting, we caught up, a handful of times each year, spending the entire day together, sometimes the whole weekend.

It was never awkward for us to reconnect, even though Kyle had become an outcast, destined to slip unseen through the spaces left behind by others. We gelled.

But none of my memories could explain his recent magical reappearing act.

An hour after I drank the water, two deputies escorted me to the bathroom, then watched while I toileted and rinsed the remainder of the blood from my forearms. Zoe's blood swirled down the drain while something unholy swirled up my windpipe.

An hour after that, Ray blustered into the interview room with unexpected news:

"Okay, buddy. Time to get you signed out. You're free to leave. Let's hit the road."

Chapter Twenty-Three

Headlights blinded me, searing my optical nerves all the way to the back of my skull. I pulled down the sun visor, but it failed to block them out.

"Thanks for this," I said to Ray as we drove south on 41 in his black Escalade.

It was after two in the morning, with everywhere closed. I reeked of iron oxide and sweat, but Ray didn't pass comment or ask me not to dirty the leather.

"I don't know what favors you called in to persuade them to drop the charges, Ray, but I'm grateful. I owe you."

"Well, I'm happy to take the pat on the back, but I can't take all the credit," he said. "Wasn't just my doing. I had stupidity helping me out." He pressed a button on the steering wheel, and Willie Nelson began to croon quietly from the backseat about lost love. "Put it this way: the DA and Sheriff Torres didn't need much in the way of convincing. Seems they were already on to Pinkerton long before I raised the alarm. Turns out he's studying to be a half-wit, and I'm afraid he ain't gonna make it."

He must have seen my hopeless expression and said, "Sure you're okay talking about this, Greg? I don't want to push a leaking boat out into deep water and all."

"Ray, it's what I do for a living. Why should talking about myself be any different?"

The truth was, I didn't savor the chance to be on the wrong side of the interview, to lie, figuratively speaking, on the analyst's couch and have my life examined, exposed. It made me want to pull in my head and hide.

"The guy made three fatal mistakes," Ray explained. "First, the murder weapon. Forensics failed to lift a single print from the handle, which either points to the killer wiping it down after he used it, or he wore gloves. And the whole sheriff's office saw those bloodied mitts of yours. No one in their right mind would believe you handled the knife."

"I'm surprised they ran the tests that quick."

"For a cop killing, they'd hire NASA if they thought it'd do any good. Word is, they've got the entire crime lab doing overtime. The good news is, so far the only places they've found your prints are on a wine bottle and a photograph."

I swallowed thick phlegm.

"Secondly, they have an eyewitness—some maintenance guy in the neighbor's yard—who claims he saw a man fitting Pinkerton's description fleeing the scene, less than a minute before you showed up."

Pinkerton had been driving the white sedan that had nearly run me off the road, I realized.

"The third mistake is the real clincher," he said, "so sit back and brace yourself for this one, buddy. If you were wondering how the cops showed up as soon as they did, it's because someone placed a nine-one-one call, from Zoe's cell."

"Pinkerton?"

"It's looking increasingly likely. As a courtesy, they let me listen to the tape. You can clearly hear it's a guy trying to mask his voice, probably with the back of his hand, and not very well. It didn't sound like your girly soprano. No insult intended. Combine all three errors in judgment, and it's enough to knock you out of the prime-suspect spot." He elbowed me chummily on the arm. "Smile, buddy. You're off the hook."

I did produce a smile, but it lacked conviction.

Knowing I was no longer under the spotlight didn't change the fact that Zoe was dead. It only acted to focus every negatively charged electron within me against Pinkerton.

From the speakers, Willie Nelson began to lament about blue eyes crying in the rain.

Absently, I watched the deserted strip malls and the darkened roadside restaurants pass by, feeling slightly out of sync with my environment. I knew this feeling, this hollowed-out disquiet. It had carried me along for months in the wake of Scarlett's death, enabling normal bodily function in spite of my brain wanting to opt out. It was cold shock, keeping the world at arm's length. Survival at the expense of everything else.

"Have they found him?" I asked.

"Who, Pinkerton? No, not yet. I hear they're working on it, though, which—between you and me—is copspeak for they have no idea where he's at."

"Can't they trace his phone or Zoe's?"

"Maybe. So long as they're powered up. From what I hear, Detective Thompson tried calling Pinkerton from the crime scene, to break the bad news about his wife. This was before Pinkerton became a suspect. The number came back unreachable. Thompson called Pinkerton's office, again without a response. So they sent a deputy over, only to find the place locked up for the weekend. They have no clue where he's at."

But I did, I realized suddenly, and for completely selfish reasons, I didn't mention it.

Only once had I made the mistake of asking Zoe what her husband did for a living. We were both tipsy at the time, at Donovan's, playing a pretty diabolical game of Truth or Dare and giggling like teenagers. After revealing he was a personal trainer working out of a rented office,

Zoe had realized her blunder and then expertly redirected, politely reminding me of our nondisclosure agreement.

But Zoe had let something else slip just recently, again without realizing it.

She'd told me that her husband was out of town on business, at a power-shake convention in Sarasota.

Pinkerton had set himself up with an alibi.

As far as any interested party was concerned, he was elsewhere at the time of her murder, gone the whole weekend. Zoe had alluded to her husband having left for Sarasota yesterday morning.

I imagined he'd driven to the hotel that was hosting the convention, checked himself in, made a fuss, ensuring that he was visible, memorable, dumped his personal effects in his room, and then snuck out the side door.

Six months ago, during a drive past Zoe's home, I'd noted a red Dodge Charger parked in her driveway, in front of her motor pool vehicle. One of those macho muscle cars to match Pinkerton's bodybuilder physique. But he hadn't come back to Bonita Springs to commit the foul deed in his very noticeable Charger. He'd returned in a nondescript white sedan. An unremarkable and unmemorable car, and probably one he'd picked up from a local rental agency in Sarasota.

Then, later in the afternoon, he'd lain in wait inside their home. He'd surprised Zoe, confronted her. Maybe they had argued. Maybe he had told her all the things he'd told me, all about his anger and the pain that never went away. Maybe he'd vented his jealousy. Things would have gotten heated, giving Pinkerton the very excuse he had needed to reach for the chef's knife and stab her to death.

A shudder ran through me.

"You okay there, buddy?"

"I think I need food."

"Snickers in the glove compartment."

I thanked him but declined.

On Wednesday, wearing his Toomey guise, Pinkerton had agreed to a second consultation, knowing he would be elsewhere at the time, knowing that if he canceled at the last minute it would free me up to see Zoe. It was all premeditated.

"Only a matter of time until they track him down," Ray was saying. "He can't run forever."

Even so, I knew he wasn't running. He was in Sarasota, probably sharing jibes and jokes in the hotel bar and looking forward to the power-shake convention in the morning. He wasn't running, because he believed he had an airtight alibi.

And all he needed to untangle himself from the murder charge was to raise a reasonable doubt.

For Zoe's sake, I couldn't let that happen.

We turned off 41 onto Terry Street.

"Sure you want to do this?" Ray asked.

"No time like the present." My tone was flat, dull.

Shock doesn't just disable, it enables us to act, to go through the motions in ways unimaginable after it wears off.

"There's no rush here. You could do this tomorrow, after you've had some rest, got your head together."

But I knew if I didn't do this now, I'd come up with a hundred excuses by the morning not to.

"It'll be fine," I told him as he stopped at the intersection with Harbor Drive.

"You sure?"

"Yeah." I wasn't. But I had no choice.

I took a deep breath, climbed out, and said my thanks, then asked him to keep me updated if he heard any news from the sheriff's office overnight.

"Get some sleep," he told me in return. "I'm on this."

Then I walked the rest of the way to Zoe's house with my fists curled and my breathing shallow.

A few hours ago, this quiet cul-de-sac would have been a completely different scene, lit up like Times Square and crammed with sheriff's cruisers and EMS vehicles. Neighbors watching from their front walks as emergency personnel scurried to and fro. Detectives assessing the scene before giving the go-ahead to the forensics technicians to catalogue the macabre. Deputies combing the property, while assistants from the coroner's office wheeled out Zoe's exsanguinated body on a gurney.

Now, it was as if nothing terrible had happened here. It looked like just another sleepy suburban street, blanketed in darkness. But there was no mistaking the crime-scene tape forming an *X* across Zoe's front door. It was the sign of the plague, warning of evil within, visible from the street.

My car was where I had left it. I pulled open the door and fell inside. I let out a long, troubled breath. Then, comforted by the familiarity of my surroundings, I closed my eyes.

"I was going to drive it home, but you took the keys."

I twisted around, pulse pounding, to see a shadowy figure in the back.

"Relax," came the voice again. "It's me."

The figure leaned forward, so that a face emerged from out of the dark.

"Kyle?"

"Hey." His tone was calm, soft. "How's it going? I was beginning to think they wouldn't let you go."

Impulsively, I grabbed him by the neck of his shirt and hauled him toward me.

"Take it easy, man," he yelped. "No need to get all physical. We're on the same side."

"What are you doing here?"

"What does it look like? Being a pal and waiting for you. Like I said, I would've driven—"

"I mean what are you doing here, in Bonita Springs?"

"What do you mean?"

"Don't make me spell it out for you, Kyle."

"I was worried about you, man."

I stared into his sunken eyes, trying to see deeper than the obvious. "Why on earth would you be worried about me? It's been eighteen years. We don't even know each other. Not as adults. We were boys back then, kids. We're as good as strangers."

He took hold of my wrist and levered my hand free, then smoothed down his shirt. "Don't bait me, man. I'm not getting into this with you. Sure, it's been a while. But we made an oath, remember? We slit our hands and shared blood. Friends for life, we said."

"We were thirteen when we did that! And only because we saw it in a movie and thought it was a cool thing to do!"

"Maybe so. But I've always valued your friendship."

"We haven't spoken since we were teenagers!"

"Didn't stop me thinking about you, hoping you were doing okay. Can I get in the front?"

"No!"

His mouth turned down at the corners.

I shook my head, as if by doing so he would vanish. "This can't be real. There's no way you can be here. No way."

Kyle reached out a hand, extended a finger, and flicked the tip of my nose. "Does that feel real?"

I blinked.

He snickered. "C'mon, man. I mean, have you lost your mind or something?"

"It's debatable."

"Well, I'm as real as you. More real, probably, since I don't hide behind my fancy possessions or my good community standing."

I was tempted to defend myself, but I frowned instead. "What happened to you, Kyle? That last time I saw you, we were seventeen. You turned up in a stolen SUV."

He snickered. "Oh, sure. We took that thing off-road, didn't we? Into the woods. Spent the whole day running gullies. Fun times, man."

"It was dangerous. Insane. I didn't want to."

"Sure you did, Greg. You didn't take much persuading. You never did. We both enjoyed it."

"Even so, I never saw you again after that. So tell me. What did happen to you?"

"In a nutshell, the judicial system happened to me." His frame seemed to settle in on itself, like wet clothes on a drying rack. "I did things back then. Stuff you don't know about and don't want to know about. Things I'm not proud of. Things that would make your toes curl. For a while, I got away with most of it. Just petty stuff here and there. And the more I did, the more risks I took. Then lady luck ran out on me. Next thing I know, they're sending me to juvie."

I leaned against the steering wheel. "Juvenile detention."

He nodded sheepishly. "For too long, man, I was in and out of one institution after another. Something like that sticks, you know? Each time I came out, I reoffended. I didn't want to. I wanted to go to school, get a life like yours. But the only education I got was from the other kids in juvie. The wrong kind."

"Kyle, I didn't know."

"Yeah, well. It's not something you broadcast. Prison was tough, man. I only just survived the last time."

"I'm sorry."

He shrugged. "Only myself to blame."

"It still doesn't explain why you're here now."

"That's simple. Because of Zane Murdoch."

I shrank back at the sound of his name. I pictured Murdoch enlisting Kyle to help him hunt me down, using his questionable ethics to do his bidding. "The two of you know each other?"

"Yeah. That's one way of putting it." Kyle squirmed a little on the backseat. "Man, this is the uncomfortable part, for sure. So, yeah, I do know Murdoch. But we were never friends. Not like you and me. So don't look so freaked out. We shared a cell for a while, that's all, a few years back."

Now I sat up straight. "You were in Marquette?"

"Hey, don't crucify me, man. I'm not the world's brightest spark. Not like you. You turned out all right. Look at me: I wasn't blessed with brains or beauty. My PO says I have, and I quote, 'undeveloped social skills.' He says I'm an unschooled simpleton who's getting everything he deserves. He's right, you know? It's a dog-eat-dog world out there. An uneducated guy like me uses what he can to get by, to survive. As a kid, I was good at sneaking around and stealing stuff, so that's the road I went down. He called it 'the path of least resistance.'"

"You were in Marquette with Murdoch?" My mouth was dry, with the beginnings of a cool dread spreading through my gut.

"Hey, imagine my surprise. Talk about small world! Sheesh. I couldn't believe it when they put me with him."

"Did you and Murdoch plan this?"

Kyle made a dismissive snort. "What? No! Are you for real? That creep's a number-one nutjob. Top of the charts. I never met anyone so cut off from reality before. You know what I'm saying?"

"Disconnected."

"Yeah, that's the word I'm looking for. Man, those six months I spent with him were sheer hell. Partly my own fault. First week I was in there, I made the mistake of saying I knew you. Worst thing I did. After that, he never stopped bugging me. All he wanted to do was talk about how you ruined everything for him and what he was going to do to you after he got out."

I swallowed dryly.

"He was making a big deal about you setting him up. I mean, I didn't get into the specifics with him. That guy could make the pope swear. Something they found in his trash is all I know. I closed off after a while, learned to tune him out."

For the life of me, other than their mutual drug abuse, I was never able to see what Scarlett had seen in Zane Murdoch. As far as I could tell, intellectually they were worlds apart. As different as night and day. Murdoch was a loudmouth and a high school dropout. He'd worked in his father's lube shop up until his arrest. One of those inelegant guys with rough hands to complement his coarse character. In comparison, Scarlett was a New Age hippie, an artist, a poet, happy in her tie-dyes. She believed in everything I didn't: karma, feng shui, yin and yang. But she had seen something in Murdoch, something other than just the supplier of her street drugs. Something I didn't see, couldn't, because I was seeing him through the wary eyes of a protective brother. Even so, the attraction had existed, bringing them together for the last few years of her life, effectively replacing me.

Kyle cleared his throat. "So, yeah. So, anyway, he said he had this plan. Said he had this scheme to overturn his sentence. He said he had, and I quote, 'an unshakable alibi.'"

"The home invasion."

"You know about that?"

"Thursday, I had a visit from the Michigan State Police. They checked out his alibi. They believe Murdoch was in Ontonagon when Scarlett disappeared. And now they think I killed her."

Kyle's expression crumpled. "Come again?"

"They've reopened the homicide investigation, with me as the prime suspect."

"Because they found your sister's body at Crooked Lake?"

I nodded. "Their forensics people retrieved skin from under her fingernails." My tone was oddly very matter-of-fact, like someone else was using my voice to speak. "They think it's mine."

Kyle cussed and thumped the headrest. "That's not the way things are supposed to pan out, man!"

"Right now, it's the least of my worries."

Kyle glanced toward Zoe's house, then back to me. "Hey, I was meaning to say, tough break about the girlfriend, man. Real bummer. Yeah?"

I wanted to smirk at his inability to project true compassion, but shock had fixed my face in a permanent scowl.

"I'm telling you, man, the last thing I expected to see was a murder."

"What did you see, Kyle?"

"Nothing at first. I heard them. I was down along the side of the house. They were in the bathroom, arguing. Him raising his voice. Her trying to push him away. He chased her out of the shower. So I went around to the back and saw them go into the kitchen." He shook his head. "Man, I've never seen nothing like that before. I think she was going for her gun, but he just knifed her. Right in the ribs. Just like that."

My heart was in my mouth.

"Then he left and you turned up, and I was like, man, that's what I call a coincidence!"

Kyle's misplaced excitement made my jaw tighten. "You going to explain about that, how you just happened to be there right before it happened?"

Dramatically, Kyle rolled his eyes. "Hey, man, I don't plan these things. We're all instruments of the universe, you know? I go where I'm sent. Point and press. That's me. Lucky for you, right?"

"Kyle . . ."

"Okay, okay. I saw it on TV."

"What?"

"Murdoch's conviction being overturned. It made the evening news back home. I knew after what he told me he'd come looking for revenge. And I felt obligated to do something."

"Why?"

"We're friends, man. Pure and simple." He said it like we'd never spent a day apart in thirty years. "That's why I hired my guy to find you."

"Your guy?"

"Sure. He calls himself Black Irish."

"O'Malley? He's working for you?"

Kyle gave a lopsided smile at my surprise. "I know. It's totally out there, isn't it? Me, being so *conventional*. So, yeah, I scraped some cash together and hired the best guy I could afford down here."

"Wait a minute. Your last name's Hendrickson? I thought it was Sanders."

"That's my mom's name. I used it growing up, because my loving dad was MIA so much of the time." He emphasized his statement with a grin, but I got the impression he wasn't happy with the arrangement. "Officially, it's Hendrickson."

"How did you even know I was in Florida?" I said.

"Now that goes back to my time in Marquette. Murdoch told me he'd put the feelers out years ago. He said this private eye of his had tracked you down to Bonita Springs. That's what gave me the idea about Black Irish."

"And that's how you knew about Zoe's place, too?"

Kyle nodded. "My guy was nothing if not thorough. He filled me in on everything, including your girl. Which was why I was here when the poop hit the fan."

"You were spying on Zoe?" I realized it with a start.

"No, man. God, no. I was curious. Okay? I'm not a pervert. Sheesh. Think all the bad things you want about me, Greg, but perversion isn't high on my list. Please. I wanted to make sure Murdoch wasn't hanging around her house, like he was at yours."

I held up a hand. "Wait a minute. Back up. You were at my house?"

He let out an exasperated sigh. "What are you, deaf? I saw that Murdoch was making plans to come down here—stocking up his truck for a long trip and heading out. So I made the trip before he did. Flew down ahead of him."

"To *protect* me?" It seemed absurd, the weakest motivation. Who in their right mind would drop everything and do such a thing? Kyle and I hadn't seen each other since we were boys. We didn't owe each other anything.

"So, yeah, I was there," he continued, "at your place the other night, when he came at you with the knife. I'd been there awhile, catching *z*'s in your boat."

"You were the one I saw in my backyard, the night before."

"I guess."

"Why didn't you just knock on my door, introduce yourself?"

He shrugged. "I don't know! My brain doesn't work like yours. I'm used to staying in the shadows." Then he smiled. "Man, you should've seen the look of surprise on his face when I jumped in. It was priceless."

"You intervened?"

"I had to. I thought he was going to butcher you."

I pictured the two of them scrapping, slugging it out on the wet grass in my backyard, intermittently lit by lightning, fists flying, punches landing, with me sprawled on my back in the rain, out of it.

"I whipped that knife right out of his hand and had it to his throat quicker than he could blink. You should have heard the excuses he started babbling."

I pictured an unsatisfied Kyle running the blade across Murdoch's throat, the bloodcurdling gurgle muted by thunder, the blood squirting from Murdoch's ruptured jugular as Kyle manhandled him to the swollen river, letting the storm surge take him, wash him away. Then he'd taken my boat, but not before hauling me back inside the lanai and onto the pool chair.

"You killed Murdoch." It wasn't a question. It was a prickly realization.

I pictured Murdoch's waterlogged body snagging on the ramp at the boat club, the manager finding him, turning him over, seeing the ragged slash across his throat, and Murdoch's lifeless eyes staring back at him.

"Killed him? Sure, I was tempted. He gave me every reason to. But I didn't do it. By this point he was crying. I mean, down on his knees and begging me to spare him. Said he was on a mission of forgiveness and all he wanted to do was talk. Like he'd seen the light or something. It was pitiful, man. I mean, goddamn embarrassing. He was whimpering like a baby."

As he started to poke fun at Murdoch, I hushed him, hurriedly taking out my phone and opening up a browser.

"Whatcha looking at?"

"The latest local news updates."

I found what I was looking for and stared with disbelief at the phone. Midafternoon, the body at the boat club had been identified as that of a local vagrant, not Zane Murdoch. The medical examiner had determined a blood-alcohol level four times the legal limit and indications of drowning. A spokesperson for the ME's office suggested the homeless man had fallen into the river during the thunderstorm, and that his neck wound was probably the result of an interaction with a submerged sharp object, such as a boat propeller.

Mystery solved.

I put my phone away, feeling more than a little foolish.

Paranoia makes every bad decision seem good.

"What happened to him, to Murdoch?"

"Beats me. I sent him home with his tail between his legs. Last thing I saw, he was getting back in his truck and hightailing it. If you ask me, I think he was headed for the nearest church."

On my behalf, Kyle had sent Murdoch packing. I should have sat a little straighter, felt a little lighter, but I didn't.

Kyle handed me something from the backseat. "Before I forget, you'll want this back."

I turned the bundle over in my hands.

In the days following Scarlett's disappearance, when my suspicion about Murdoch had fallen on deaf ears, I'd done everything in my power to demonstrate his guilt. Every fiber in me had wanted to make him pay for dumping my life in the trash, to do whatever necessary to appease the rage boiling away inside.

I'd been proactive, intent on making sure he didn't get away with it.

Zoe's holstered gun was a dead weight in my hands.

And all at once, I knew what had to be done.

Chapter Twenty-Four

Dawn was feathering the eastern sky flamingo pink as I pulled the car into the hotel parking lot and left the engine running. There was a metallic smell in the air and in my mouth. I rolled down the window, letting the warm breeze flow in, bringing with it a tang of damp vegetation and a distant rumble of traffic on the interstate.

Kyle was asleep on the backseat and had been for the last two hours, bleating like a baby, every now and then calling out and kicking reflexively.

The drive north up I-75 had been relatively quiet and, for the most part, uneventful. Even as we'd accelerated up the on-ramp from the beach road, Kyle had chosen to curl up on the backseat. He was snoring within seconds, leaving me to my dark thoughts and the hundred-mile drive ahead.

I didn't mind him sleeping; the silence had given me plenty of time to think.

Incredibly, he had even slept through a pit stop at the RaceTrac store at exit 170, where I'd paused to refuel and recharge. I grabbed a bag of potato chips and a hazelnut coffee, then paid a visit to the restroom, where I'd been scowled at by my unshaven face in a mirror. My tousled hair. Dried blood on my shirt. A weird calmness in my eyes.

I looked like someone who had been through hell.

No one has ever referred to me as a violent man. If I can, I'll avoid stepping on ants. Life is precious. When you lose someone close, you learn that lesson quickly. All told, I have lost five members of my immediate family and survived to undertake what many people consider to be an invaluable job; no one can argue I don't embrace life, cherish it.

I twisted the rearview mirror to get a good look at Kyle.

My plan hadn't involved bringing him here. But he had insisted, saying he had nothing to go back to, nothing except a whip-cracking parole officer and the high probability of him doing something stupid to land himself in prison again.

Repeat offenders don't get a choice, he'd said. *It's in the genes.*

Even so, I still couldn't believe he was here, eighteen years later, fully grown and yet somehow still childlike.

At a glance and in the poor light, he could have passed as seventeen; the darkness masked his bulkier body mass and the bristles coating his jaw. Otherwise, he was the same Kyle, with his reckless sense of humor and his trademark lopsided grin. As though his brain had ceased its development on the day we'd last parted ways and he was the same teenager trapped in an adult body. Here in my car.

It seemed about as believable as losing Zoc.

Our lives had followed very different courses since Kyle and I last hung out, our paths diverging drastically. Half of me was reluctant to get involved with Kyle again, to let it all back in, to rekindle a past I could barely remember and maybe for good reason.

But half of me was sympathetic, compassionate. Life had been rough on Kyle. Social pressures had forced him to eke out an existence on the other side of the tracks, living off scraps and handouts, repeatedly breaking the law and trying to avoid detection, while I had breezed through high school and college, hardly ever imagining his existence was any less smooth than mine.

One of the best-preserved memories I have of Kyle was when we were eleven. It was a freezing December evening, and I was skating on the frozen surface of Quarry Lake, acting cocky, thinking I had all the moves. It was bitterly cold, I remember, with a clear indigo sky speckled with stars, and the whole world seemingly covered in snow. I was on my own, my breath forming frosty clouds as I'd slipped and slid across the lake. Then the world had tipped over and I'd hit the back of my head against the ice, hard enough to knock me out cold. When I came to, Kyle was leaning over me. He told me he'd been watching me from the sidelines, amused by my antics. He helped me to my feet and urged me to hold a handful of snow against the welt on the back of my skull as he half carried me home, where he deposited me on the doorstep of my grandparents' house before taking off.

Three sutures and a bad concussion—that was my reward for being reckless. I remember the doctor saying had I not made it home, it might have been fatal, given the freezing conditions.

I owed Kyle for saving my life that night.

Perhaps that would mean returning the favor.

Would it be such a big imposition, I wondered, to give him somewhere to stay for a while? My house had more bedrooms than Eve and I could use. I could give him a hand up from the gutter, homeschool him, counsel him, convert him from criminal to model citizen. If we were both committed to it, I could turn his worthlessness into something valued by society.

Who was I kidding? Eve wouldn't settle for a dog, let alone a lodger.

I switched my heavy gaze to the four-story hotel rising up against the burgeoning light, to the stylized Sunny Inn & Suites logo glowing brightly against the stucco. Scattered across its flanks, a handful of windows were lit up yellowy, with signs of movement in one or two. It was a little after six, with guests beginning to stir.

"Is this it? We here? This the place?"

Kyle's head appeared, yawning, in the gap between the headrests, his gnarly fists rubbing sleep from the pits of his eyes. His mouth was a cavern filled with broken stalagmites.

I'd sat in my car outside the RaceTrac for thirty minutes, drinking coffee and using my phone to run a search for seminars, conventions, and conferences taking place in the area this weekend.

Only the Sunny Inn & Suites on University Parkway had fit the bill exactly, hosting a promo seminar for a new energy drink called Nvigor8.

I grabbed the roll of duct tape I'd picked up at the gas station and opened the door. "Stay here," I told Kyle.

"Let me help you, man," he said sleepily.

"No." I closed the door and then tapped the window. "I mean it, Kyle. Stay here."

He stuck out his tongue.

I shook myself. Zoe's blood had turned my clothes to cardboard. Rust-colored flakes were coming off in the creases. I stuffed the duct tape in my back pocket and then crossed the blacktop toward the main entrance. Only a few empty spaces were left, a packed parking lot. A sold-out crowd for the power-shake convention.

The reception area was decorated in oranges and browns, with subdued lighting, trendy furniture, and one of those walls that masquerades as a waterfall. Sixties styling reimagined for the modern era.

I aimed for a dark-haired girl pretending to look busy behind the front desk. She had a red streak in her hair and a ruby nose gem to match.

"Hi," I said with a smile. "I wonder if you can help me?"

She glanced up from her computer screen. Her gaze didn't make it any higher than the bloodstains on my shirt.

"Sir, have you been assaulted?"

"It's a long story."

She looked worried. "Do you need me to get you medical attention?" She picked up her phone, her heavily made-up eyes growing wide as they worked their way to mine.

That's how awful I looked, I realized, with my permanent scowl and Zoe's blood caking my clothes. I resembled the victim of a physical attack, as harrowing as the psychological one I'd suffered already.

"No, thanks. It's really not as bad as it looks." It was, but she didn't need to know. "Nosebleed," I said, smiling loosely.

She didn't smile back.

"Seriously, I'm okay. You think this is bad, you should see the other guy."

"Sir, let me at least call the police for you. If you've been attacked—"

"Honestly, it's no problem." I flapped my hands. "I'm okay. I don't want to trouble anyone unnecessarily. I just need your help with one small thing." I leaned on the counter. She pulled back slightly. I nodded toward the easel near the front entrance, with its big color picture of a bikini-clad girl holding up a fizzy green drink. "I'm here for the Nvigor8 conference. I checked in yesterday, but as you can see, I got into a bit of a mess this evening. In all the confusion, I think I misplaced my room key." To demonstrate, I patted my pockets. "Can you fix me up with a replacement?" I offered her the loose smile again. It was no more convincing.

Even so, she said, "Okay. That, at least, I can do. But I think you should report the assault. When it comes to customer safety, the hotel has a strict no-tolerance policy for—"

I raised my hand, cutting her off. "Just the room key. Thanks. I desperately need to jump in the shower."

She stared at me, and for a moment I thought she was going to see right through my facade. I forced the loose smile one last time, but her suspicious expression held on for long, uneasy seconds. Then she must have decided any further debate wasn't worth the effort, or was above her pay grade, and she set about tapping at a keyboard.

"What name is it?"

"Troy Pinkerton."

She frowned at her screen. "Pink . . . Pinker . . . Ah, yes, here we go. Pinkerton, room two-twelve." She fired up a new key card and handed it over. "You really should report this, sir."

"I appreciate your concern." I took the key before she could change her mind. "You've been a great help. I'll be sure to mention it to your manager." Then I turned and headed for the elevators.

A lifetime ago, in one of his many flashes of inspiration, Kyle had said, *Sanity is like the moon—we know it exists, but hardly anyone's been there.*

Predictably, I exited on the second floor, my shoes moving soundlessly on the patterned carpeting. There was no one around, but I could hear muffled sounds of showers running and toilets flushing as guests geared up for the complimentary breakfast buffet and a day of corporate brainwashing.

The air-conditioning vents were blasting an arctic wind.

Down the hall, a door opened up and a man in a blue business suit came out. He was on his cell, preoccupied, a messenger bag tucked under one arm. I turned on my heel, got out my own phone, and pretended to be deep in conversation, keeping my back to him until he disappeared into the elevator bank.

Time wasn't on my side. I knew the sheriff could pinpoint Pinkerton's whereabouts at any moment. I had to make count what little time I had available to me.

I moved on.

My hastily hatched-together plan—if you could call it that—involved taking Pinkerton by surprise, confronting him with the truth, and encouraging him to admit his guilt, hopefully publicly by way of my recording our conversation.

Despite the gaping holes in his alibi, I knew that to rest on my laurels, safe in the assumption the sheriff would find sufficient evidence to put him behind bars, would be a mistake.

Without a great deal of effort, Pinkerton could explain away his visit to my office the other day simply by saying he was curious. He'd say he wanted to weigh up the competition, check out the guy who was elbowing in on his home life.

Then there was the all-important crime-scene eyewitness, the guy repairing the sprinkler system in the neighboring yard. In passing, he'd snatched a glance at Pinkerton. Maybe he could pick him out of a lineup. Or maybe not. Pinkerton's lawyer would pull that brief glimpse apart, putting sufficient doubt in the eyewitness's mind to make his testimony essentially worthless.

I'm not sure how voice recognition works. Maybe the police forensics people could match the masked voice on the 911 call to Pinkerton's. Or maybe not.

And without Pinkerton's prints on the murder weapon, nothing other than the general presumption that the husband did it would tie him to the killing.

Lastly, there was the matter of the rental car. It would come as no surprise to learn he'd presented a fake ID to the rental agency. And the fleeing sedan would be seen as circumstantial at best and irrelevant at worst.

I imagined this is how it would go when the police finally contacted him: Pinkerton would play the devastated husband role, laying it on thickly, lavishly, dramatically. Saying it was the first he knew about it.

Zoe's dead? Oh my God. I don't believe it! Was it him, the psychotherapist?

He would tell all—or at least his version—and hold nothing back, saying how I had muscled in on his marriage and ruined everything. He would sob and scream, punch at the wall, and throw some furniture around for good measure. Then he would unfold the fantasy already in the back of his mind, a piece of fiction about how he and Zoe had reconciled, planning to get back together, to make a go of things again. He would tell Detective Thompson that Zoe had arranged to have me over, with the intention of breaking the bad news to me in person, while

Pinkerton was engaged elsewhere, giving her the space she needed to cut me loose.

Given enough room to maneuver, he would spin it all around, turning himself into the victim and me into the killer.

The hotel staff would confirm he had checked in on Friday morning, hours prior to the vicious attack on his wife.

With a canny lawyer in his corner, Pinkerton would get away with murder.

And the investigation would return to me, the jilted lover.

I couldn't allow that to happen.

I hesitated at room 212 with the key card poised at the lock, glancing guiltily up and down the hallway.

Sure, I had my reservations, my self-examining questions, my *whys* and *what happens if*s. I could turn back, I knew. No lines crossed yet. No one holding a gun to my head. This was all free will, my will, the will of righteousness. I could leave with my tail between my legs, return to the car, and drive away, let things take their natural course. No one ever knowing what dark thoughts had been coiling like serpents in my head.

Or I could make a difference.

I dipped the key card in and out of the lock. The little green light flashed, and I eased the door inward, stepping through and closing it quickly but quietly behind me.

The first thing I noticed was a smell of sweat and musk that some people associate with manliness. The second sensory input was visual: it wasn't completely dark inside room 212. The drapes were drawn, and the bedroom was a cave of indistinct shapes, but the light in the bathroom was lit, specifically the one above the shower cubicle, where the sound of running water drowned the thudding in my chest.

I had expected to find Pinkerton cocooned in his bedding, dreaming sweet dreams about how smart he was to have pulled off his wife's murder.

But here he was: a big slab of steaming meat, fogging up the shower glass, inharmoniously whistling what sounded like a poor rendition of "Always Look on the Bright Side of Life."

A rumble of retribution rose in my thorax, and I slid Zoe's gun out of the waistband at the small of my back.

Hours earlier, this man had slain his wife in cold blood, and now here he was, soaping himself up like he was getting ready for a date night.

"Pinkerton!"

The whistling faltered.

"Get out here!"

Now it stopped altogether. I saw his big pink shape swivel in the shower, a hand squeak across the pebbled glass, an eye blink at me through the mist. The glass door swung open to reveal Pinkerton in his water-speckled birthday suit. I heard his voice grunt, "What the—?"

"Hello, Troy. Or should I call you Gus?"

His big brow furrowed up. "You?"

The first thing that struck me was that Pinkerton worked out. And I don't mean a couple of twenty-minute sessions at the gym each week. I mean a hundred bench presses per minute, perhaps even one-handed. There wasn't an ounce of fat anywhere. His sculpted physique would please Michelangelo's eye and win the Mr. Universe title. I'd already known Pinkerton was in shape—I'd spent an hour facing him in my office on Wednesday, seen those clamp-like hands and those pliers for fingers—but to see him in the flesh was . . . intimidating.

The second thing that struck me was Pinkerton.

He launched himself out of the shower cubicle, wet feet slapping against the tiled floor, teeth clenched, saliva flying. In every way the snarling Terminator, with its power-tool hands outstretched and aiming for my throat.

Ray had warned me not to play with guns, predicting I would shoot myself in the foot if I tried.

Pinkerton didn't give me the chance to prove him right.

He was on me before I could do anything to protect myself, his iron fists knocking me backward against the wall. Pain ricocheted down my spine as air whooshed from my lungs.

Zoe's gun sprang from my hand.

No one this big, this dense, I thought, *ought to be able to leap like a ballerina. It defies classical mechanics.*

But Pinkerton was a law unto himself. A hulking mass of meanness, intent on ripping me apart, and I realized with horror that I had woefully miscalculated.

Even as I was sliding down the wall, he was grabbing my shoulders with his grappling-hook fingers, lifting me off my feet. I squirmed, thrashing out, defending myself in the only way someone with no physical training can: laughably.

Who was I kidding? I was no match for Pinkerton. This was a reimagining of the David and Goliath encounter, where Goliath disarmed David of his slingshot and came out the victor.

In a flash, I saw how this would all play out: Pinkerton would tell the sheriff how I broke into his hotel room, how I tried to kill him with Zoe's handgun, how he was forced to defend himself to the death. My death. And I had played right into his big butcher hands.

Pinkerton head-butted me, his brow cracking, rock-hard, against mine, and fireworks exploded behind my eyes. It was like being hit with a wrecking ball. I recoiled from the enormous pain, not quite believing what was happening. Then, before I could recover, I was sailing through the air headfirst. I hit the side of the bed in a tangled mess and crumpled to the floor.

Naïveté and stupidity were standing in the corner, laughing at me. The two things that were about to get me killed.

I heard Pinkerton's bare feet pound across the carpet. The thud, thud, thud of a *Tyrannosaurus rex* in a rush to finish off its kill.

Weakly, I rolled onto my back, my brain bombarded with thoughts. *Get up and run! Get up and fight! Just get up or you're going to die!*

Before I could do any of that, Pinkerton dropped to his knees and straddled my chest, so that his weight was crushing down. He was big, wet, slippery, with water dripping from his hair and into my eyes.

I gasped, "Don't," and raised a puny hand to ward off what I knew was coming next.

His pile-driver fist batted it aside, cuffing me on the jaw, and more immense pain erupted in my skull, along with blood in my mouth and stars sparkling in my vision. The piston arm hoisted up its big bag of knuckles, aimed, and fired again. I twisted my neck, and the fist connected with my cheek, scuffing off my skin.

Everything was spinning, spotting. My ears were beginning to ring.

I couldn't move, couldn't breathe! My vasovagal syncope was about to suck me out of reality, and I was helpless to prevent it.

The fainting goat, placing its fate in the hands of others.

Through all the mush, I heard a knocking noise, but I thought it was my brain banging against my skull or the precursor to the impending blackout.

Pinkerton must have heard it, too, because he paused my pummeling to glance at the door to the room.

The knocking sounded again, this time louder, more urgent, accompanied by someone shouting, "Hotel security! Open up!"

Enraged eyes swung back to me. "Say one word, Doc, make one squeak, and I'll snap your neck."

I believed him.

Jesus Christ. He's going to kill me!

With a steel-reinforced forearm, Pinkerton exerted pressure on my chest, hard enough to squeeze every last ounce of breath from my lungs, before catapulting to his feet.

My chest was on fire, my diaphragm pancaked. Desperately, I sucked in air, raking flaming oxygen over the cinders of my lungs.

Through tunnel vision, I saw Pinkerton stride to the guest room door, naked as the day he was born, every muscle moving fluidly. I saw him lean on the handle and pull the door open. I heard him bark something.

Vaguely, distantly, as though I were looking through a telescope the wrong way, I saw the shape of a man silhouetted against the brighter light in the hallway. Vainly, I tried hollering for help, but all that came out was a hot, fizzling wheeze and maybe a trickle of blood.

Then the strangest thing happened: I saw Pinkerton fold at the waist, stumble backward into the room, seemingly clutching his testicles, and fall to the floor in a big pink heap.

The blackness came rushing in, and I lost consciousness, but not before seeing the man in the hallway come into the room and stomp on Pinkerton's head.

Chapter Twenty-Five

A torrent of icy water gushed over me, and I broke the surface, spluttering and gasping, momentarily confused to find I was lying on a bed in a room with the drapes drawn, the upper half of me soaked with freezing water, and slushy ice cubes everywhere.

Then it all came flooding back: the Sarasota hotel room, Troy Pinkerton's attack, the intervention of hotel security, and my blackout.

I pushed up on an elbow, brushing bits of ice from my face.

Kyle was standing next to the bed, an empty ice bucket in his hands and his trademark lopsided smile hooking up his lips. "Welcome back," he said softly, discarding the ice bucket. "Sorry about the rude awakening, but you would've slept all day if I'd let ya."

I sat upright. "What happened?"

"Aside from saving your bacon yet again, I caught an adult movie on the hotel pay-per-view while you were sleeping." He saw the confusion knot up my face and added, "I'm joking, man! I'm your backup guy, remember? The brawn to your brains. You didn't think I'd let you wrestle the bear on your own, did you?"

Invariably, fainting makes my thinking sluggish, but the ice bath was beginning to sharpen things up.

"Pinkerton?"

"Ah, don't worry about him." Kyle flapped a hand. "We've been getting along like a house on fire. He's a funny guy when you get to know him. He's been cooperating nicely."

I got to my feet. The floor felt uneven.

Kyle reached out a steadying hand. "Take it easy, man. You took a bit of a hammering back there."

Automatically, I touched the welt on my cheek and winced, tasted coppery blood in my mouth, worked my aching jaw, then probed my tongue around my teeth, comforted to find them all intact. "How long was I out of it?"

"Couple of hours—I wasn't counting. You were twitchy for a while. At one point I thought I heard you shout 'Kill the priest.'"

"Very funny." I scanned the room. "Where is he?"

"In the car."

"What's he doing in the car?"

"Waiting for us." He said it like it was obvious, like it warranted a *duh!* suffix. As though we were three buddies about to embark on a road trip.

He tugged at my sleeve. "C'mon, man. We gotta leave."

Wordlessly, I followed Kyle out of room 212, shivering in the hallway as the icy air-conditioning blasted at my wet skin. My rude awakening, as Kyle put it, had softened up Zoe's blood, turning my stiff shirt into a clinging bib. I wiped at it, horrified by it, only to come away with her blood smeared on my hands.

Kyle took the stairs, and so did I.

When I first started my therapy practice, I was alarmed at the number of people who appeared to have no conscience, or if they did, it was buried so deeply under their repressed emotions that it was as good as ineffective, anyway. In the workplace, a conscience is an obstacle, keeping supercompetitive people from their goals. In relationships, a conscience is a limiter, preventing infidelity. In life, a conscience is God's fail-safe, stopping superselfish people from committing the vilest acts. The trouble with people disconnected from their conscience is they never consider consequences.

I wondered what had come over me, thinking I could manhandle Pinkerton into a confession.

Then I realized the answer wasn't my disconnection; it was my connection—to Zoe. My own conscience was clear.

We exited into the lobby.

I could smell eggs and hot skillets, the lingering scents of the in-house breakfast. There were a few business types milling about. Some talking in small groups, some on their phones with their eyes roaming the ceiling, some drinking the complimentary coffee and checking their watches. Mostly, they were youngish men in pressed chinos and pastel shirts one size too small. Tanned muscular types with red-ribbon lanyards swinging from their thick necks.

Never mind a power-shake convention; this looked like the Chippendales were in town.

Head down, Kyle hustled me across the lobby.

"That's him," I heard a woman cry out.

I glanced toward the front desk, to see the girl with the nose gem pointing a finger in our direction. "He's the one!"

Several heads turned our way—including the head of the green-uniformed sheriff's deputy who was standing at the counter in front of her.

I heard Kyle mutter a curse at the same moment the deputy said, "Sir, I need you to hold up and stop right there."

Kyle didn't. In fact, his gait increased, taking me with him, and we burst through the glass doors, out into the parking lot and the intense sunshine.

Adrenaline was searing my gut.

Rationally, I knew I should have dug in my heels and done the deputy's bidding. Ignoring his official request spelled trouble. It would wreck my chances of getting an unbiased hearing. But I didn't slow; I knew whatever it was that Kyle had done to cause the girl to call the police had to be serious, and I was implicated in it by the sheer fact that we were leaving together.

Irrationally, I ran.

There was a white sheriff's cruiser parked in the shade of the porte cochere, blocking our escape.

"This way!" Kyle dragged me off to one side.

My car was parked a few spaces away from the entrance, on its own. Among other things, Kyle had moved it while I'd slept.

"Get in the passenger seat!"

I pulled open the door, just as Kyle turned and raised his hand toward the hotel entrance.

At first, I thought he was giving the deputy the finger. Then a series of loud bangs echoed off the hotel walls, and the glass doors exploded into a million pieces.

I think I heard someone scream.

The adrenaline scorched my throat.

When Kyle turned back, I saw Zoe's gun in his hand.

"Get in!" he shouted, waggling it. "Get in!"

Mouth agape, I did, and so did Kyle, but not before shooting out the rear tires on the sheriff's cruiser.

Then he dropped into the driver's seat, twisted the keys, threw the vehicle into drive, and planted his foot on the gas.

"You have reached the point of no return," he said chirpily. "Buckle up and hold on tight."

The deputy came crashing through the remnants of the shattered door, weapon drawn, as my car squealed out of its space and fishtailed across the blacktop.

Above the sound of the screeching tires, I heard another couple of whipcracks and ducked in the seat, instinctively, as one of the deputy's bullets buried itself in the back of my headrest.

Kyle let out an insane whoop as we bumped out onto University Parkway and accelerated in the direction of the interstate.

I do not believe I have ever felt my heart beat harder than it did in that moment. So hard that I thought it would surely burst. But instead, it kept pumping hot epinephrine-enriched blood into my panicked brain, feeding the frenzy.

Beyond salvation. This was one of two predominant thoughts clawing their way through the chaos as we raced up the ramp and onto I-75. Kyle had gone one step too far once again, taking my plan and twisting it into something unrecognizable.

The other thought competing for dominance was that Eve would be massively disappointed.

Sincerely, she'd tell me it was my own fault, my own doing, my mannish stupidity, saying I should have foreseen that nothing good would come of trying to force a confession out of Pinkerton.

The ramp gave way to sun-bleached pavement and a spattering of traffic headed north. Kyle nudged the car up to the speed limit and held it there.

I let out a yowl. "Damn it, Kyle. You shot at the sheriff! I can't believe you actually shot at the sheriff."

"But I didn't shoot the deputy," he answered with a chuckle.

"This isn't funny. You can't go around shooting at cops. This is anything but funny."

"Hey, don't blame me, man. He gave me no choice."

"He didn't shoot first!"

"Calm down, man. You're not seeing the bigger picture here. He would've shot first if I hadn't. I was being preemptive."

I was surprised he even knew the word, let alone what it meant. Even so, his logic was warped, flawed.

I told him to pull over.

"No way, man. We've got a good head start."

"I mean it, Kyle. Stop this car right now."

"That's never gonna happen."

I grabbed the steering wheel. "I said pull over!"

"I don't think so!"

Kyle tried to wrench my hand free, but I clung on. The car pitched. Someone honked. Kyle pulled. I pushed. The car lurched. We veered onto the shoulder, grit clattering around the fenders.

"Let go, man! You're gonna get us both killed!"

"I think you've already managed that one for yourself, Kyle. Now stop the damn car!"

He fired off a long barrage of expletives and then hit the brakes. The car slid to a stop on the shoulder, and the second it was stationary, I was out and on the roadside grass, pacing and cursing. I raged noisily, venting frustration, flexing my fists and clenching my teeth.

"Take a chill pill, man," Kyle shouted through the open passenger door. "It was either him or us."

"We had a chance, Kyle. Right there in the hotel lobby. We had an opportunity to end this. But you blew it." I was animated, angry.

"Yeah, well, shine a bad light on me all you want, Greg. But I didn't see you giving yourself up."

I stopped my pacing and gaped at him.

He shrugged nonchalantly, as if saying, *Nothing to do with me.*

I rushed back to the car. "Can you actually hear what you're saying? Jesus Christ, Kyle. Are you delusional? You shot at the police! What's wrong with you? You can't go around doing stuff like that! We're not kids anymore, breaking windows at the old sawmill. You just made us fugitives!"

"Greg, seriously, man, you need to take a breath and calm down. You're gonna draw attention."

"You shot at the police! It doesn't get any bigger than that!"

I slammed a hand against the car roof, then slammed it again and again, hard enough to leave dents and make the bones in my hand ring. Then I grabbed the doorframe and let out a frustrated howl.

"C'mon, man," I heard Kyle saying. "Stop making a scene and get back inside the car. We'll work something out. They know we have a hostage. They won't try any funny business."

I closed my eyes and willed myself to disappear. I pleaded for some benevolent universal force to take pity and suck me out of the predicament I was in.

This wasn't just crazy; it was potentially fatal.

For long unanswered seconds, traffic roared by, its din indistinguishable from the roar inside my head. I stood there, kicking and screaming internally, while the kiln-like heat glazed my skin.

Then I rolled the tension from my shoulders and leaned inside the car. "We need to go back."

"Okay. And hope they take mercy on us? Are you serious?"

"Kyle, this isn't a game."

He shook his head. "Sorry, man. No can do. There's no way I'm going back to the pen. I'd rather die."

I reached in and plucked the keys out of the ignition. "This ends here. We need to fix this."

He took a swipe at my hand, but he wasn't quick enough. I retreated onto the grass as he stormed across the shoulder, waving Zoe's gun at me.

I backed up some more. "What are you going to do, Kyle— shoot me?"

"I don't want to."

"We need to turn ourselves in, do the right thing."

He stopped at the edge of the grass. "Man, don't put me in this position. I'm on parole. My PO doesn't even know I left the state. Now this? They catch me, they'll throw away the key for sure this time."

"I'll make a character statement, speak up for you."

"You'd do that for me?"

"Sure. I'll tell them you need medication."

"I do? Hey, that might work. People respect you. Your opinion must mean something. You'd do that for me, put in a good word?"

"Sure."

"You're crazy, man! You think they'll believe anything you say after what we've done? We kidnapped your girlfriend's husband!"

I went to say *estranged* but held back.

"That was you and me, Greg. You and me. We broke the law. And this was all your idea."

"Wait a minute. I just wanted to talk with him."

"With a gun in your pocket? Now who's delusional? We drove two hours out of our way to be here. We brought duct tape! This isn't one of your therapy sessions, Greg. We came here for one thing and one thing only: justice. You think the cops are gonna believe you just wanted to *talk* with him?"

Kyle had a black-and-white way of highlighting my lack of forward thinking. I didn't like admitting it, but he was right. Shock had shuffled my thought processes and dealt me a bad hand. From my warped perspective, I couldn't think straight.

"Have you even seen what we did to him?"

For the first time, I noticed the big man shoehorned into the backseat.

A naked Troy Pinkerton was bundled up into the back, eyes and nostrils flared wide. Behind him, I could see a pair of cracked holes in the rear window, and a ragged gouge in the upholstered roof where the deputy's second bullet had torn through.

Pinkerton had been an inch from getting his head blown off.

I returned to the car and leaned in. "You okay?"

It was a stupid question, of course. One born out of the madness of the moment and a very human need to behave normally in extreme circumstances.

Panicked people are dangerous, unpredictable. They trample over their neighbors in a crowd and run off the tops of buildings.

I took a breath, and another, then repeated my question.

Pinkerton didn't answer. Not because he was furious at being abducted—which he was, undoubtedly—but because Kyle had wound duct tape around his head several times, completely covering his mouth. Another band was noosed around his neck, holding him upright against the rear headrest, preventing him from moving. More of the silvery tape bound his wrists and ankles.

"What did you do, Kyle?"

"He resisted a bit." He slid back into the driver's seat. "But he soon came around to our way of thinking. Didn't you, big guy?"

Pinkerton growled, straining against his leash. A bubble of snot inflated and popped at the end of one nostril.

One of his eyes was swollen and closed, the skin puffed and glowing pink, rimmed with blood. There was a crook in his nose I hadn't seen previously. And several long lacerations crisscrossed his bare chest, like devilish claw marks, with trails of trickled blood all down his torso and staining his boxers.

"You tortured him?"

"Only a little. We didn't waterboard, if that's what you're worried about. I know all about the Geneva convention! We just got to know each other's weaknesses a little better. Isn't that right, big guy? If it's any consolation, I got his confession. Check your phone, man. It's all on there. Everything you need to know about how to plan and execute the perfect murder. Even stuff we didn't know about. Now get back inside and close the door."

I did, realizing I was in far deeper trouble than I'd thought.

Kyle gunned the car along the shoulder, then rejoined the steady stream of traffic heading north.

Behind us, Pinkerton was snorting and stamping his feet like an enraged bull.

I have said it once, and I will say it again: the law isn't my forte. But I do possess enough of a grasp to know that no court in the land will admit a confession made under duress. It's called coercion. Worse still, I knew Pinkerton knew it.

"Kyle, listen to me. We don't have a choice. We're in a no-win situation. The cops will be on us any second. We can still end this peacefully, without further bloodshed."

He looked at me sideways. "Has anyone ever told you you'd make a great therapist?"

"Kyle . . ."

"Lighten up, Greg! You're such a killjoy. I'm a pro at this, remember? There's always a way out. So here's what we'll do: we'll get off the interstate at the next exit, dump the car on the way to your house, and steal another. They'll never know it was us. Simple."

But, as usual, Kyle's logic was fatally flawed. He wasn't taking into account the witnesses we'd left behind at the hotel, or the likelihood that our escape was recorded by security cameras.

Apparently, lacking a conscience comes with imperfect foresight.

"They know this is my car, Kyle."

"So, we torch it."

"They'll still know it's my car!"

"So, you say it was stolen."

"Besides," I said, "the next off-ramp is in five miles, and we're headed north, not south." The frustration rattled in my throat.

"And you know this how?"

"Because it's late morning and the sun is behind us. Plus, we just passed a sign for Tampa."

"Damn it!" He banged a fist against the steering wheel. The car swerved. "Okay, okay. Let me think."

"Go for it, Kyle. See if you can arrange for those two brain cells to have a meeting."

"Sarcasm is the lowest form of wit, man. You, of all people, know thinking isn't my specialty—it makes my head hurt."

I leaned forward and looked in the side mirror. In the distance, several sets of red and blue lights were gaining on us, weaving in and out of the traffic.

"Okay," Kyle said, "so how about this: we put some distance between them and us, get some breathing space, and then we figure something out." He leaned on the gas pedal, as if he believed that my no-frills car could outrun the Florida Highway Patrol in their state-of-the-art Chargers.

"Sounds like a great plan, Kyle. Except for one thing. Running makes Pinkerton look innocent."

He dipped a hand to his waistband, brought out Zoe's handgun, and balanced it on his shoulder with the muzzle pointing at Pinkerton. "We could always shoot him."

Pinkerton let out a snotty whimper.

I grabbed Kyle's fist and wrested the gun out of his grasp.

"Why'd you do that?" he said.

"Consider it damage control. Because killing Pinkerton makes me the prime suspect again."

We sat in silence for a minute or two. I checked the side mirror again, to see the sheriff's cruisers much closer.

"Exit coming up," Kyle said.

Traffic leaving the interstate was almost at a standstill, cars slowing, brake lights gleaming. Kyle slid the car into the exit lane and eased off the gas. Then, unexpectedly, he stood on the pedal again and the car swerved back on the highway.

"Cops," he stated flatly.

As we shot past the exit, I saw a pair of black cars parked on the grassy triangle next to the off-ramp, their roof lights blinking, a trooper waving checked vehicles through.

"What now?"

I was thinking furiously.

Fizzle or bang.

The truth was, my head was all over the place, and I was angry with myself for letting things spiral out of control.

"What now, Greg?"

"I'm thinking!"

"Sheesh, don't pop a blood vessel on my account. And there I was thinking I was the idiot in this duo."

"Keep driving," I said. "Just keep driving."

For the next couple of minutes, Kyle drove with his foot down, avoiding other traffic while the sheriff's cruisers decreased their distance and increased their numbers behind us. We arrived at the long bridge spanning the Manatee River, tires slapping against the white concrete. Blue sparkling water on either side, fringed with emerald-green trees and boat docks.

Up ahead, dozens of brake lights were popping on simultaneously and staying lit. Vehicles were changing lanes, all moving to the right, heading for the exit at the end of the bridge. I could see police lights flashing all along the curving off-ramp, officers out of their cruisers, directing the decelerating traffic toward the Ellenton exit and off the interstate.

The police had been quick to mobilize their forces after the incident at the hotel, I realized. People get killed in car chases, and clearly they wanted to get everybody off the highway. I imagined all the police cars within a ten-mile radius had responded to the call and were now converging on I-75. Ultimately on us.

Sooner or later we would come to a dead end.

"Suckers," Kyle laughed, keeping his foot down. He steered the car into the empty fast lane, missing the median wall by an inch.

As we tore past, I glimpsed startled drivers, no doubt all wondering who the crazy person was.

They would know soon enough, as soon as they watched the TV news.

The bridge gave way to the regular road and we accelerated out onto the pavement with no other vehicles in our way.

I looked back, to see officers scrambling to their cars, sirens already blaring as they took off in hot pursuit.

Up ahead, as far as the eye could see, the entire northbound interstate was completely deserted.

Kyle put his foot down, a big lopsided grin splitting his face in two. "Looks like we made it!"

I could sense his whole mood lifting into celebratory orbit.

I dropped my gaze to the gun in my lap, with no idea how I was going to retrieve the situation, or if it was retrievable at all.

Chapter Twenty-Six

Ten minutes later, we were at the summit of the Sunshine Skyway Bridge, tires shrieking as the car bounced off the wall and fishtailed to a stop, a smell of burnt rubber eating up the oxygen. My head snapped back against the headrest, and I stared, in disbelief, at the sheer number of police vehicles blocking the roadway up ahead.

In the ensuing silence, a bullhorn crackled: "Get out of the car! Get down on the ground! Hands behind your head!"

If there was ever a definition of a surreal moment, this was it.

Kyle burst into a fit of ripsaw laughter and rolled out of the car.

I joined him, shoving Zoe's gun in my waistband and out of sight.

My mind was in overdrive, on the verge of a full-scale panic.

What now, brainiac?

We were on a narrow ribbon of reinforced concrete suspended two hundred feet above the azure waters of Tampa Bay, with what must have been a hundred members of law enforcement boxing us in on either end.

A few miles back, the massive motorcade had forced us off the deserted highway and into a bottleneck from which there was no escape. At least, no conventional escape. For the second time today, we had reached the point of no return.

I saw Kyle's eyes scan the police roadblock, saw him cup his hands to his mouth, and heard him shout, "Stay back! We have a hostage here! Come any closer and he's dead meat!" He pointed at the police helicopter hanging in the air about a hundred yards out. "And call off your attack dog!"

For a moment, nothing happened. Then the helicopter pulled back, rotors slapping the air as it climbed.

Kyle turned to me and said, "Okay, let's get him out."

I opened up the door to the backseat and ripped away the duct tape pinning Pinkerton to the rear headrest. He tried shaking me loose, kicking and thrashing, as I grabbed his bare flesh. Kyle came over and helped haul him out, stand him up. Then, between us, we hopped him over to the edge of the bridge and sat him down on the knee-high wall.

"Stay put," I told him, "or else."

The panoramic seascape was dizzying, magnetic in an unnerving kind of way.

Kyle elbowed me playfully in the ribs, pointing it out.

But I was too busy peering into Pinkerton's eyes, trying to detect evil and figure out what unraveling process had turned him from doting husband to wife killer. Was it all my fault? Was the very fact that I had fallen for Zoe the reason he had fallen too?

A dark hate smoldered in his eyes.

Unarguably, something deep inside me wanted to rip into Pinkerton right here on the bridge, letting the animal loose, making him pay with pain for murdering Zoe. But my analyst's brain needed to understand, to decode the chemical change that had transformed man into monster.

Were we both beyond saving?

Kyle elbowed me in the ribs again, this time harder, while making more childish observations, and I decided then and there that I'd had all I could stomach of his immature devil-may-care attitude.

This mess, this predicament, this disaster, it was all his fault. He'd driven me here, to this. There was no going back to normalcy after what we had done. Not after playing a part in kidnap and torture.

It was very possible my life was over because of him.

The realization knocked the air from my lungs and filled me with a bone-crushing dread I had never felt before.

Jesus Christ. I could go to prison!

Physics shows that everything has its breaking point. All it takes is enough pressure exerted in the right place and . . .

I snapped. I didn't expect it; I'd thought I had more stretch in me, more to give. But who knows at what point a fuse will overload and blow?

My hand, seeming to act autonomously, clutched Kyle by the throat and, before I realized what was happening, I was stepping up onto the low wall and hoisting him up there with me.

It was cool this high up, windy, as if invisible hands were trying to pluck us off the bridge. The wall was just inches thick, beyond which lay nothing but thin air and a fatal drop, all the way down to the sun-speckled water below. This was no place for the weak-kneed or the faint of heart, or for anyone in their right state of mind.

"Killing me isn't the answer," Kyle squeaked as I held him over the blue abyss.

He tried to push me away, but I pulled him back.

"Wait," he gasped. "You're forgetting our unfinished business: Pinkerton. He needs to pay for what he did. You need me for that. And I know exactly what to do."

Staring into Kyle's manic eyes was like looking at my own damned reflection.

His sneakers scrabbled for purchase. "Greg, you gotta trust me on this one. This is my area of expertise. I know a way out of this. For both of us. No one has to die today."

The wind blew at us, flapping noisily at our clothes.

It had all come down to just Kyle and me.

Two hundred feet up in the air.

Standing on the edge of the world, with only the twitch of a muscle deciding our fates.

Beyond his challenging eyes, I could see the tiny white flecks of pleasure craft plying the cerulean waters, and my stomach buckled.

Some people believe the act of falling is enough in itself to induce death. *The fall will kill you first!* they say. Of course, that isn't the case. You need only to ask skydivers about free-falling, and they will categorically deny that they died on their first jump.

Other people subscribe to the theory that water breaks a fall. *Land in water and you'll survive!* they say. Like water has a cushioning effect on the fragile human frame, when the truth is, if you jump from this high into water you might as well be landing on concrete. Bones snap like twigs. Skin sheers off. Internal organs slam into each other, rupture, pop. People end up mangled bloody messes, or even unrecognizable as being human. Those unlucky enough to survive will usually drown in agony. Those who don't, wish they had.

Then there is a third group. The believers. *God will take your soul before you hit the ground!* they say. They have faith in divine intervention, so if they do survive the fall, it would be at the grace of an angel.

I had a good idea which category Kyle was in.

My grip was weakening.

"Let's hear it," I said. "This better be good, Kyle."

"Oh, it's the best. Man, you're gonna love it."

His hand came up in the gap between us, and in it I saw Zoe's gun, taken from the small of my back, the muzzle pointed at my chin.

You befriend a lion and one day it'll bite off your head.

In unison, we stepped down off the wall and disengaged, putting space between us, Kyle with the gun trained on me, and me with my bloodied hands in the air.

"So what happens now, Kyle? Look around us—you won't get a dozen yards. This is as dire as things get."

A phone rang.

I stared at him. He stared at me.

As bizarre as it sounds—out here in the middle of no-man's-land, on this thin sliver of concrete strung between heaven and earth—a phone rang.

The warbling noise came from a red box on a pole bolted to the wall a few yards behind Kyle.

I nodded. "You going to answer that?"

He snickered. "How much are we betting it's a cold-caller? Wait right there, Greg."

Keeping the gun trained on me, he backed up to the call box, opened its door, and pulled out a handset. I saw him put the receiver to his ear, listen, nod, say something too low for me to pick up, nod again, and then glance in my direction. "It's an old flame," he called, motioning with the gun. "Go ahead and entertain yourself with something else for a minute or two."

Pinkerton growled, and I turned my attention to him. He was still sitting on the wall, fists balled and toes curled up against the smooth concrete. He looked like he wanted to snap my neck, and probably would if he could. I reached out. He pulled back, making muffled sounds. I reached again, told him to stay still, found the end of the duct tape with my fingernails, and then unwound it from his head.

"Why did you do it, Troy? Why did you kill Zoe?"

He spat out gluey saliva. "Screw you."

I wasn't intimidated; I knew that extreme trauma had a way of prioritizing fears. I nudged him with the toe of my shoe.

He tipped back a little, closer to the edge, then immediately caught his balance. "Hey, watch it!"

"I have to know. Why did you feel you needed to kill her?"

"You're crazy."

"Just tell me."

"Yeah, and you can go ahead and screw yourself."

I grabbed one of his ears and twisted it. His face shriveled up, and a yelp leaked out.

"Listen to me, Troy. You're this close to making me push you over the edge. I'll do it, too. I won't hesitate. You took Zoe from me. Grief has made me crazy. The cops will understand. I'll push you over without thinking twice. The worst that will happen to me is I'll get a prescription and a few months of counseling. Now talk!"

I twisted the ear some more, then released it.

Pinkerton hissed out steam. "Because she was cutting me out of my own life!" he shouted.

"Wrong answer. Couples divorce all the time. You could have hired yourself a mutually beneficial attorney, divided things equally, and gone your separate ways with no hard feelings. You didn't need to kill her."

He eyed me with a deep and unsettling distaste, as though I were something revolting he'd stepped in. "Spare me the therapist's speech. She was a bitch. Okay? What do you want me to say? She deserved it. How about that?"

His words bit into my protective layer of shock, letting in a little of the cold reality. I resisted the urge to nudge him harder. "Zoe told me the split was amicable."

"Is that what she told you? You shouldn't believe everything you hear, Doc. Sounds to me like you weren't told the whole story. Sounds like you only got her self-righteous half. Now *there's* a surprise. Trust me, there was nothing friendly or harmonious about the split. She was showing me the door, throwing me out of the house I paid for."

"But *murder?*"

"She was squeezing me dry!"

It was a pitiful excuse, and not actually an excuse at all. Right here, right now, part of me regarded him as something less than human, the reason my own life was now a total shambles. And yet, I also felt sorry for Pinkerton. It was clear he had resented Zoe for finding happiness, probably because he couldn't find it himself. Instead of cutting his losses and walking away, he'd let that bitterness consume him, convincing him that Zoe's death was the only cure to his cancerous feelings. While his genes had concentrated on blessing him with the physique of an Adonis, they had forgotten to beef up his brains.

"Your turn," Kyle called, and I looked around to see him setting down the handset.

"Me?"

"Well, sure. The hostage negotiator wants to talk to you, man. Don't ask. The guy's a premium-cut dick."

We swapped places. Kyle caught me by the arm as we passed, coming close and looking me in the eye. "Listen, Greg old pal, I just want you to know this didn't pan out the way it should've. I never meant any of this to happen. Believe it or not, I came down here with good intentions, out of loyalty, to protect you. In my own narrow-minded way I was trying to do the right thing, be honorable. But I screwed up. It seems to be the story of my life. Everything I touch turns to crap. Like I have bad blood and I contaminate everyone."

"Kyle—"

"Greg, please let me finish—we don't have much time. Getting you in trouble wasn't part of the deal. That's my screwup. It's on me. You're a good and decent guy, and I'm only half the man you are. You shouldn't be here with me, with Pinkerton, like this. You're a dreamer. You're not designed to handle this kind of real-world pressure. That's my job, always has been. I should've dealt with Pinkerton on my own, protected you better."

"Kyle—"

"Almost done." Another lopsided smile flickered across his face. "After this is over, you're gonna hear some pretty dark stuff about me. Some of it'll be lies, for sure, but most of it'll be true. Stuff that'll make you crazy. From the horse's mouth, I want you to know, right from the start, you're the only person I've ever felt connected with, deep down. I don't know how to describe it, man. I don't have the words like you do. It's all weird and supernatural to me. Spooky. I can't tell if it's destiny or fate—I always get the two mixed up. What I do know is you're the only true friend I've ever had, and for that I thank you from the bottom of my heart."

"Kyle—"

"That's why it kills me, man, you know? It cuts me in half, to know I've let you down big-time, and I'm . . . sorry. Genuinely sorry, for everything. And I hope you can forgive me, in time. I love ya, man. Whatever happens next, you gotta remember that."

It was the most lucid and coherent speech I had ever heard him make.

Then, out of nowhere, he hugged me. And I hugged him back, hesitantly as first and then fully, as though we were long-lost brothers, actually committed by blood. I heard Pinkerton make gagging noises and tell us to get a room.

"Now go speak with the premium-cut dick," Kyle said with a smile as we separated, "before he wets himself."

I plodded over to the call box. A sign on the metalwork read "Emergency Crisis Counseling," and beneath it, a scuffed plaque had a message for any soon-to-be lost soul before they leapt to certain death: "There Is Hope."

I smiled at the irony and grabbed the phone. "Hello?"

No reply. Not even a dial tone or static. Just an empty nothingness. I hung up and picked up again, then repeated my greeting.

Still nothing.

"They hung up," I said, turning back to Kyle.

He was standing in front of Pinkerton, covering him with the gun, his face eerily vacant.

"It's dead," I called.

"Must be catching," Kyle called back. Then he pushed Pinkerton off the wall.

Just like that, Pinkerton's exaggerated upper body mass making it the easiest of actions.

For a heart-stopping moment, I was rooted to the spot, riveted, as though my shoes had been nailed to the bridge. I couldn't believe my eyes. I was unbreathing, disbelieving, with all sorts of similar adjectives colliding with my frontal lobe.

Pinkerton tipped backward, his feet came up, and then he was gone, his absence accentuated by a long and terrified wail as gravity sucked him down.

The telephone receiver fell from my grasp.

Before I could react or even breathe, Kyle had stepped up onto the wall, turned his back to the drop, spread his arms out wide, straight as airplane wings, and tilted his face to the sun.

I heard him shout, into the wind, "I'm coming home!"

Incredibly, I broke free from my transfixion spell and sprang straight for him, hands reaching out, boiling panic launching me forward, and fear fueling the leap. I saw his eyelids close and his chest swell as his lungs drew in a deep breath. Then he was tilting backward like someone performing an innocent bungee jump—unbelievably serene—falling from the bridge.

I grabbed at his legs as they angled away, my fingers clawing uselessly at his pants. My insides were aflame, my brain bursting with fright. It was insane! Somehow, miraculously, my fingers snagged on his sneakers, hooking into the laces of both shoes, and I dropped to my knees, slamming up against the wall, ribs creaking, as Kyle's momentum flattened me partway over the concrete precipice and threatened to drag me down with him.

My intervention broke his fall, and very nearly my spine.

Then Kyle's full weight cracked against my arms, almost wrenching them out of their sockets. The pain was excruciating, beyond any other physical pain I had ever experienced. I screwed my eyes shut and held on with all my might.

"You gotta let me go, man!" came Kyle's voice.

But the only thing I let loose was a fiery breath. I opened terrified eyes to find an upside-down Kyle gazing at me and a backdrop of dazzling sapphire water two hundred feet below.

Unreal, and one of the most frightening moments of my life.

I was on my stomach, draped over the wall, knees butted up against it, arms dangling over the drop, with white-knuckled fingers hooked into the very last loops in Kyle's shoelaces, struggling to fill my lungs and to stop Kyle's weight from taking me with him.

"Hang on," I said. It came out a scorching wheeze, and a fresh wave of muscle burn swept up my arms. "I can haul you up."

Of course, the stark truth was, it was taking every bit of strength I had just to hold him where he was, and we both knew it. My strength dwindling by the second. Fingers being deprived of blood. Plus, the laces were old and worn, grayed, liable to break at any moment. Our predicament was less than hopeless, and it was only a matter of time before something snapped.

Distantly, I was aware of someone barking orders and the sound of police boots pounding across the bridge.

I dug in my fingernails.

Kyle swung like a pendulum, arms dangling. "Sure thing, man. Whatever you say. You're in control. Wow, this view is to die for."

"How can you joke at a time like this?"

"Beats crying."

He swung some more, deliberately, and my hips grated against the cement. "Stay still! It doesn't have to end this way. I know you, Kyle. You don't want this. We're caught in a bind, and you think this is your only way out. But you're wrong. We can get through this, together. You'll be okay."

Now he laughed. "Your Jedi mind tricks won't work on me! You gotta accept things for what they are. It's no big mystery. You and me, we've come as far as we can go. It's time to cut the proverbial cord and move on. You need to make your peace, man, because, God knows, I've made mine. My conscience is clear. I'm ready to take my leap of faith. Are you?" He wriggled, twisting.

My fingers felt as if they were about to be severed. "We can work this out. I do this for a living. I talk people down before they jump."

He laughed. "Save your energy, man. I think we're past that point, don't you?"

Now he kicked, trying to work his feet free of my grasp.

I clung on, resisting, arms complaining, sinews straining, not knowing for how long I could continue without losing all my fingers. The edges of my vision had already begun to darken, and I knew that even if I could hold on until help arrived, the likelihood was that my imminent blackout would kick in beforehand and ruin any chance we both had of coming out of this in one piece.

Then Kyle made his final, fatal move. Using deep ab muscles, he folded at the waist and hoisted himself up, reaching until his hands were on the tied bows of his shoelaces.

"I'm serious, Greg. It's time to let me go. The world won't even notice I'm gone."

"I will."

He smiled lopsidedly. "Thanks, man. Means a bunch to me. You won't realize this right now, but I'm setting you free." He yanked at the ends of the laces. "See you on the other side, old pal."

There was a moment of surreal hesitation in which we stared at each other, wordlessly communicating a lifetime of hopes and dismays, as the knots slowly unraveled. My hands were otherwise engaged; there was nothing I could do. Then, soundlessly, his feet slid out of the shoes and he dropped away.

His weight was lifted, but it crushed me flat.

If I yelled, *No!* I didn't hear it; my brain was too busy screaming obscenities at me.

And so he fell.

Down and down he went, while all I could do was watch, stunned, as he tumbled head over heels, plummeting toward the sparkling water and instant death.

There was no wail, no cry of terror. At least none that wasn't my own.

Kyle fell without a sound, getting smaller and smaller, his arms at right angles to his body. A dive-bombing kamikaze, I imagined, with his lips peeled back, challenging his target to do its worst.

And, somewhere inside of me, I fell with him.

If he made a splash, I didn't see it; strong police hands were suddenly hauling me up from the brink, bundling me to safety and denying me a last glimpse of Kyle as he hit the waves.

Through ringing ears, I heard my rescuer shout, "Take it easy, sir. We've got you now. Sit tight—the paramedics are on their way."

As his colleagues rushed in, I expected to black out, right there in the police officer's lap, to escape myself, as usual.

But the blackout never came.

And never did again.

Chapter Twenty-Seven

Aside from an armada of attentive medical staff, I had a handful of visitors during my forty-eight hours under clinical observation at Tampa General, including Ray Stitt, as my legal representative; Zoe's partner, Detective Thompson; his information-gathering counterparts from the Tampa Police Department; and finally, wonderfully, Eve—but not necessarily in that order.

The second Eve had heard of my misadventures with Kyle, she had dropped everything and rushed to the hospital, temporarily overcoming her agoraphobia by virtue of the fact that her fear of losing me outweighed her fear of leaving our home.

Phobias are psychological in nature and disproportional to the posed danger. In high-stress situations, the mind sorts our fears in order of risk.

And so Eve had weathered the storm and appeared, wearing a green head scarf and large dark sunglasses, reminding me of Audrey Hepburn in the movie *Charade* and bringing a needed smile to my face.

I had expected her to chew my ear off, to expose my foolishness with hard-hitting phrases such as *I told you so* and *I could have told you that wouldn't have worked out,* but she surprised me by expressing nothing except a deep concern for my welfare, refusing to leave my side and acquiescing only when other visitors demanded my undivided attention. Later, I knew, after her own shock wore off and we were back in our own environment, she would broach the subject of my stupidity, and I would not argue back.

Simply by her being there, my whole dark mood was lifted a few shades lighter.

Omitting my scuffed cheek and busted lip, outwardly I was in otherwise good health. Not exactly fighting fit, but in no worse shape than anyone else who had been used as a punching bag. Grappling with Kyle had left me bruised and sore, but nothing was broken, and medication was numbing my aches and pains, which I was happy with. My being slightly addled and sometimes incoherent had frustrated my police interviewers, but my doctors weren't overly worried, so neither was I. I answered my interviewers' questions honestly and openly, which was why I could neither explain their frowns nor their exchanged looks of bewilderment when they heard my tale.

Inwardly, however, there were concerns. *It's to be expected,* the doctors said. They made a point of stressing that I'd been through a life-and-death situation, been involved in a murder/kidnapping scenario with a deadly outcome. It was affecting my thought processes, so a little mental muddle was understandable.

Things like this can mess with the mind, they said. Essentially, events can screw us up, with liberal helpings of posttraumatic stress to come.

It wasn't anything I didn't tell my own patients.

Nothing is more selfish than the unconscious component of our psyche. It will manufacture all manner of psychological defenses to prevent the conscious part from imploding. Its one folly is, it isn't very good at seeing the bigger picture.

In the short term, our psyche copes as best it can: It cleaves to what it knows, finding comfort in the familiar. It undergoes risk assessment, rearranging anxieties in terms of imminent threat. It creates buffer zones, and it focuses on navel-gazing. In other words, it self-protects, sometimes at the cost of our sanity.

In the longer term, there is always a possibility of PTSD, of physical side effects, of self-incrimination for failing to live up to our own lofty expectations.

One by one, my bedside attendees reminded me I had witnessed death firsthand. Ordinary people are normally excluded from that party. I had discovered my girlfriend dying and then witnessed the killing of her husband and the suicide of a childhood friend. I'd survived exceptional circumstances. Right now my mind was erecting barriers, doing what it must to preserve itself.

It helps explain your present confusion with events, they said. *Counseling will be a compulsory factor in your convalescence.*

That first night in the hospital, I'd slept fitfully, dreaming of Scarlett on repeat as I often did. This time, she was in water as black as tar, being swept around and around in a whirlpool—a fiery sun orbiting a black hole—while I was on the outside of its influence. Scarlett passed by, tantalizingly out of reach, imploring me to take her hand, before finally being sucked into the vortex, gone without so much as a scream.

Each time the dream had ended, I'd woken in the dark, keeping perfectly still as hot blood revived my petrified muscles. The swaddling darkness feeling safe, womb-like. As I always did, I replayed the dream, as though if I applied enough external logic I could change its outcome. Awake but not fully separated from it. A boy leaning over a tide pool, fascinated by the beautiful creatures within, poking a stick into the miniature world, stirring it up, wondering what exotic sights lay hidden in the darker recesses beyond reach.

Eventually, I'd gotten up and padded into the bathroom for a pee, each passing second taking the dream and Scarlett farther away.

Midmorning the following day, Sunday, a request had reached me in the form of a message from Detective Sergeant Dunn. Can you believe, in all the mayhem, I hadn't thought about him once? He wanted a meeting. I informed Ray of Dunn's wishes, and he advised me to have him present, which I did.

"I'd offer you refreshments," I said to Dunn as he closed my hospital room door behind him, "but we're all out of caviar."

He ignored my icebreaker and nodded salutations to Ray, who was standing at the foot of my bed, arms folded defensively.

"Mind if I grab a seat?" Dunn asked. "Standing plays havoc with my lower back."

"Help yourself."

Noisily, he pulled a chair over to the bedside. "So, Greg, here we are. You've had a hectic couple of days. How are you feeling?"

"Never better." Of course, that wasn't the case. But Dunn didn't need to know how, for at least fifty-nine minutes of each waking hour, I'd been beating myself up. "With a bit of luck, I'll be discharged this time tomorrow."

He nodded, causing his handlebar mustache to tremble. "Whatever they offer you, take it. Don't refuse anything. I've experienced my fair share of trauma. It's not good. Talking helps, but you already know that. Have they arranged counseling?"

"Ironic, isn't it?"

"I guess whatever it takes to fix things, Greg." Dunn seated himself.

It was an invitation for Ray to do the same, on the opposite side of my bed.

I saw Dunn's gaze rove the room, taking in the blank and silent monitors and the lack of get-well cards standing on the empty tray table over the bed.

He said, "Both your doctors and my colleagues with the local PD tell me you're having difficulty remembering things."

"They do? Not at all. It's crystal clear."

"Which contradicts the impression they gave me."

"I can't speak for them."

"They say you've confessed to the killing of Troy Pinkerton."

"For the record," Ray said, "my client has answered all their questions without reservation. He hasn't been charged with anything. He's been totally transparent. He's not even under arrest."

"So I understand. I've read Greg's police statement, Mr. Stitt, and I can see why it's caused a bit of confusion. At first, they thought he'd taken a blow to the head, but a CT scan ruled it out."

I hitched myself up on the mattress and puffed out my chest. "That's because I'm fine."

"You don't look fine."

"And you don't look like a doctor."

His mustache twitched. "You're defensive."

"No, just a bit tired of being prodded and poked. There's nothing wrong with me. I have no idea why your colleagues insisted on the scan."

"Perhaps because you haven't been making much sense."

I sighed. "Look, if you're worried about my mental health—"

"Please don't misinterpret my curiosity for worry."

"I've spoken with a resident psychiatrist here," I said. "He's a nice guy. I've agreed to work with him."

"That's good. Things are moving in the right direction. I hear the sheriff's office has closed the case on your girlfriend's murder, posthumously charging her husband with the killing."

Grimly, Zoe's partner had updated me. Thompson had located the rental agency that had leased Pinkerton his getaway car, and traffic camera footage had put Pinkerton in Bonita Springs on the afternoon of Zoe's murder. Plus, Thompson had retrieved Zoe's cell phone from Pinkerton's hotel room in Sarasota, hammering home the last nail in the coffin.

"About what happened with me and Pinkerton," I began, "there's nothing to confuse. I was candid. I didn't hide a thing. I told them all I knew, and I didn't leave anything out."

"You said you acted on your own."

"I did."

"That you consciously tracked down Troy Pinkerton with a view to causing him harm. That you beat him, abducted him, and ultimately killed him."

My throat was full of cotton balls. "That's right."

Something had happened to me as the ambulance had rushed away from the Sunshine Skyway Bridge, lights flashing, my thoughts popping. Some people call it enlightenment or a revelation. I'd seen it as a damning acceptance and a coming to terms with a cold hard truth.

Kyle was an illusion.

In my shocked state, it was the best explanation I could come up with to support the coincidental and convenient appearances of my childhood friend—my *imaginary* childhood friend.

I had a bunch of memories of the two of us together, spanning a twelve-year period. Hot summer days whittled away as we explored the places declared out of bounds by adults: the abandoned sawmill, the high school rooftop, the cement mix plant. Doing stuff that made us feel like the first ones ever to do it. Freezing treks into the snow-laden woodlands, following deer tracks, and carving rudimentary spears. Waiting on the railway bridge for freight trains to come along, each daring the other to stand his ground, then leaping into the river at the last second as the train thundered by overhead. Summer evenings sprawled on our backs on the sports field, talking about greater things beyond our tiny sphere of influence while the stars penetrated the blue-black canopy above us.

But no memories of Kyle and me *and somebody else* who could corroborate our interactions.

Aside from that first day in kindergarten, I had no memories of us in a public setting.

How could Kyle exist and yet be unseen by everybody except me?

Crazy as it sounded, as damning as it was, the obvious answer was that I'd completely made him up.

Look, I treat clients who live with complex visual hallucinations all the time, clients who will swear under oath that the imaginary people they see are as real to them as members of their own family. People like Doris Tucker. Dig deep enough and you discover a common cause at the root of their first appearance: sudden emotional trauma. Usually, but not always, this traumatic event occurs in early childhood. To protect itself, the young mind creates a confidant, a fictional friend, someone who can relate, give support, make sense of the pain. Scarlett and I had lost both our parents, tragically, when we were toddlers.

Had I conjured up Kyle to compensate?

In ten years as a psychotherapist, I have only scratched the surface of how deeply our immature minds are affected by such emotional disturbances.

Until very recently, my memories of Kyle were all childhood ones, faded snippets, sketchy and largely unreliable.

I'm not alone in this: if I ask my clients to recall their earliest memories, the ones they recollect tend to be sparse and mostly those etched more deeply in the mind by heightened emotion.

Long-term memory isn't stored like information in a filing cabinet. You can't pull open a drawer and flick through to the relevant folder. It takes effort for the brain to store memories over a long period of time. That's why we remember the extremes more than the incidentals. When it comes to memory, the brain doesn't differentiate between pain and pleasure. Both trauma and bliss imprint themselves with equal amounts of mental ink. We remember our first kiss and our first heartbreak with the same amounts of fondness and sadness. It's the everyday stuff we forget. The inconsequential constancies. Sometimes, however, for self-protecting reasons, the mind deliberately deletes some of the important stuff.

How far can I trust my own brain?

Delusion or illusion—it was the only explanation that made at least some kind of sense. Kyle was no more real than my fertile imagination.

Through talk therapy, I have helped people with similar hallucinations, people on psychotropic drug prescriptions, perfectly functioning but still struggling with their memories of phantom friends, still trying to understand how and why their minds had fooled their every sense. The reality is, some people possess a natural disposition to psychological fracture, to let their darkness leak through the cracks, to let their shadow come to the fore in times of crisis.

Was this my answer?

Somehow, the realization felt *right*.

I imagined, at some point very early in my development—probably on that momentous first day in kindergarten, thrown into the social mix for the first time and faced with the disturbing prospect of being bullied—I had created an alter ego, someone to save me, someone to take over. In this case, Kyle. He was my darker half, the side of me that trod where angels feared to, conjured up by my protective subconscious to deal with the aspects of life I shied away from.

And the more I had thought about it, while riding in that ambulance, the more the pieces had fallen into place.

Kyle had only ever made an entrance during and after intense emotional turmoil, occasionally on the back of a blackout, and never in the company of others. My imaginary friend had manifested whenever my mind had needed him, probably to distract or act. Then college had come along and I'd matured, grown more confident and less in need of saving. And as a result, Kyle had taken a backseat.

Until now.

Eighteen years later, he'd come to my rescue once again, to deal with Murdoch in my backyard. It had taken the threat of imminent death for him to reemerge, for him to take control and thwart my attacker. While I was in blackout mode, Kyle had dealt with my problem, slipping back inside my mind the second the danger was past.

Fear had kept him close, just beneath my consciousness, ready to leap to my assistance at the first hint of distress.

My grandmother had said, *Ninety-nine percent of the big stuff is subconscious, hidden in the spaces between our elementary particles.*

Hence, Kyle had resurfaced yet again upon my discovering Zoe bleeding to death in her kitchen. Then once more, in the tumultuous aftermath, when a darker kind of strength and resolve had been required to deal with Pinkerton; Kyle had driven me to the brink and executed the inconceivable, helping me throw Zoe's murderer off the bridge.

Kyle hadn't fallen. My mind had.

But it was a bitter pill to swallow, to accept that my own brain had lied to me so easily and with such realism, had conjured up a complex visual hallucination tangible to the touch, with its own distinct personality.

Yet, for the life of me, I couldn't think of any other explanation to account for the synchronicity.

So I had told the police that I'd acted alone, with no mention of Kyle.

I imagined, from their viewpoint, they had seen me driving my car with Pinkerton bundled on the backseat. Me, talking to the man in the rearview mirror. Me, talking on the telephone with the hostage negotiator. Me, pushing Pinkerton off the bridge.

Ray brought me back into the hospital room by saying to Dunn, "Whatever happened up there on that bridge is beyond your purview, Detective. So what can we do for you? I'm pretty confident this isn't a social visit, or a last chance to say farewell before you fly back to Michigan."

Dunn placed a manila folder on my bed. "Those DNA results came in. You'll recall our conversation the other day, about our forensics team retrieving viable epithelial cells from underneath the decedent's fingernails?"

"You mean my client's sister," Ray said. "Why don't you just say her name?"

Dunn looked offended. "I'm not purposely avoiding saying anything, Mr. Stitt. It's just the way I speak, is all."

"It's uncompassionate. If your intention is to inflict further emotional pain on my client—"

Dunn dismissed him with a sharp shake of his head. "Don't go getting your boxers in a bunch, Mr. Stitt. It's nothing of the sort. Those DNA results came back, and my thinking was, since I was still in town, you'd like to know the outcome in person."

"Was it a match to Murdoch?" I said.

"No."

Ray looked at me, unresponsive, waiting until I made a move.

Slowly and deliberately, I said, "For the hundredth time, I didn't kill my sister."

"Just like you didn't kill Troy Pinkerton."

"But I did!"

Dunn's gaze was unreadable, so it came as a complete surprise when he said, "Greg, each and every way, you didn't kill Mr. Pinkerton. And I believe you didn't kill your sister."

I sat upright and stared at him.

"And not just me either," he continued. "My fellow investigators also agree. We're all of the same opinion, Greg. We don't believe you killed your sister. So, please, relax some, will you? You're no longer under our microscope."

I was speechless, light-headed, as though until this moment I'd been wearing a hat made out of lead, and now gravity had less of a hold on me.

"You have a match for the DNA," Ray said, ahead of me by several steps. "Someone other than Greg's."

"We do."

"Which is as good as saying you know who did kill her."

"DNA never lies, Mr. Stitt."

Again, Ray glanced at me.

My eyes were pinned on Dunn. Hardly breathing, I watched him open up the manila folder and leaf through its contents.

"Now here's the difficult part," he began, "and you'll see why my colleagues are all scratching their heads over your confession." He slid a photograph out from among the papers, turned it around, and placed it gently on my lap. "The DNA we recovered was a one hundred percent match to this person, who we now believe to be your sister's killer."

It was the photo of a man's head and shoulders taken against height markers on a plain gray background, instantly recognizable as a police mug shot. In grubby fingers, the man in the picture was holding up a booking number and wearing an expression that spoke of someone who hadn't expected to be caught.

It wasn't Zane Murdoch.

Ray leaned over the bed. "Now who the heck is this character?"

"According to his multiple arrest dockets, a frequent flyer with the Michigan and Minnesota penal systems. Perhaps Greg can fill us in?"

The cotton balls in my throat had thickened into a hard, asphyxiating wad, and my thoughts had hit a mental wall. Mind reeling, I stared into the dark eyes in the photo, grasping for words, preferably something eloquent to explain what my eyes were seeing. But all that leaked through was:

"It's Kyle."

Jesus Christ. How can this be?

It was impossible. Hallucination or hoax—take your pick.

Every self-analyzing check I had undertaken since being hospitalized had told me I was in full retention of my sanity. But this was insane. No argument. Impossible, and yet unarguably *real.*

"His full name's Kyle Hendrickson," Dunn said. "He's a resident of Naubinway in the Upper Peninsula. His youth was misspent, in and out of detention centers. As an adult, he's served time twice in the Marquette Branch Prison. Interestingly, he shared a cell for a while with Mr. Murdoch."

My jaw was on my chest.

Ray took the photo from my hands, looked it over, and then passed it back to Dunn. "That's some coincidence, Detective. But great news for Greg, right? You're quite sure this Kyle character is good for Scarlett's murder?"

"Absolutely." He slid the photo back into the file. "Hendrickson was a person of interest in the original investigation. His history of burglary and criminal battery was known to the investigators, and he was interviewed a number of times."

Ray said to me, "Did you know any of this?"

Stiffly, I shook my head; it was all news to me, written in bloody headlines. I was still struggling to accept that, in a heartbeat, not only had Kyle been proven to be real, but he was also connected to Scarlett's death.

Dunn spoke again. "Eyewitnesses placed Hendrickson in a bar in Manistique until around one a.m. the night your sister disappeared. He was unable to provide an alibi for his whereabouts after that."

"So how did the focus switch to Murdoch?" Ray asked.

"In light of Greg's police statement, Mr. Murdoch was also a person of interest. Isn't that right, Greg?"

I found my scratchy voice. "What? Yeah. Sure. Murdoch was Scarlett's boyfriend, but they split a few weeks before he killed . . . before she died. He blamed me for the breakup, but I had nothing to do with it. I think Scarlett had just come to her senses. She'd started doing normal stuff again, seeing her old girlfriends. Making up for lost time, I guess. Murdoch didn't like the fact she was getting on with her own life without him in it. He got drunk and made a few wild threats in public—said he was going to kill her and then me."

"And then there was the anonymous tip," Dunn said, "which led to the discovery of the knife in his trash."

Ray nodded. "With Scarlett's bloodied blouse."

"That's correct."

I gagged.

They both looked at me.

I flapped a hand and swallowed. "Excuse me. It just brings everything flooding back."

They both nodded.

After the knife's discovery, the police had come to my home for Scarlett's hairbrush, so that they could tweeze out hair follicles and hopefully retrieve viable DNA to compare against the bloodstains on both the supposed murder weapon and the shirt it had been wrapped in. I had handed it over, knowing their tests would prove an exact match.

All her life, Scarlett had suffered from nosebleeds, sometimes a trickle, sometimes a torrent. Always connected with her migraines or her menstrual cycle.

The day before she'd vanished from my world, she'd had one of her more explosive events. Mount Vesuvius episodes, she called them. Blood all down her shirt, enough to wring out. As usual, she'd dropped the bloodied garment in the washing machine and left it for me to deal with. I'd intended to. But then my world had ended and I'd forgotten all about the blood-soaked blouse—until a dark thought had come to mind days later.

Right from the get-go I'd been convinced that Murdoch had done something terrible to Scarlett, and as the days had passed, I'd made plans to cement his guilt.

The insane idea had come from nowhere, probably deep down in my hindbrain.

In gloved hands, I'd taken her shirt from the washing machine and drizzled just enough water onto it to moisten the blood. Then I'd rubbed an old hunting knife over the shirt, stabbing it through the place where her heart would have been, tearing through the cotton. Committed, I'd massaged more of the blood into the seam where the blade joined the handle. Then I'd wrapped the knife in her shirt and secreted it in a garbage can outside of the Murdoch family home.

I'd been an angry brother, not thinking straight. I hadn't regarded it as framing Murdoch. I'd thought of it as a way to strengthen the growing suspicion against him, to persuade the police about his guilt, which I would have staked my life on back then. It had been purely reactive. All my thought processes bent out of shape by rage and fear.

Any which way, I had wanted my pound of flesh.

Of course, I'd had no idea what tests the crime lab would run or how thorough they would be. I was confident Murdoch had done something despicable to Scarlett—he'd vowed as much in the aftermath of their breakup—and I didn't want him to slip through the net on a technicality.

I had spied my chance, and I had taken it.

Murdoch had been arrested.

And I had campaigned to get him convicted.

Desperation is a dangerous animal. Caged, it's controllable. Unleashed, it lashes out.

I couldn't tell Ray or Dunn that I had planted the knife in Murdoch's trash, or that I had been the anonymous caller pointing the police to its existence.

They wouldn't understand. Who would?

I'd figured it was a gamble worth taking. It's what desperate people do.

But now . . . Now I was struggling to accept the truth.

"Kyle killed Scarlett?" I said, each word slitting my throat on the way out.

Dunn nodded. "You'll recall him speaking with the hostage negotiator on the bridge? Hendrickson confessed to everything, the whole shebang, right before taking his own life."

I'd heard about people racked with guilt, offloading before they died. Priest or no priest, it all came pouring out, like an exorcised demon.

Ray asked the awkward question: "Did he provide details?"

"Just the basics. He said he came into contact with Greg's sister by chance that night. He was drunk, he said. He made inappropriate advances. She fought him off. One thing led to another, and the unimaginable happened."

"Kyle killed Scarlett?" I repeated, incredulous, heart pounding.

A mismatch of disbelief and acceptance formed a nauseating amalgam in my stomach. The idea of my childhood friend being responsible for Scarlett's death was like a collision between radioactive elements, and my brain was the supercritical mass about to go nuclear.

In my silence, Dunn said, "Hendrickson told the negotiator he was the one who called in your sister's whereabouts following Mr. Murdoch's release."

Ray stopped sucking his teeth and asked, "Why? If anything, that would have led to him incriminating himself."

Dunn closed the file folder with a finality that made me jump. "We can only assume he didn't possess the capacity of foresight, or figure we'd recover his DNA from the body. Who knows what goes through the mind of a mentally unstable career criminal like this?"

It sounded like Kyle: impulsive, reckless, cutting off his nose to spite his face.

As if from a distance, I heard myself say, "What about what happened at the bridge?"

Dunn's eyes came back to me. "See, this is where Hendrickson's confession and yours don't quite add up. You say one thing while he said another. My colleagues at Tampa PD are equally baffled. Repeatedly, they've pointed out their observations and the discrepancies in your statement, but you've been unwavering in your account. I'm hopeful it was the shock talking and now that you've slept on things you can set the record straight. Above all else, you need to recant your statement, so that it realigns with the facts as they stand."

"Okay."

"Before leaping to his death, Hendrickson told the negotiator you were there against your will. He admitted to abducting both you and Mr. Pinkerton from the hotel in Sarasota. Witnesses there have confirmed his story. He also mentioned that he forced you to drive him there at gunpoint. He didn't say what motivated him to do so or why he chose to kill Mr. Pinkerton. Unfortunately, those explanations died with him." Dunn leaned his forearms on the mattress. "So help me out here, Greg. During the time you and Hendrickson were together, did he mention anything about his reasoning behind those tragic events, such as a motive or anything at all?"

I shifted uncomfortably in the bed, in sheets that were suddenly clinging to my skin.

My thoughts were in disarray, my heart palpitating wildly. I was still trying to process Dunn's revelation, and badly. I couldn't accept that Kyle had killed Scarlett. It would take time to absorb it, make sense of it. Maybe I never would. I couldn't deny it either; the irrefutable evidence was there in Dunn's dog-eared folder. It was a conflict of concepts that left me unbalanced on a tightrope.

I swallowed the acidic phlegm in my throat, and said, "No, he didn't say a thing. Not a single word. It all happened too fast."

Dunn looked disappointed. "Well, that's a shame. I was hoping you could put this to bed once and for all."

"So," Ray said, "are we done here, Detective?"

"Seems so. For now. Regarding the formal identification of your sister's remains, Greg, I'll be in touch." Dunn got to his feet, appearing to be closing up shop, then hesitated halfway to the door. Slowly, he turned back to face me, massaging his handlebar mustache as he did so. "One last thing. And this may be a tad unorthodox, Greg, so please forgive me if I speak out of turn here. Just to satisfy my own curiosity: You're a psychotherapist. You work with unhinged people all the time. You must have seen cases like this before. From your professional point of view, why do you think Hendrickson kidnapped you and then killed Mr. Pinkerton?"

"That's asking a lot, Detective," Ray said. "Can't you see my client is in shock?"

"He'll answer if he wants to. Greg?"

Both Dunn and Ray stared at me, hanging on my response.

Growing up, I'd had as many friends as the next guy, mainly those I went to school with. Those who had been permanent features in my life. Constants. Friends I'd played sports with, partied with, watched girls with. Those who had left stronger impressions in me, overshadowing Kyle's transiency.

My relationship with Kyle—if you could call it that—was always fleeting, never of any real substance. Sure, I'd enjoyed the times we'd spent together. Kyle was my opposite. He'd given me a kind of false courage, enabling me to do the things I would never have dreamed of doing on my own. I was drawn to him. He was a pariah, whose existence outside of the school system, and in some cases the law, was attractive to an impressionable child like me. But he had never figured high on my friend list, which didn't seem to be the same in reverse.

By his own account, Kyle had valued my friendship more than I had his.

I suspect he hadn't had very many friends at all, with those acquaintances he did have being a result of mixing with undesirables in juvie and later in the penitentiary. Fair-weather friends with ulterior motives. Never the best type. Never the lasting kind. Those you owe for all the wrong reasons.

To Kyle, I must have represented a mainstay. A little bit of normalcy in his mad world. Someone who led the kind of life he would have wanted for his own had he had the same degree of stability in his, the same all-important ingredient required to bake a good human being, which is love.

Every now and then he would hunt me down, to get his normalcy fix. Hanging out with me would have made him feel less alien, less conspicuous. A wolf in sheep's clothing, momentarily deferring his predatory nature, happy to rub shoulders with the prey for a while.

Dunn's right. I have treated people like Kyle. Men, especially, who have grown up in broken households, single-handedly raised by mothers doing their best while battling disabling addictions. I remember Kyle telling me his mom loved her liquor, and that's why he was left to his own devices much of the time. Add that to the fact that his father didn't figure in his upbringing, and is it any wonder Kyle became wayward, shunned by society?

Unless an intervention takes place, wounded children make for defective adults. Sure, most can be fixed. It's never too late. Apply the right counseling, the right support mechanisms, sometimes the right medications, and the fractures can be healed, or at the very least patched up. Of course, the subjects need to be willing, with the desire to change. More importantly, they need to rediscover their humanity along the way. But it is doable.

Even so, one thing that many of the psychologically damaged have in common is a stress-induced thinking pattern aligned more toward the feral than the civilized.

And that's why they act impulsively sometimes, without any obvious rationale.

So, what was Kyle's reasoning?

Dunn's simple question deserved a complex answer. But I wasn't prepared to sit here in my hospital bed and go through all the intricacies of how social imprinting and, to some extent, genetics can screw up an immature mind.

So I formed a clueless expression, the kind I make whenever Eve puts my failings into words, and said, "The truth is, in all the time I've been doing therapy, the one thing I've learned is you can never predict the actions of a crazy person."

And that seemed to do the trick.

Epilogue

Wise beyond her years, Scarlett had once said, *Reality is a mirror, reflecting who we are on the inside.*

"*I'm still not entirely sure this is a good idea,*" Eve confessed as her gaze flitted across the room's sparse contents: the filing cabinet, the wooden desk with its office paraphernalia, the leafy peace lily languishing in the corner.

"It'll be okay," I assured her, and not for the first time. The drive down to North Naples had been a tug-of-war, and we had stopped several times along the way to debate. "We need to do this."

She nodded—reluctantly, I sensed—as she continued to scan the room, as though seeking a back door should things go awry.

I puffed out my chest, steeling myself, even though I felt like slush inside.

Eve wasn't the only one with nerves in her belly. On several levels, this was a first for both of us, a milestone in our journey together. A few jitters were to be expected. But I knew mine were minor compared with hers; she was out of her comfort zone by several miles.

"You can't stop progress," I added after a few seconds.

We were at a clinic on Naples Boulevard, seated and waiting in the shipshape office of a psychologist named Charles Fechner.

I imagine frailty is the first thing people think of when they meet the shaven-headed Fechner, at barely five feet tall and under one hundred *pounds, with his blue velveteen suit and matching bow tie. Frailty and then farce. Judgmentally, they will peg him down as a lightweight, ill-equipped to last the full round and lacking any real punch. A ventriloquist's prop.*

But Fechner is no dummy. Ten years of talk therapy have taught me that looks are always deceptive. You don't need height or girth to have stature. It's all about posture and technique and sometimes plain old balls. Remember the boy David with his slingshot? Despite his outward appearance, Fechner is a heavyweight, a hard-hitter, whose knockout words have the kind of gravity that can lay you out cold with one expertly placed jab.

Over the past five weeks, Fechner had taught me how to let go. It hadn't been easy, more so for me than for him. Doctors make the worst patients. I was full of old tricks, ingrained, inert, both heels dug in deep. I'd been an unwilling participant, resisting opening up new veins with someone I regarded as competition. Silly, I know. But gradually, as I'd warmed to Fechner and he to me, I'd softened my defensive stance in favor of a more cooperative partnership, and Fechner had reminded me that spilling a little blood can often ease the pressure, which it had.

I'd talked all about the recent harrowing events until my throat turned raw, and about how all my feelings felt unboxed. My sense of loss and hurt over Zoe. My sense of shock over Pinkerton. My sense of betrayal over Kyle. Fechner had suggested ways to compartmentalize, to pigeon-hole and box them back up, so that I was better equipped to take stock.

Coping mechanisms never fix the problem, but they can help us put things in perspective.

And so, with everything labeled, I'd worked through the blame, the guilt, the grief, the heartache, and the self-recrimination, and come through relatively unscathed. I say *relatively* because every experience changes us. Sometimes superficially, sometimes monumentally. Always unexpectedly.

Now, I was feeling more focused than I had in ages, fitter both physically and mentally, ready to live in my altered reality, which is how things are when we lose somebody close.

But I did go through a blip.

Two weeks after leaving the hospital, a large manila envelope arrived by courier from a mailing address in Jacksonville. Inside, I found a typewritten note from O'Malley, the PI, together with a smaller sealed envelope from Kyle. The note explained that Kyle had left specific instructions for this envelope to be forwarded in the event of either his detention or his death.

With an uncomfortable lump in my throat, I read Kyle's handwritten message, squinting at the spidery scrawl and frowning at the juvenile spelling. I could tell from the scattered and rambling way he'd put it together that it hadn't been easy for him.

I think he had intended it to be a confession, but it read like an apology.

Essentially, Kyle explained what had happened the night Scarlett died, when all hell had broken loose and tipped my world off its axis. He'd been passing though Manistique on his way home from Marquette, pausing to celebrate his recent release from his first major stint in big-league prison. He'd stumbled out of the bar, planning to pay me a surprise visit, the first in eight years. And that's when he'd run into Scarlett.

Thankfully, he didn't go into detail—I don't think I could have held it together knowing exactly what had happened to her—but he did say he'd never intended to take her life, that the dastardly deed was done in his drunken stupor, before he'd realized what was happening.

Alcohol is no excuse. Sure, it lowers inhibitions, but it doesn't raise killers. It just gives the ones already inside a platform to perform.

Kyle went on to say he'd wanted to come clean about what he'd done, but fear of authority and the prospect of life imprisonment had held him back. Then Murdoch had been charged, tried, and incarcerated, and in Kyle's mind an admission of guilt had seemed superfluous. My word, not his.

It was only when he'd heard about Murdoch's release that he'd felt compelled to make amends. Maybe he did feel guilt. Maybe all this time he'd been looking for a way to broach the subject of my sister's murder and his part in it. Maybe he saw this as his last chance to seek atonement. Who really knows? He'd spent six months behind bars with Murdoch; he knew Murdoch was looking for me. Whatever his underlying motivation, he'd decided to act.

Anonymously, he'd called the police, revealing where he'd buried Scarlett's body. He didn't say why he did so, or why he'd backtracked the night of her murder to dispose of her body at Crooked Lake. But I suspect the first was done thoughtlessly and in a rush of guilt, and the second was in an attempt to bury her as far away as possible from his home in Naubinway.

It was clear that Kyle's thought processes weren't linear. He was one of those people whose mind could go from *A* to *B*, but not without taking a detour to all the rest of the alphabet on the way.

Then Pinkerton had killed Zoe, forcing Kyle along an altogether different path, and I could only surmise he'd seen killing Pinkerton as his way of redressing his past sins, doing so the only way he knew how: unlawfully.

His suicide wasn't planned, but having received his letter, I knew death was something he'd planned for.

Kidnapping Pinkerton had sealed his fate, and the thought of returning to prison on a permanent basis must have been too much for him.

In his mind, leaping from the bridge was his only way out.

Later, I learned that the Coast Guard didn't find his body. The police assured me there was no way he had survived the fall, more likely that a rip current had swept his corpse out into the Gulf before it could be recovered. They told me it happened on occasion with some of those desperate souls who took the same leap of faith.

Reading that untidy letter of Kyle's made me want to hate him, despise his very soul. But, surprisingly, my heart wasn't in it, and all

I could do was cry. Not for his loss or even for what he'd done, but because my whole belief system to this point had been based on a lie.

As for Murdoch, I hadn't heard anything more from him. Not directly, anyway. The week after I came out of the hospital, I did Dunn's bidding and caught a plane to Sawyer International, all expenses paid. He collected me in person and chauffeured me straight to the Marquette County medical examiner's office, thankfully without too much probing conversation along the way.

The grim lines of our mouths spoke more than words.

Robotically, I went through the motions of identifying Scarlett's corpse.

Sure, it sort of looked like her—or some melted, twisted freak-show version of her—but I told myself it wasn't her, just to get through, just to stop the panic from rising and forcing me to flee.

More food to fuel my nightmares.

I pushed the experience as far to the back of my mind as I could.

During my ride back to the airport and almost as an afterthought, Dunn told me he'd heard that Murdoch had made it back to Manistique in one piece, whereupon he had set up a soapbox in the center of town, selling God and heavenly futures to anyone within earshot.

"We're all just spiritual icebergs," Eve said reflectively, bringing me back into the moment, "with just the tips of us poking into reality."

It was something Scarlett might have said, and it made me smile.

I glanced at Eve, wondering what the future held for us.

Her gaze had settled on the coffee table. On its glass surface was a Polaroid instant camera and a photograph. The picture was of me, seated on the very couch where we were now sitting, with the word *before* written in red marker on the white space beneath the image. A suspicious-looking me of five weeks ago, clearly giving off anxious vibes.

Thankfully, my discharge from Tampa General had come with a clean bill of health, and I had returned home to Eve, to a prescribed two weeks' sick leave, so I could lick my mental wounds and convalesce.

Even so, my attending physician had recommended a follow-up course of counseling, principally to trudge through the fallout left behind after what he described as a devastating chain-reaction event.

People don't die from getting a splinter, he'd told me. *But if left unchecked and an infection sets in, sepsis and death are only a small step away.*

It wasn't a great analogy, but I understood the meaning. All the same, I had been reticent to go along with the cheery doctor's suggestion. The thought of being the subject rather than the therapist had seemed utterly alien. I was the first to admit that a lifetime of listening, asking poignant questions, and offering constructive advice had made me inflexible and dogmatic. I wasn't sure I could do it.

Okay, so I had gotten it wrong about Kyle. It was perfectly understandable, given the high-stress situation I was in at the time. When the mind is out of its depth and treading water, it will head for the nearest bit of dry land, even if it turns out to be an active volcano. In extreme circumstances and under intense emotional pressure, I had made an innocent mistake. It didn't necessarily follow that I was losing my marbles.

And so I'd spent the first week after Zoe's funeral puttering around the house and getting back on my feet, complaining about boredom and the soaring late spring temperatures. Basically, doing all I could to stop my brain from overanalyzing everything and, more importantly, from thinking about Zoe.

As an expired member of the grief club, the last thing I wanted to do was renew my membership.

Still, there was only so much daytime TV to watch, only so much lazing about at the poolside to do, only so much deflecting I could handle before it had all become too much and I began to freak out over every little thing.

Relaxing, it turns out, is stressful stuff.

In a last bid to unwind, I'd taken my recovered Yellowfin out into the bay to fish the flats each afternoon of the following week. Alone. Just me, the boat, and the mirrorlike water. Chilling out in the heat, with my feet up, beers crowding the cooler and the gentle bob of the current lulling me into a meditative state.

Perfect escapism.

But the trouble with meditation is, it ushers in introspection.

And so, as the week had worn on, I'd begun to think more and more about my ruinous role in other people's lives. It was inevitable; consciences have loud voices, and mine was no exception. Time and again, I'd listened to its arguments, hearing how my selfish decisions had hurt others and how I'd played an instrumental part in the deaths of two people I loved the most. Both the sheriff's office and the Tampa Police Department believed I was innocent of any crime. But in my mind I was as guilty as Kyle or Pinkerton. Maybe not for wielding a killer knife, but culpable of their murders nonetheless. And the truth was immutable, hardwired, written into every bit of me like bad DNA.

Not only had I failed Scarlett, but I'd also failed Zoe, and no amount of self-cleansing could wash their blood from my hands.

So I had given in, agreed to undergo the suggested six-week psychotherapy plan, to come here voluntarily each Monday morning, to spar with a man half my size but twice my worth. Unexpectedly, I'd built up a healthy rapport with Fechner. I hadn't yet invited him out on my boat, but it was on the horizon, after I was done with treatment. In spite of his sobering truths, Fechner was a good-hearted man and would be a great friend, in due course. Even so, I was hoping that today would be the last time we would meet under these conditions.

The door opened, and I took a deep breath.

Fechner hustled in, arms loaded with case files stacked higher than his head. "Sorry for the delay," he murmured from behind the pile.

"Annual audit on its way. Reams of red tape and paperwork to get through. One of those days." He closed the door with his heel.

"We all have them, Charlie. It's character-building. Need any help carrying those?"

"Relax. I think I've got this covered." Unceremoniously, he dumped the files on one end of the desk, steadied them as they started to spill, and managed to catch several before they slid to the floor. "You brought Eve with you?"

Supportively, I squeezed Eve's hand. "Just like you asked." Automatically, I looked at her, unable to contain my smile. In the morning sunlight slanting in through the window blinds, her skin was radiant, her hair ablaze, her freckles glimmering like flakes of gold. "She took some convincing. She can be a hard nut to crack. But here she is."

Fechner straightened his bow tie, came over, and sat himself down in the leather chair facing us. "This is excellent news, Greg. A huge step forward, and such a lovely surprise. To be honest—and you know me, when it comes to telling it like it is, I'm brutally honest—I didn't think you'd pull it off. I kept thinking to myself, he'll never make it. He'll be in two minds over this one, pulled from pillar to post. So, yeah, I know exactly how difficult it must have been for you." He reached out with a hand and fist-bumped mine. "Congratulations," he said. "You're one step closer to certified sanity."

"Makes me feel all warm and fuzzy inside."

"Now, that could be the medication." He smiled. "Okay, let's get right down to business." He picked up the instant camera from the table.

"So this is it," I began, "the end is nigh?"

He popped the flash. "All good things come to an end, my friend. What we do after is the true test." He put the viewfinder to his eye. "Smile like you mean it."

I did, pulling Eve into me.

The camera flashed, leaving a nuclear explosion on my vision. I shook my head and blinked, but the white-hot glow had scorched my retinas. I heard the camera's discharge mechanism whir and heard Fechner say:

"Seen the light, Greg?"

"Just about." Vaguely, I had an impression of him placing the camera back on the side table with one hand and shaking the developing photograph with the other. I performed a long blink. "Blinded by it, more like."

"Keep blinking. The shock will subside. Did you tell Eve the reason I asked you to bring her here today?"

"I did." The glow was beginning to dissipate. "She knows everything."

"Way to go, Greg." He blew at the photograph, as though his hot moist breath would encourage the activating chemicals. "Sharing is all part of the healing process. You want to get that diamond out of the ground, you've got to dig deep and be prepared to get your hands dirty doing it. Eve is an integral part of where you're at, both emotionally and psychologically. Seriously, you wouldn't be here if it wasn't for her. You said it yourself, several times—she's your rudder."

"Steering me along the straight and narrow."

"He exaggerates," Eve said, "and always has. I just remind him of the things he already knows but is too knuckleheaded to acknowledge."

Fechner glanced at the resolving photograph, frowning. "It never fails to amaze me how these things work."

"It all comes down to chemical reactions," I said.

He nodded. "Doesn't everything?" He continued to scrutinize the developing image, as though he were a laboratory technician inspecting a culture growing in a petri dish. "If it came to it, Greg, do you believe your psyche could survive intact without her?"

I blinked, this time for different reasons. "Seriously?"

"It's just a thought."

The makings of a frown were beginning to form on Eve's silken brow, but I smiled the frown away. "I guess I could, if I had no other choice. But I wouldn't want to. By far, she's the best part of me. I know it sounds schmaltzy, but I'm a better person with her in my life."

"Don't believe a word out of him," Eve said. "He has this idealistic image of me in his head, which is hard to live up to, basically because I'm nowhere near perfect. Greg likes to make out that I am, and it's cute, but we have our differences of opinion, sometimes heated. We disagree all the time."

Fechner looked at us over the top of the photograph. "Greg, you said Eve threw you a lifeline ten years ago. She saved your life."

"That's right. I was in a bad place, drowning and going under. She was my lifesaver. I have no idea what might have happened if she didn't turn up when she did."

"Do you think suicide was a possibility?"

Now I felt my cheeks heat up. "I don't know. It scares me to think it could have been, that I might have been a whisker away from it. Thankfully, I didn't get to choose."

"Because Eve intervened."

"Yes."

"Don't let him fool you," Eve said. "Greg did all the hard work. I threw him the lifeline, but he pulled himself out of the mire." She looked up at me and smiled. "The credit's all his."

Fechner was still admiring his photography skills. "Say, this one isn't bad. I'm improving all the time. No red-eye." He shook it some more. "So, switching it up a little, Greg, do you believe in me, what we've achieved here these last few weeks?

"Sure. I have to hand it to you, Charlie. You know your stuff."

"Do you believe in yourself?"

It was a surprise question, but I didn't have to think about an answer. All my life, I had relied on Gregory Cole to get the job done, and I told him so.

Fechner placed the photograph facedown on the flat of his hand. "Last week, you told me about the time Scarlett assigned you Native American names. Yours was Fainting Goat, right?"

I nodded, all at once unsure where Fechner was headed with this.

"What was Scarlett's?"

"I think I told you."

"So tell me again."

I drew a long, tremulous breath.

Scarlett loved the water. It was as though she had a symbiotic relationship with it. Mutually life-giving. She was the fastest kayaker I knew, quicker than me by a figurative mile. She possessed both the strength and the technique of an Olympian. I wasn't jealous. Not much, anyway. No more than any loving brother who always came in second. When we were out on the river, just the two of us, I loved nothing more than to sit in her slipstream, in awe of the rapid rotation of her arms, of her long and fluid strokes as she rocketed across the water with her flame-red hair trailing behind her. She would taunt me about it all the time—her being by far the faster kayaker.

"We were kids," I murmured quietly. "It wasn't meant to be serious."

"What did she call herself, Greg?"

I smiled shakily. "It was just a bit of fun."

"What name did she pick for herself?"

Now I swallowed uncomfortably and felt Eve stir nervously.

"Greg?"

"Even with Rocks. She called herself Even with Rocks."

It was juvenile, I know, and silly, but apt. In her kayak, Scarlett was a combustible whirlwind of pure energy, giving off sparks, uncatchable. She'd say, *I can outpace you any day of the week, Greg, even with rocks in my boat.*

Fechner was nodding. "But you shortened it, didn't you, Greg? When it was just the two of you together, what did you call her?"

I glanced at Eve and opened my mouth as if to speak, but no words came out.

Fechner saw my inner struggle come bubbling to the surface and held out his upturned hand with the facedown photo on it. "It's time, my friend. Your sanity awaits. Go ahead and take the picture."

I didn't move. Instead, I saw Eve's fingers reach out.

Teasingly, Fechner withdrew his hand a little, causing Eve to pause. "Before you leap," he said, holding my gaze, "know that you will not fall. You will not go down in flames. I've got you, Greg. These past weeks, we've put in place mechanisms to help you parachute to safety. We've erected a safety net. You will be okay. Have faith, my friend—you can do this."

Apprehensive, I said, "Can I get a drumroll?"

Fechner smiled. "Stop delaying and take the picture."

Eve took the photograph and turned it over so that we could both see.

It showed the flash-brightened image of a man who looked exactly like me, seated on the couch in Fechner's office, on his own, with a big confident grin plastered on his face, looking like someone who had won life's lottery and was ready to embrace the positive change it would bring—the significant part being *he was on his own.*

I looked at Eve, snuggled up next to me on the couch, at the vibrant woman who had replaced Scarlett in my affections, with her auburn hair and her sisterly smile—most of all, at her soft Cole family features, which were unmistakably the female version of my own. In every way, my fraternal twin.

In my ear, she whispered, "I think we may need a second opinion."

And we burst out laughing, uncontrollably.

Acknowledgments

For your steadfast support, your honesty, your truth. For your endless words of encouragement, your positivity, your patience. For all the small things that make the big things matter. For giving me your time, your thoughts, your love. For being my muse and for being my wife.

Thank you, Lynn—for without you, I am just a dreamer.

My family is the most important thing in my life—so a special thank-you to my lovely daughters and sons-in-law, Gemma and Sam, and Rebecca and Ruben, for your limitless love and support. And fondest grandpa cuddles to my four wonderful granddaughters, Willow and Perry, and Ava and Bella, who swing from my every limb at every opportunity, sometimes all at the same time. Warmest hugs to my mum and dad, June and Bill, and to my dearest mother-in-law, Lillian.

Together, you are my world.

A huge thank-you to Emilie Marneur, editorial director at Amazon Publishing, for your continuing faith in my writing, and for being a good sport. Thank you to Charlotte Herscher, my eagle-eyed editor, for pointing out that my box has eight sides, with the outside being the most important. Thank you also to Elizabeth Johnson, my copyeditor, for thoroughly Americanizing my work. And a big thumbs-up to everyone else who has helped shape this novel.

Thank you to all my loyal readers worldwide, some of whom have been with me since the start. Your e-mails and social media support are always sincerely appreciated!

Lastly, thank you for reading my book. I hope you enjoyed it.

Keith Houghton, England, February 2016

About the Author

Keith Houghton spent too much of his childhood reading science-fiction books, mostly by flashlight and tented under the bed covers, dreaming of becoming a full-time novelist.

When he was thirteen, his English teacher—who was fed up with reading his space stories—told him he would never make it as a science-fiction writer. Undeterred, he went on to pen several sci-fi novels and three comedy stage plays, while raising a family and holding down a more conventional job. But it wasn't until he switched genres and began to write mystery thrillers that his dream finally became reality. These days, despite his head still being full of those space stories, he keeps his feet planted firmly on the ground, enjoying life and spending quality time with his grandchildren.

Keith Houghton is the author of the three Gabe Quinn thrillers, *Killing Hope*, *Crossing Lines*, and *Taking Liberty*, as well as the stand-alone psychological thriller *No Coming Back*.

To read more about Keith Houghton and his writing, please visit www.keithhoughton.com.